THE DEMON LORD

Borderland Legacy Book One

NIKKI FRANK

To Charlotte,
Keep Reading :)
Nikki Frank

SOUL MATE PUBLISHING

New York

THE DEMON LORD

Copyright©2018

NIKKI FRANK

Cover Design by Fiona Jayde

Published in the United States of America by
Soul Mate Publishing
P.O. Box 24
Macedon, New York, 14502

ISBN: 978-1-68291-662-9

ebook ISBN: 978-1-68291-636-0

www.SoulMatePublishing.com

For Brewer and Briley who keep me young.

Acknowledgements

Much love and gratitude for my husband, Richard Walker, without whom my characters would be snarkless and demure. Thank you for believing in me and my writing, even when my own faith flickered. You listened and read and gave me time to work in peace, a rare commodity with small children. I couldn't have done this without you.

I owe a debt of gratitude to my mentor, fellow writer, William Greenleaf. You found me at my rawest as a writer and still saw my potential. For taking me under your wing and teaching me, you have my thanks. Your advice and friendship has meant so much to me.

My heartfelt thanks to my faithful beta readers and critique partners. Foremost to Joan Walker for hours spent reading and hashing out details. Your insights and unfailing support has been invaluable. I'm honored to have you in my life.

Thank you to all my friends and family who rallied around me as I undertook the adventure of becoming a published author. My parents and siblings, who love me unconditionally. My sister-in-law, who has never read a book, but will read mine. My nephews and nieces who think it's cool that I write. That's high praise from teenagers. Nicole, Heather, and Joy, busy moms who are never too busy to offer a hand, an ear, or a shoulder. You have waited years, sharing my joys and anxiousness. I'm so happy you've all stuck around on my journey, and I hope to continue on this path with you for many years to come.

Of course, my editor, Cheryl Yeko, for picking up both me and this story and dusting us both off. Thank you for helping us shine. And I couldn't forget the rest of the talented staff and artists at Soul Mate Publishing who have helped turn this dream of mine into a reality.

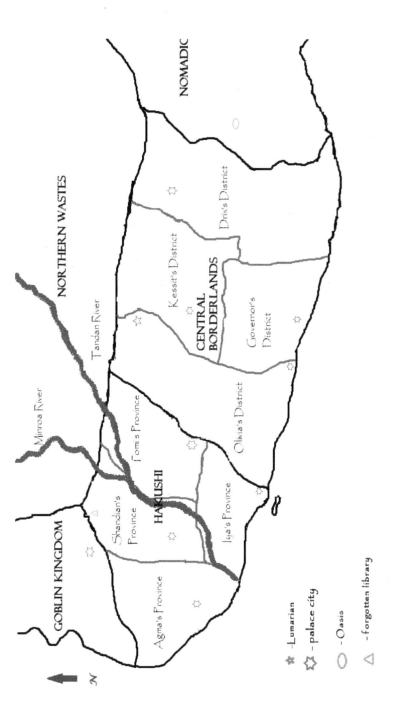

N

NORTHERN WASTES

NOMADIC

GOBLIN KINGDOM

Minroa River

Tandan River

Shandian's Province

Tomi's Province

Agma's Province

Iya's Province

HAKUSHI

Kessit's District

Drix's District

CENTRAL
BORDERLANDS

Olivia's District

Governor's
District

☆ – Lumarian
⛉ – palace city
◯ – Oasis
△ – forgotten library

Chapter 1

534,478,961 children worldwide wished their brothers or sisters would disappear last year. I had to take some of those children. I am a kidnapper. Sometimes I work as an assassin, when my schedule allows. I don't have much free time for such things, though. Like most seniors, my life is starting to get really busy.

As hard as I try to be a normal teen, sometimes I feel like there's not really anything interesting about me. I have mediocre grades and flat brown hair which hangs in my face. My eyes are brown. I have olive skin. My height's average. My ears are slightly pointy, same with my third teeth, top and bottom. And oh yes, I happen to be an imp. That's a secret.

No one at school has ever mentioned the various points on my features. But then again, they're not really noticeable unless I'm hunting children. This may sound cruel, but as an imp it's something I need to do, like a hawk hunting its prey.

"Hey, Olivia," my friend Emmett called to me. He and I have been inseparable since third grade when he moved to my school. He'd be eighteen in two months. I'm not sure where the time went, and I hated to see it go. Imps tend not to make many friends. I dreaded not being accepted to the same college.

"You wanna come out for pizza and video games? I'll drive you home after."

I shook my head. Riding the bus would give me a little quiet time to mentally prepare for hunting later. I needed to center myself because I don't like what I do. But kidnapping is not a choice for me. I send the wished-away children to the Goblin Kingdom in exchange for a ration of magic, something like plugging in for a recharge. If I don't get the magic, I'll die.

Emmett caught and held my hand until the bus door closed, and it started to roll forward. He grinned at me knowing I could no longer worm out of going home with him. Hitching his backpack higher onto his shoulder, he turned toward the student lot. He kept my hand until I tugged it back, falling into step beside him.

I plopped into the passenger seat of his black coupe. Inside smelled homey, like used car and Emmett. I had to admit, riding with a friend beat being on the bus.

He pulled into the driveway at my house, a blue bungalow with no outstanding features. My home fit me perfectly in that respect: average.

"Are you sure you don't want to hang out?" Emmett gave me brown, puppy eyes and I wavered.

"I can't."

I grabbed my bag and got out of his car before I caved. I'd do pretty much anything for Emmett. Receiving such devotion was part of being special to an imp. But if I played before I hunted I wouldn't get any sleep. Going to bed early kept a late night from being even later. Tomorrow would suck if I didn't rest.

"I always *want* to hang out, but I have to do this. Don't make me feel guilty. I thought you wanted us to move toward being more adult. Following through with obligations should be important, right?" I gave him a superior, but teasing look.

He grinned widely in return and waved on his way out of the drive. Inside the front door, I kicked my shoes into the hall closet. I walked the creaky hardwood hall to the kitchen where Mom and Dad sat at the table, papers spread in front of them. They must have work. They only planned this way before they left for an assassination.

"Oh, Olivia. You're home." Mom smiled up at me. "Here's the name and address of tonight's job. You'll be fine if you go after 10:30. Your dad and I are going to be gone a couple days on this assignment, so I selected an older child for you. The capture ought to be worth enough to tide you over until we get back."

I took the slip of paper she held out. "When do you guys leave?"

"This hit is important, so we head out tonight," my dad said.

"Wow, that's fast. What's the assignment?"

"Political elimination. Seems there's an alpha dispute in a pack of arctic werewolves. We're taking out the superfluous one. Pays in diamonds, though. Getting to the northern reaches of Siberia is going to be the real beast."

I shook my head. Sometimes my dad was a little too glib. Assassinating a werewolf . . . no biggie compared to getting from Redding, California to Siberia. My parents are also imps and assassins. Killing is how they made a living. Even an imp has a mortgage to pay. Rarely did we ever take a hit on humans. Mostly we eliminated magic folk. Hey, we can't all be born fairy princesses. Coming to terms with the fact that imps are considered less . . . savory . . . magic folk had taken work on my part.

I went through a rebellious phase a few years ago where I languished over the injustice of not having been born something everyone loved, like a mermaid. But I'd eventually gotten over my feeling of being crapped on by fate. Life became much easier when I accepted what I was. I took all my negative feelings and put the energy to work making myself as good a person as I could be, for an imp.

"You be careful," I told Mom. "I don't want to get a box of pieces in the return mail."

Mom stood and pulled me into a hug. "We're always careful. You know we love you, right?"

My dad chuckled. "We'll be fine. You just look out for yourself, all right? You'll be good tonight?"

I waved the paper in his direction. "Piece of cake."

Halfway to the stairs, I thought of something and turned to go back to the kitchen. I paused. My parents were deep in discussion.

"What about taking the silver daggers?" my mom asked. "Furduk has a reputation for being ruthless."

"Probably not a bad idea. But don't pack too much. I don't want to haul around the luggage. Besides, it's only one werewolf."

My mom let out a low growl. "And however many of the pack support him. You need to take this mission seriously."

"We can pause time if we get cornered."

My mom's chair screamed against the floor before toppling over. Angry footsteps crossed the room. Though she kept her voice low, every word rang clear. "Don't you *ever* suggest *that* magic. You know using a time pause is a death sentence. There's no way I could get you sufficient magic fast enough to save you."

"If you were in danger, I wouldn't care what happened to me." My dad's voice was low and full of emotion. "I'd do anything to protect you."

Mom growled again. "Do you think I could live without you?"

I turned to go. My question could wait. I understood the emotion in Mom's voice. Imps may not make very many friends but the few we do we're fiercely loyal to. The connection is even stronger between partners, and I couldn't scratch the surface yet of what a pair-bonded couple might feel.

I dashed up the stairs to the attic bedroom, my favorite place in the house. The room took up the whole attic and had windows looking out on all four sides. Polished wood floors smelled aged and cozy. I'd decorated the whole thing in my favorite yellow and spring green. Ever since I was tiny I'd always been happiest when surrounded by those colors.

Plopping on the bed, I unfolded the paper and did a doubletake at the name. Poppy Stedman. Oh no. Poppy was the eleven-year-old little sister of the hottest guy in my class, Cory Stedman. Why would he want her gone? What if I bumped into him on the job?

He would know me if he saw me. We had Biology class together. As far as datable females went, I doubted I registered on his radar. Cory would never look twice at a girl as plain as me. I spent a good deal too much time looking at him. You have to be special to find a place in an imp's heart and I had Emmett, who left me perfectly satisfied. I had never thought I had the need for other friends or boyfriends. But in the last few months when I stole glances at Cory I found myself wondering what it would be like to be asked out.

The buzz of my alarm woke me at ten. Outside the door to my room everything sat in silent darkness. My parents had obviously already left. I pulled on yoga pants and a specially made chameleon fleece. Pricier than human designer clothing the expense was well worth it. To humans the wearer looked like a shadow. My parents had shelled out for the fleece as soon as I'd started hunting for myself.

I pulled on my Hermes shoes: an awesome gift from my parents for my birthday last winter. The shoes allowed me to move in utter silence and with nearly blinding speed. They resembled something like black ballet slippers. I loved the way they hugged my feet and promised freedom.

Fully dressed, I looked like any of the shadows wavering in the moonlight beyond my front door. I slipped outside and took a deep breath of the warm, fresh air. Mid-August nights in Redding had yet to cool for autumn and the air still smelled of summer and freedom. We'd only been back in school for a week.

Poppy's address took me all the way across town but with the Hermes shoes, I didn't care. At the edge of my sidewalk, I crouched like a sprinter at the starting line and took off. The wind made my eyes water and tore at my ponytail. I loved the feeling of nearly flying and the freedom I had while I hunted. The trip to the Stedman's house took only a few minutes. All the windows were dark, like my parents had said they would be. According to the slip of paper, Poppy slept upstairs on the south-facing side. I found her window, crouched and used the Hermes shoes to leap with total silence onto the roof beside her dormer.

A bit of magic undid the lock and I slid the window open. Poppy lay completely unaware in her bed, a host of stuffed animals along the wall next to her. From here, kidnapping offered little challenge. I pulled out a small bag of goblin-dust and sprinkled a pinch over her head. Then I blew a kiss at her. She vanished from her bed, a new captive of the Goblin Kingdom.

I paused for a moment as the fresh rush of power surged through me. Obtaining magic had no comparison with any of my more mundane, humanish needs. The flow left me tingly and refreshed and invigorated. Feeling a bit high, I crept to the window and leapt lightly back to the ground. I didn't worry about closing the window. Who cared how they thought she got out? Brushing the dust off my hands I put the bag back in my pocket and raced home. Mission accomplished.

~ ~ ~

I wasn't surprised at all the next morning to arrive and find the school buzzing about the disappearance of Cory's little sister. I took a jab in the sides by two fingers, nearly toppling the books I'd been stacking in my locker. Emmett tucked a stray wisp of my hair behind my ear then leaned casually next to me, shooting me a toothy grin.

"Too bad you can't comfort poor Cory," he teased.

Poor Cory, yeah right. The jerk had wished his sister away in the first place. I found him much less attractive knowing he willingly asked to be rid of her.

"Some things were never meant to be." I pulled out my books for first period. "I—"

"Would Olivia Skotadi please report to the principal's office."

Emmett gave me a wide-eyed look and I shrugged. Like I knew what they wanted. Eyes followed me as I trudged through the hall to the office. On my way in I passed the new girl, Buraee Iyer, on her way out. She'd just transferred to our school. She turned her head away as I passed, a sheet of long black hair hiding her face. As if I wanted to talk to her either. She struck me as the stuck-up, prissy sort.

The secretary jumped when she saw me and ushered me into the principal's office. Inside sat a man in a navy polo and khaki slacks with a badge on his chest. The principal, a middle-aged woman with over-dyed blond hair and a pinched face, stood and pointed me toward a chair.

"Olivia, this is Detective Parks. He'd like to talk to you for a moment."

"About?" My voice came out squeaky.

The detective cleared his throat. "We've been trying to contact your parents. You wouldn't know where to reach them, would you?"

I shook my head. Cell reception in Siberia was unlikely. "My parents are gone on a business trip right now and will be unavailable for a few days."

The detective frowned. "Do you have a guardian while they're gone?"

"Um. I'm staying at my house alone but the Keelers are my emergency contacts."

The principal pushed the intercom. "Lynette, will you

get Mrs. Keeler on the phone for me? Let me know when you have her."

"Did something happen to my parents?" Worry scratched at my stomach. After all, they were hunting a werewolf.

"I assume they're fine, but can you tell us *your* whereabouts last night?" Detective Parks asked.

My heart gave a funny flop. "At home."

He nodded. "Did you happen to visit the Stedman's last night?"

"No." My throat tightened. How could they possibly have information on that? I should have been all but invisible to humans.

"Someone seems to have seen you there around ten-thirty last night." Detective Parks shifted in the chair. "You're going to be turned over to the custody of the Keelers. We're not sure at this point if you're a witness or a person of interest, but you'll be under house arrest until your parents return and take responsibility for you. When do you expect them back?"

"A couple days at most. May I go home and get a change of clothes first?" I needed to get my chameleon fleece and shoes. Then if I had to hunt or run for any reason I'd be prepared.

"Yes. We can get your things."

I blinked at gathering tears as I listened to the phone conversation with Emmett's mom. The detective asked if she was willing to care for me. If she said no, I'd be placed in state care until my parents claimed me.

When all the arrangements were made, I followed Detective Parks out to his unmarked car. The whole time I sorted through furiously swirling thoughts, looking for answers. But I only raised more questions. Who wanted me arrested? Whoever sold me out, they were magic folk. A human couldn't have seen me. And they had to know me by sight. But being turned in by magic folk seemed so unlikely. We tended to watch each other's backs unless one of us abused our power or risked exposure. I had done neither.

Suddenly the image of a sheet of black hair hiding a disdainful face popped into my mind. What did I know about Buraee? Was she magic folk? Conceivable. She certainly didn't like me. But what would she possibly gain from my arrest? Or what had I done to her to deserve being sold out?

Nothing fit together. We pulled into my driveway and Detective Parks followed me around as I gathered my things. Just in case I needed to feed before Mom and Dad got back I grabbed the name generator: a small coiled shell which had been enchanted to spit out the names of our victims. The children we hunted came out in green. Assassination targets came out in red.

Thankfully the ride between my house and Emmett's is short. Every minute in the detective's car stifled me, making me want to scream in frustration. Before I cracked he pulled into the drive at Emmett's two-story farmhouse with the wrap-around porch. My other home.

Detective Parks escorted me in and placed me in the care of Emmett's mom. With no wasted conversation, he turned and left me standing miserably in front of Ivy Keeler. She gave me a hug and a kiss on the top of my head as Detective Parks backed out of the driveway and pulled away.

"Don't worry," she soothed. "They just want to know where you're at. You're not accused of a crime and when the little girl is found you'll be cleared." Ivy gulped. "I know you didn't do anything."

For the first time in a long while I felt guilt over my role as an imp. "I . . . can I be alone for a while?"

"Sure, Dear. I got Vanessa's room ready for you."

I took my bag and headed up the familiar stairs, stopping at the door next to Emmett's. Normally the room belonged to Vanessa, his older sister, but she was away at college. I flopped down on Vanessa's very purple bed and got a whiff which reminded me of Emmett, kind of, his laundry detergent at least. He'd smelled the same for as long as I'd known him. This last year he'd muddled the scent with his new body spray. I'd given him crap about that.

I stayed sprawled on the bed even when Ivy dropped off a sandwich and chips for lunch. I couldn't eat them. I couldn't even find the will to get off the bed. I rolled through self-pity, burning anger, and apathy by turns. Time blurred with no real sense of passing until the door opened and Emmett came in. School had already ended.

"Livy?" He sat beside me on the bed. "I brought your homework."

I stared at the ceiling waiting for him to give up and go away.

"Cory never came to school today."

I still ignored him.

"I went by his house and tried to cheer him up."

I scowled at his lie. Emmett hated Cory.

Emmett leaned back on his hands, giving me a melodramatic look. "Yeah, he was in bad shape, distraught and all. Cried on my shoulder like a baby. One thing led to another and then we started making out. So sorry. You can't date him. He doesn't like your type."

I hit Emmett with a pillow. "Knock it off. Even if you thought Cory was a respectable human being, you wouldn't make out with him. I've seen your browsing history and I doubt Cory has boobs to satisfy your tastes. Perv."

"Oh, so you are alive." He leaned over, grinning at me. "Hi there. I missed you."

I smiled back. "I see you still believe in me."

"Of course." He flopped down next to me. "Why would they even think you'd be involved?"

I sighed. "Supposedly someone saw me there last night and the police think I'm either a witness or a suspect. They haven't decided which. But they can't say foul play until they find evidence of such. So, I'm simply in custody until I have legal guardians again."

"That's ridiculous. You don't have a car and your parents took theirs. Buses don't run in the middle of the night. How would you even get there?"

I shrugged. Better not to tell Emmett too many blatant lies. I stuck to a few core lies to make my story easier and more consistent. He stayed for a bit, but I wasn't very talkative, and he left to go do his homework. I kept my eyes on the door until it clicked shut, kind of wishing he hadn't gone. Loneliness had already set in. Emmett's presence soothed me somehow. He'd never brought out those feelings before and I pondered the oddness for a bit.

Chapter 2

I woke late the next day. If I had to be under house arrest at least I got to sleep in. Ivy and I were the only ones left in the house. I wandered around in an increasing state of agitation. Something wasn't right. Malevolence hung over Redding like smog. The aura overwhelmed me. I knew the only beings who gave off this kind of power were extremely evil. But such creatures shouldn't be allowed on Earth, so where or who was the miasma coming from?

I paced the living room in thought. Was being put under house arrest just in time for a malevolent being to arrive really a coincidence? Too fishy for my taste. Was I being held for my own safety? Maybe someone thought they were helping since my parents were out of town. But the somebody could have simply told me to lay low. Besides, as an assassin I could handle myself against nearly anything out there. Maybe not a full-grown dragon or a demon lord, but this aura wasn't strong enough to come from one of those.

I stopped in front of the window. Unless . . . I hadn't been locked away for safety's sake. Maybe the whole arrest was to get me out of the way. But if some other magic being had a task involving one of the students, I wasn't likely to interfere. Why would a hawk care what a fox ate unless . . . *shit*.

Emmett.

I raced back to Vanessa's room and jerked my fleece and Hermes shoes out of my bag. Only one person at school meant enough for me to bother interfering. I don't care what job another creature had been given, no one was taking

Emmett from me. They'd have to pick a different target. Without saying anything to Ivy, I tiptoed to the door, opened it, and took off faster than she'd be able to see.

I went to my house first. I would be a fool to go up against an unknown, evil-being unarmed. After strapping a dagger to each thigh, I slipped a vial of poison in my ponytail. I couldn't imagine needing more weapons to get Emmett to safety.

Getting in and out of my house took less than five minutes and in the same amount of time I stood in the shadow of a tree in front of the school. The grounds appeared quiet, but the evil presence was definitely centered here. I gave a low hiss and my teeth lengthened. They aren't fangs. I'm not a vampire. But they are hunting teeth like any other predatory mammal. I sniffed at the air. Emmett and the creature were on the far side of the school and they were together.

I hoped I'd gotten there in time to save him. Depending on what type of creature was hunting him, they could disappear in an instant. I sprinted to the source of the stench and skidded to a stop. I'd arrived in the middle of first lunch. Students sat all around the courtyard enjoying the open campus and the sunshine. On a bench sat Emmett and Buraee. I stalked, largely unseen, across the courtyard. An observant student might have noticed a moving shadow, but I knew if Buraee could see me it would confirm she was magic folk.

"Get away from him," I hissed at her.

She wore surprise first and then a wicked smile spread across her face. "I knew the cops couldn't keep you penned in. But calling them on you was worth a shot. I guess we do this the hard way. I do get why you've been keeping him to yourself. Imagine figuring this out as early as you did."

Buraee stood and pulled a pin out of her hair. A moment later she had the glossy length twisted up and out of her way. "Do you have any idea what you're up against?"

I scowled at her. I didn't, but I wasn't going to admit I lacked knowledge.

"I'm a diablita," she whispered with a giggle. "But with his power I won't be forever. I'll be free and a garden variety imp like yourself will be dead."

I gasped and took a step back. A diablita was a moderately powerful demoness. One who should be locked in service to a demon lord and stuck in the Borderlands. Unless her overlord ordered her out, she shouldn't be moving freely on Earth.

"Well, you're smart enough to know the difference in our abilities. So, why don't you run along and leave my prey to me."

I tried to catch Emmett's eye, but he ignored me, staring at Buraee like she was water in a desert.

"What did you do to Emmett?"

She giggled again. "A little spell to make him easier to handle."

Shit, she'd given him a love potion. Now I'd have to get her to expose her true form in his sight to crack the love spell. And I'd have to get her to release her form before I killed her, or he'd pine for her forever. This extra step made a tricky situation even worse. I hoped I had enough reserves to finish the job. I should. I'd fed well enough for another few days of normal magic use, thanks to Poppy. Besides, when I said I'd do anything for Emmett, I meant *anything*.

I took a step back, planting my feet. I still had no idea why she wanted Emmett, but she'd have to fight me for him. Luckily for me she had no way of knowing I wasn't a "garden variety" imp.

Her eyes narrowed as she watched me take my defensive stance. "Are you stupid? In the middle of the school? And you do understand what you're up against, right?"

"I'm *not* giving you Emmett."

No need to waste breath sparring words with her. Instead I slipped off my fleece. I'd be visible, but cooler and mobile. I couldn't hide without a barrier, anyhow. I also couldn't afford the magic to put one up. All around us students gasped at my sudden appearance.

She gave an exaggerated sigh. "Fine. Give me your best shot."

I'm a quiet hunter. I like to stalk my prey like a tiger, invisible through the grass. On the odd occasion they saw me coming, I found using the same strategy tended to unnerve my opponent. I slid one slippered foot in front of the other toward her. She hissed at me and backed up.

"You seriously want to do this without a barrier? You don't care if everyone here watches you die?"

I gave a little push with my Hermes shoes and slid to a stop behind her, wheeling to face her back. In my hand I gripped the hilt of one of my, now, bloody daggers. Buraee shrieked and wiped at the blood on her cheek. I'd sliced her on my way by. I had to piss her off enough to get her true form out.

I actually wanted to see her other form myself. I'd never seen a fully released diablita. As I said, I'm visually unimpressive. My ears were very pointy now, as were my teeth. Only once had I ever lost control enough to sprout a tail. Yes, imps have tails if we're fully uninhibited. But I've heard the diablita's a flashy critter. There's a reason they aren't let loose on Earth. I mean, aside from the evil, flesh-eating, cousin of the succubus thing.

The teachers tried unsuccessfully to clear the courtyard, which played perfectly into my plan. On my next pass I took her hair off at the scalp. In addition to lots of gasping from the students when I hacked off her ponytail, came raucous laughter. I had to get her to show herself before the police arrived and interrupted. I might not get a second shot at her. I needed to publicly humiliate her to get her to cave. I knew she wouldn't take much more provocation. She already trembled with rage. One humiliation more ought to push her far enough.

I slid in, like lightning, and slashed her dress open in the front. In nothing but her panties her face turned red and the scream she let out caused the windows in the courtyard to shatter. Unprepared for the speed of her released form, she managed to grab me by the neck. She pressed her knee on my chest as she pinned me to the ground.

Relief. I'd gotten her to reveal herself. That's what really mattered. Besides, I could get out of this.

In her released form Buraee's skin shone white as ice and nearly as smooth. As if she didn't already look evil enough, she'd sprouted a set of leathery bat wings. Not your mom's purse, boring brown leather, but blood-red, shiny, patent leather. Her jet-black, soulless eyes glared at me. I knew only one of us would survive this fight.

I ignored the screaming in the courtyard. I'd worry about the humans later. Rolling, I threw my weight against her, grabbing a hold of her arm as she fell off me. Using her momentum and my weight I drove a punch through the center of her upper arm. Since we moved in opposite directions the blow snapped the bone in her arm and she screamed. Twisting, she managed to sink fangs into my arm. Dammit. Were diablita venomous?

I had to end this now. She rolled to her feet and I used my Hermes shoes to give me one last boost. I rammed into her chest, blade first, and gave her neck a quick snap for good measure. Her body flared up in black flames. A moment later I sat on a pile of burnt salt. Good thing I'd had my blades blessed.

My ears perked. Sirens were closing in on the school. I needed to get out of there before I got snared in a mess which required breaking any human laws. This situation already had disaster written all over it. The story ranked no better than tabloid fodder. If my parents and I left town the incident would be like one of those mass UFO sightings. The news would cover the story long enough for the nation to laugh at them and speculate how they doctored the photos. Then the whole thing would be forgotten when something else weird happened—I hoped.

I stood and brushed the salt off my knees. The sirens had stopped. The cops were here. I held my hand out to Emmett.

"We've gotta go."

He shrank back from me as if I might kill him next.

I rolled my eyes. "Emmett. Now. I can't protect you here anymore."

He still didn't respond. Snatching my fleece off the ground, I yanked it on. I grabbed Emmett and swung him onto my shoulders in a Deadman's carry. Putting what I had left into getting us out, I leapt to the roof and dashed off as a swat team or something of the sort burst into the courtyard.

I ran clear across town with Emmett on my shoulders. A mile or so past the far edge of the city I collapsed. I'd managed to shove Emmett off the road and into the woods, before I gave out, completely drained of energy. I doubted my remaining magic would even allow me to use my shoes for a kidnapping. I'd have to do a job the hard way and hope I didn't get caught.

Before I'd regained my breath, Emmett came to his senses. He screamed and scrambled back against a tree. "What the hell are you?"

I rolled to my back panting. "That's my question for you. What the hell are *you*?"

"I'm human. I thought you were, too. But you've got . . ." He blathered as he gestured at his ears. "And . . ." More dithering as he snapped his teeth.

"You're not human." I had to heave to get the words out. Why was I having so much trouble breathing? "Whatever you are, you're strong enough to attract a beast like Buraee and slick enough to hide from hunters like my parents. So fess up. I'm an imp and you are . . .?"

"I'm human."

His yell held anger and fear, but no lie. In which case what was he? And how did he not know he held enough magic to lure in a diablita?

He gave a sob. "You killed her. I don't even know what she . . . that was . . . but you just played with her and *killed* her."

"I had to kill her to save you. I told you she planned to eat you. She was a diablita. A demon in human terms. But she served a much stronger master than herself and I have a feeling you're not done being hunted. You're not safe, unless you stay with me, and if we're taking on a demon lord we're gonna need my parents help."

Emmett rubbed his face and knocked his head back against the tree. "I'm not going to pretend I understood any of what you said except the part about getting your parents' help. So, let's go with that. How are we going to get them? I thought they were away on business. Out of range."

"They are. They're assassinating an alpha werewolf in Siberia. I have an emergency contact method, only for life and death situations. But I think this qualifies. I'll get them back and we can go from there."

"I wanna go home," he whimpered.

I tried to sit up and my head spun. "Emmett, you can't." This had to be so hard on him. Imagine an attack by a diablita being your introduction to the world of magic folk. I patted his ankle and he flinched. "I'm so sorry. But there's lots worse things out there than Buraee. For now, I'm wiped. I'll have to rest and . . . uh . . . take care of myself for a bit tonight. Then I can contact my parents. I'm out of magic."

I took the fact he hadn't run off yet as a positive sign. Good thing, too. I knew I didn't have the energy to chase him down. I lay on the forest floor, letting myself decompress.

Emmett's silence suited me perfectly, though I knew he must have a million questions. The world around me continued to spin, frustrating me. I should have better stamina than this.

"Emmett." My voice came out scratchy. "Something's not right. I'm not recovering normally."

"Could the trouble be your arm? You're bleeding."

My heart sank. "Yup, that's the problem. Buraee bit me. The bitch was poisonous." I heaved a sigh, wincing when the air made my chest burn. "I'm in deep shit without help." I waved my hand at him to get him closer. "Help me sit up. I'll try calling my parents anyway. I'll probably be unconscious afterward. When they get here tell them I've got diablita venom in my arm."

He grabbed me around the shoulders and sat me up. I flopped against his chest and had to fight the urge to sink my teeth into him. He smelled like raw power. *"Oh my God. What are you?"*

I had my face pressed into his shoulder. I'd never felt the urge to prey on a live person until now. I wanted to eat him. To drain every last drop of his blood. To somehow ingest his power. We hit the trunk of the tree with a thud. I'd managed to shove him back, even being nearly out of magic.

"Livy?" Fear made his voice tight.

His alarm didn't affect me like it should have. I was starving, dying really, thanks to the venom. He could fix me. Something deep in my gut knew that to be fact. But how to get at the magic without hurting him? I wasn't so far gone I would harm Emmett. I still had some control over my base instincts.

Without thinking my body reacted. Keeping him pinned I lunged forward and kissed him. I used the kiss to pull his power out. The flow of magic I drew from him satisfied far better than any ration I'd ever had: water for thirst, and no kidnapping needed.

Emmett struggled beneath me and I scrambled backward, horrified. We'd never been involved. I considered Emmett my right arm or my brother or something else unromantic. What would he be thinking right now? I stared closely at him. He'd gone pale and clammy.

"Are you okay?" I asked.

Emmett nodded and gulped. "I . . . uh . . . yeah. You're . . . you're full of surprises today."

"Oh, Emmett. I'm so sorry. I reacted without thinking. I had to have you. I don't know where you got those reserves of power, but thanks. You saved my life."

He scratched his head. "I saved you by letting you kiss me?"

"No. I wasn't kissing you. I mean I was, but not for . . . you know, romantic stuff. I just needed to draw on your magic to replace my own. Sucking the power out seemed a better way to get it, at the time."

"Better than what?"

"Eating you."

He yelped. "You eat people?"

"No, no, no. I've never eaten anyone. But you smelled so strongly of magic and I needed power so badly. The thought of eating you *did* pop into my mind. But that's why . . . you know . . . with your lips and mine."

The recharge I'd gotten from Emmett wouldn't last forever. He probably still had issues, but I needed to move on for now. I dug in my pocket and pulled out a leather pouch marked with a red cross. Pinching a bit of the white powder inside, I held my wounded arm out to Emmett.

"Squeeze the bite until it bleeds for me."

"I can't do that. I'll hurt you."

"Please. I can't pinch my arm and sprinkle the medicine at the same time."

Emmett grabbed my arm and pressed either side of the holes, looking the other way as he did. I tried not to make a sound or flinch even though touching the wound hurt like hell. I refused to make Emmett any more uncomfortable. When two ruby drops appeared, I sprinkled the powder on each.

"Let go," I ordered.

Emmett dropped my arm and enough of the blood retreated into the holes to take the medicine with it. The rest I did by magic, spreading the drug around my own bloodstream. Once the medicine started working, relief enveloped me. I'd still need more help, but keeling over wasn't such an immediate threat.

Time to call my parents. I tugged my necklace out: a blank disk of gold on which I could write a single word. When I finished, the message would show up on Mom's necklace. The chain would shrink into a choker, so she couldn't miss my call. I wrote, *help*. They would travel back by magic and hopefully they wouldn't take too long.

I leaned back against the tree next to Emmett. "They're coming." I took in his pale face. "Are you *really* okay?"

He turned a halfdead look on me. "Did I ever say I was okay? How am I supposed to be okay? You're some sort of creature. You attacked and killed a monster. You drank magic from me. How the hell you carried me in one leap onto the roof and through the city like a human bullet train is beyond me. Truth be told, I'm waiting to wake up and go back to reality."

"Me, too." I shuddered. "Ever since my parents left life has been like a nightmare." I'd gotten so hot. I went to pull my fleece off and stopped. "Wait, you can see me right now?"

"Duh."

I pulled the shirt off. "Well, you just proved you're not human. This shirt is designed to make me look like a shadow to humans. How do you think I got into the school?"

"I don't know why you need confirmation since you

used me like a power smoothie." He rubbed tiredly at his head. "Should I feel like you sucked half my soul out?"

"Ew, *no*." I jerked upright and scooted away. "I'd never touch a soul. I'm sure you feel off because of the drain on your power reserve. I wonder what your source is? You should need—"

"Olivia?"

"Olivia?"

The panicked voices belonged to my mom and dad.

"We're in the trees." I waved my good arm. The one with the bite throbbed too much. My parents crashed through the brush and then I was in my mother's arms. She petted my hair, squeezing me a little too hard.

"What happened? Why aren't you two at school?" She glanced at Emmett before eyeing me seriously. "You know what your father and I had to do to get back here like this . . . right?"

"It's fine. You can speak freely. Poor Emmett got one hell of an introduction already. He got attacked by a diablita."

"A diablita?" my dad asked, glancing around in alarm. "Why? Where is she?"

"Everything's fine. I took her out. But we're gonna have to move. The situation happened in the middle of school and I only have so much power. I had to pick between killing her or making a barrier. I chose to kill her. So, half the school saw the fight. I got bit."

I held out my arm which my mom immediately started working on. "I'm not sure why she targeted him. It's not like Buraee and I sat down for girl talk before we tried to kill each other. But she said she was surprised I'd found him so early and she didn't blame me for keeping him to myself. He swears he's human, but he's loaded with magic."

"Did she bite him, too?"

"No, but she did put a love spell on him. Don't worry, I got her to release her form before I killed her. Only trashy news outlets are going to believe anyone from the school. Wow, a diablita's one hell of a beast, red wings and everything."

My dad beamed and ruffled my hair. "That's my girl. Taking down a demon before you're full grown and without a partner even."

"Why does poor Emmett look so pale?" Mom asked. "Is he in shock?"

Heat crept across my cheeks. "I . . . uh . . . I kinda drained him." Both my parent's gazes snapped down on me and I blushed even harder. "I used nearly all my magic and he . . . well . . . I couldn't help it. He smelled so good and he saved me. Because of him I'm not passed out or worse right now."

My dad crouched in front of Emmett who shied away from him. "You really had no idea you carried magic?"

Emmett shook his head and pressed back against the tree. "What are you?"

"An imp, like Livy." Dad reached out a hand for Emmett's forehead and Emmett dodged. He must have been really scared still. My parents were Emmett's other set, too. "Don't worry, Emmett. I'm going to try and get a read on what you are. Each creature has a separate power signature and there isn't much living on land I haven't met. A quick touch and we'll know."

Emmett nodded silently and sat still as Dad laid a hand on his head.

Dad frowned for a moment before letting out a deep breath. "Well, no wonder. You're gonna be on the top of everyone's collection list. You're human, but you're what they call a source. A special type of human who has an opening in their being allowing them to freely channel magic. The good news is no one is going to kill you, you're far too valuable. The bad news is every magic being between here and kingdom come is going to be after you."

Now my curiosity was piqued. "Why?"

"For the same reason you already figured out." Dad's expression urged me to keep up. "He's the magical equivalent of a battery, a magical bank account which never runs out. With him you'll never need to send anyone to the Goblin Kingdom again. No need to work to earn your own magic, ever. And the same applies to any type of magic folk lucky enough to have him."

My eyes grew wider, until they almost fell right out of the sockets. "Well, that certainly explains a lot. But how come we didn't know sooner? We could have protected him better."

Dad helped Emmett to his feet. "These things usually ramp up during puberty like—"

"Gross, Dad. Don't say puberty. I feel dirty when you say weird words about growing up and crap."

He laughed at me. "Okay. Will adolescence work?"

I nodded.

"Anyway. Just like everything else in your body revs up and matures, so does the channel for the magic. Before, the connection was like a leaky faucet: drip, drip, drip. Now the flow is like a hose on full, but by the time he's grown, who knows; a stream, a river? The magnitude depends on his potential. But Emmett being a source does explain why you were drawn to him as a little kid. You would have been unconsciously aware of the leak."

"So, I've been leaching magic off him for years," I shrieked. "I'm a parasite?"

"No, no," Mom soothed. "The relationship between a magic being and a source is reciprocal. You taking the excess energy keeps him balanced. Such natural partnerships are common. For example, those little birds that ride around on the back of a rhino. The bird feeds on parasites which doesn't hurt the rhino, it actually helps him. In return the bird gets food and protection. You guys are natural allies."

Mom's explanation comforted me, especially about sucking Emmett dry, but something still nagged at me. "Then, will he be hunted for this power for the rest of his life?"

My mom frowned and slid a glance at my dad. One of those looks which said something I couldn't pick up on. I hated being deliberately left out.

"Probably not," he answered. "There are ways to create a permanent link between partners. But I'm not really familiar with them. Human sources are quite rare. I've only ever met one other." He gave Emmett a sad smile. "Emmett, I'm really sorry. I think you would be safest if you came and lived with us for a while. At least until we figure out how you bond with a magic being. Then you will need to choose a partner, but we can advise you there, as well."

"What about my parents?" Emmett choked out.

"We'll go back to your house now and we'll explain things to them. But if something nasty comes looking for you again. Not only will you be safer where the three of us can protect you, but at home your parents would be in danger. They're human and defenseless, not to mention disposable to a lot of creatures."

Chapter 3

Mom and Dad led us back through the trees to a sedan parked beside the road. I'd never seen the car before and I didn't ask. We rode in silence back to Emmett's house, tension taking up all the spare room and spilling onto our laps.

His mother answered the door in a panic. I got an immediate kick of guilt. I'd been left in her custody and then run off. I knew the school would have called about Emmett being missing. She was smart enough to connect the dots and worry herself. She grabbed us both and hugged us, fury and relief in each squeeze.

Dad gently pushed her inside. "Ivy, we need to talk. Something unfortunate has come up."

She dropped Emmett and I, chewing her tongue for a moment before letting loose a tirade. She ranted about wild stories of kidnapping from the school and me being a knife-wielding psycho who leapt off with Emmett.

Dad pressed Ivy into a chair and knelt in front of her. He stared into her eyes as if trying to hypnotize her. "They weren't wild stories, Ivy. Everything you heard is true, except one fact. Livy wasn't kidnapping Emmett. She was saving him."

Ivy shook her head. "But there's no way those stories are true. How could Livy pick up Emmett and leap onto the roof?"

"Magic."

"Isn't real . . ." she added hesitantly.

Dad shook his head. "Come on, Ivy. I'm trying to do this the easy way. Work with me here." He stared harder at her, definitely using magic on her mind, but she resisted.

She'd broken out in a sweat. "None of this can be real. They said Livy killed a devil-looking woman and a student had turned into the monster. Like a possession. A devil."

"A demon, not a devil," Dad corrected, giving Ivy a pointed look as if waiting for her to catch on.

Still Ivy shook her head. "Doesn't matter, neither is real. What am I supposed to think of all this?"

"Okay then." Dad sighed. "I'll show you. Before I do, I need you to understand Emmett is in grave danger. But we're going to protect him."

Dad nodded at Mom and I and all three of us let our appearances go. Mom and I let our teeth and ears get pointy. Following a popping noise, Dad's tail swished behind him. Ivy covered her mouth on a scream and even Emmett startled a little.

He looked up at me. "Do you have a tail, too?"

"Yeah," I said, without taking my eyes off his mom. "But like Buraee's wings and stuff we don't let them out unless were really pissed, or off our guard. He's just proving a point."

"How is Emmett in danger?" Ivy asked, through her hand.

Dad explained, but I doubted she really understood. Emmett at least got the danger aspect. He'd seen Buraee in person. When Dad finished Ivy had a different look of fear in her eyes.

"How are the three of you supposed to keep him safe against monsters?"

"We're specially trained hunters," Mom said. "We'll be the best shot he has currently."

Ivy blinked at tears. "How far are you going to go and when can he come home again?"

"We'll bring him home as soon as his situation is settled. How long that will take, I don't know," Dad answered honestly. "As for where we're going, it's best for you not to know. I'd hate to find you being used to get to Emmett. Making a human spill the truth is easy and harmless. If you know nothing, you ought to be left alone."

"My boy." Ivy sobbed.

My mom hugged her. "I understand. We'll take good care of him. We have untraceable spells on our phones. He can call as often as you want."

"Does this mean I'm getting out of school?" Emmett smiled, a little.

Both mothers scowled at him.

"Absolutely not," my mom scolded. "I'll homeschool you and Livy until we're settled and can enroll you somewhere."

"Bummer." Emmett slumped against the couch again.

Ivy asked more questions as Emmett and I went upstairs to gather a few bags of stuff. We'd summon the rest by magic after we got settled. Emmett plopped on the end of his bed and looked at his room morosely.

"Think of our trip as an adventure," I said sitting next to him. But the brightness of my voice came off as fake even to my ears.

"Yeah . . . right."

I reached over and gave his hand a squeeze and was rewarded with absolute tension on his part. I let my arm drop. "Are you stiff because you're leaving, because I'm an imp, or because I kissed you?"

"Yes. All of them."

"I'm sorry. For everything. I won't take your power from here on out. I had no idea what was going on and like I said, you saved me. So, I'm grateful. And if the kiss made you uncomfortable, I'm sorry for that, too. I wasn't starting anything . . . I mean, I don't feel . . . I mean, you don't have to—"

Emmett held up a hand. "You can stop. I get it, but I need some time to sort my feelings."

"I'm still me." I tried to reassure him. "We're still us. We can be the same as always."

I shuddered at the dark glare Emmett gave me. "No. We can't. I have to get to know you all over again. I mean, you're not even human. You're always going on about how plain and boring you are and then you turn around and kick some demon chick's ass. Which, if I hadn't been scared shitless, should have been hot. But you're not supposed to be hot. No offense. You're like my sister. Then you pull that kiss. To top everything off I'm now some honorary part of your family and we're moving."

He broke off, panting with agitation. "Our life is *not* the same. It can *never* be the same. You're nothing like I thought you were. Deep down I know even though you're actually an imp, you always have been one. So . . . yeah, you're the same as you were . . . but everything *feels* like it's changing so fast and I . . ." He shrugged and ran a hand across his head, ruffling his light brown hair. "I don't know. You're still my best friend, but I need some time to come to terms with this new you. Then maybe I'll relax."

I shuffled next door to get my stuff in silence. I didn't know what to say. He had a point. I felt some of those same feelings myself. I'd always assumed he was nothing more than Emmett, yet he turned out to be some sort of source and a target for collection. I imagined the difference must be even more staggering from his side.

I took the assignment shell and kept it out. The shell had grown warm, meaning it had a message to deliver. But my parents were home now, so I'd let them worry about the incoming assignment. Downstairs, I handed the shell to my mom. She asked the device for the information and nearly dropped it when the paper came out blue.

"What does blue mean?" I asked.

"A job, but not an assassination. It's bodyguard duty and it's for you." She handed the paper to me.

"Huh? We do that, too?"

"We do pretty much whatever we're assigned," Dad said.

I read the paper and squeaked involuntarily. "Emmett. The Fairy Synod knows about him?"

"Evidently," Dad said shortly. "I'm not sure I like this. Normally high-profile guard duty is assigned to adults. Not to mention pairs. I'm surprised the assignment didn't come in for your mother and I. But don't worry, we'll provide you backup."

He turned on Emmett. "The Fairy Synod is our Central Borderland's governing body, headed by the Lord High Governor. They have acknowledged your existence and gifts, as well as your dangerous situation by assigning you a personal bodyguard. Livy will be with you twenty-four hours a day until you are appropriately placed, or a new guard is assigned. For your own safety you are not to ditch her or us at any time. A determined hunter can take you in a matter of seconds if you wander off. There are places and contracts from which even the Synod can't get you back."

Emmett shuddered and nodded, his face pale.

Dad slapped his shoulder. "All right, kids. Warnings are through, we need to get on the road. You two caused quite the commotion. We need to get you both someplace quieter."

We gave Emmett and his mom a few minutes to say goodbye. His dad wouldn't come home for a couple hours yet and my dad didn't want to risk waiting, so he'd have to call later. I didn't want to imagine how that conversation would go. Emmett's dad didn't even get the luxury of seeing my dad's tail. He'd have to believe everything Ivy told him on blind faith.

As Emmett's guard, I waited right outside the front door with it cracked to see him and his mom, but not overhear.

They deserved that much privacy at least. He came out rubbing at his face and I knew better than to ask if he was crying. I fell into step behind him and instead of saying anything I simply put my hand between his shoulder blades.

We got into the back of my parents' stolen car. Emmett either didn't catch this or didn't care, climbing in and putting his forehead against the window to stare blankly outside. I left him alone. When he was ready to talk, he would. Emmett had always been a slow thinker, processing everything before opening his mouth.

The car slid down the road, seemingly unnoticed by other traffic but far faster than a normal car would be able to go. In just under an hour we crossed the state line. But my parents didn't stop there. The afternoon turned into evening as the countryside flew by. As dusk started to turn dark we pulled into a hotel parking lot. Nothing fancy, an average motor inn.

I yawned and stretched. "Where are we?"

"Middle America," Dad said. "But I don't want either of you to let anything slip. If you didn't read road signs, so much the better. Your mother booked us adjoining rooms. You two are in one, but we'll be a doorway away if you need us."

I caught my dad's sleeve and pulled him down, so I could whisper in his ear. "Can we talk alone for a minute?"

My dad gave Mom one of their private hand signals and pulled me a little way off from the car. "What's up Livy?"

"What am I up against, really?"

Dad's eyes shifted to the side and I clicked my tongue.

I crossed my arms and glared at him. "Don't lie, that doesn't help Emmett or I. And don't say you don't know at least some of what's going on because I know Mom texted most of the way here."

His ears got pointy in agitation. "The diablita you took down was a minion of Zaemon."

"The demon lord? What could he want with Emmett? Zaemon can manufacture his own magic."

"Prestige? To keep Emmett out of the hands of someone else? Who knows. He didn't issue a press release of his plans. We managed to trace Buraee to him." My father sighed and laid a heavy hand on my shoulder. "You already know the types of creatures a demon lord keeps in his retinue. Any one of those nightmares could be sent out next. The worse Zaemon wants him, the nastier the creatures will be. Beyond hired hunters, any and everything else might be after him."

I gulped, sweat beading out on my forehead. "So how do I keep him safe?"

"Kill only those who won't back off. But be ready for anything. Feed as often as you need. Your mom and I will watch him for you when you need to go out. There's no shame in asking for our help. In our whole partnership, your mom and I have only done a handful of solo missions. You know we work best in pairs. I'm sorry we haven't arranged a partner for you. We wanted to wait and let you pick later since they usually end up as—"

"Yeah, yeah."

I brushed off the rest. I didn't want this conversation to turn into some awkward father-daughter "chat". Due to the closeness of a partnership between assassins they tended to be lifelong and exclusive. Usually meaning the human equivalent of marriage. The trust between a pairing had to be implicit since both lives frequently depended on it. Such closeness made bringing an outside spouse in very difficult, though some pulled it off, usually siblings.

I had no brother or sister, so when I reached adulthood, nineteen for magic folk, my parents would start setting up interviews and trial missions until I decided on a partner. The freedom to choose was a kind gesture on their part. Most assassins started taking jobs in their mid-teens and plenty of parents arranged their teammate for them. The kids had no choice but to deal with whoever their parents selected. Not that tons of assassins exist, even in the Borderlands, hence the need for a setup. Parents would naturally want the pick of the limited choices.

My parents had carefully made sure none of my missions had been deadly enough to need a partner so far. But Emmett and I would have been much safer if I had faced the diablita in a pair. I probably wouldn't have been bitten and Buraee only qualified as a minion. In which case, what bad boys might be sent out next?

Dad hugged me. "We'll get through this."

I nodded and whispered my next question into his chest.

"Huh? I didn't catch that."

My face flamed as I backed away, so he could hear. "I'm not going to get in trouble for staying alone with a boy?" I muttered. "I know that's against the rules."

He shifted uncomfortably. "Do you want the adult answer or the dad answer?"

"Which is the least likely to embarrass us both?"

"Neither. I'll give you the adult answer since the situation is what it is. Emmett's a good boy. Not to mention a source. If you two kids . . . you know . . . Well, with him you wouldn't need to kidnap, and you could both get nice safe human jobs and live a much less dangerous life than you were brought up for. Your mom and I . . . don't mind."

My dad had turned a shade of red a boiled lobster would be proud of, and I wanted to sink into the concrete. "So, this is match making?"

"No, no, no." Dad stared at a pothole in the parking lot. "As a single bodyguard, you have to stay with him at all times. Unless you wanted him to sleep with me and you can room with your mom. But we thought that would be weird for everyone."

"Yes, hoping we end up together isn't weird at all, *Dad.*"

"No, you're still misunderstanding, Livy. We're not *hoping* for anything, but we wouldn't oppose a relationship, if it happened. Sweetie, you're always free to choose. We'll help find appropriate partners because we have the connections to find singleton assassins in your age group, but . . ." He looked helplessly at me. "I made this worse, didn't I? Can I give the dad answer instead?"

"I'm pretty sure the damage is irreparable, but go ahead. What the hell?"

He started with an apologetic smile. "I meant to say: of course, this isn't okay with us, but you have no partner and your orders are to stay with him. Any sign of hanky-panky and we'll be forced to tie Emmett to a chair for the night. There, was that better?"

I gave my dad a grudging laugh. "Until you said 'hanky-panky'. You have a special talent for making terms like that seem extra dirty. Just quit trying to be cute."

He eyed me for a second. "Fine. If I catch you fondling one another you won't like the punishment."

"Oh my God, *Dad*." I stalked off toward my room leaving him laughing behind me.

"Livy honey, don't ask questions if you don't want to hear the answers," he called after me.

"The original question was yes or no," I yelled back.

I let the door to the room slam on his laughter. Emmett looked up from one of the two double beds. "Your mom said I should sleep further from the window." He looked at the door. "What's so funny? I could use a good laugh."

"Don't ask. No laugh is worth repeating what I had to listen to. I promise." I laid back on the other bed and gave a sigh which caught in my throat.

"Are you okay, Livy? I mean is your bite hurting you?"

"I feel better. Thanks. I'm like you. I've got a lot on my mind."

"Wanna talk about it?"

"Nope. How about you?"

"Nope."

Silence fell over us. In the next room my parents were watching TV. I sighed and got up to go tap on the connecting door. I wanted a kidnapping job. I needed more magic if I expected to excel at being a bodyguard. Mom gave me a name and address and promised to come take my place at three AM to let me go. Emmett never even looked in my direction.

During all of this I still hadn't told him how I replenished my magic. I thought I'd come to terms with what I was and what I did, but I was wrong. The idea of telling those details to my best friend filled me with shame. I sighed into my pillow and turned my back on him. Luckily, exhaustion still rode me hard and sleep came quickly.

Chapter 4

Fatigue pulled at me so badly during my kidnapping I swear I made enough noise to wake the dead. But somehow, I got the eight-year-old boy off to the goblin kingdom without a hitch. I half expected to run across Buraee waiting on the kid's dark lawn as I crept back out the window. But the night remained cool and empty.

Tapping my mom on the shoulder I took her spot in my bed, grateful she'd kept it warm for me. Sleep nearly had me when Emmett's muffled voice carried across the room.

"Where'd you go?"

I swallowed on the choking feeling in my throat. "You don't want to know."

"Is it gross?"

"Emmett, go back to sleep."

"I can't sleep. So, is it gross?"

Damn it. He'd reached the point of needing to talk in the middle of the night. I sighed to let him know he'd roused an unwilling conversational partner. My bed creaked as he climbed in.

"This way we can talk quieter. I don't want to keep your parents up."

"But it's okay to keep me up?" I didn't even bother trying to sound friendly. The numbers on the clock glared 4:12 at me. I just wanted sleep.

"You were already up. Was it some imp thing?"

"Yeah. Emmett, please don't ask anymore."

Next to me, he tensed. "It's not dangerous, is it?"

"No." I hurried to reassure him. "Mom and Dad wouldn't have slept through anything serious. You're fine. I had to take care of some . . . personal needs."

"Oh." The tension hadn't left his body. "I want to know if I'm in danger. I don't like the idea of you out there fighting things for me without at least knowing what you're doing. Even if all I can do in return is thank you." His body trembled.

I rolled so I faced him. "How scared are you? Really?"

Emmett opened his mouth and snapped it shut as tears started rolling.

I sighed and wrapped my arms around him, patting the back of his head. "You're safe here."

"I worry about you, too." He sniffled. "What if I hadn't fed you the extra power? Would you have died? If Buraee had known more about you, would the fight have gone down in your favor? She seemed surprised at your skill."

I gave him another squeeze. "Don't worry about me. I've been raised for this. Assassination will be my profession, like my parents. I've been handling weapons since I was five. I've been hand fighting since three. Not to mention, imps . . . well, we're technically classified as malevolent magic folk. Mostly meaning we're predatory. A little worse than our closest relatives, the fairies. Fairies aren't very nice either, but they're more tricksters who prefer mean pranks. Imps pretty much don't care who gets hurt."

"Really?"

"Really. We usually have a few family or friends we care for, and those get our full protection. That's why I fought a she-demon for you." I squeezed his arm. "You, your parents and my parents are the only beings on the planet I'd go to such trouble for. I can't even guarantee I'd save your sister. But I would easily have ignored the incident if Buraee had taken any other kid at the school."

"Really?"

"You sound like a broken record. Yes." I hung my head. "You probably think I'm awful."

He shrugged. "Not really. Plenty of humans can't even manage that much caring. But I guess the imp-thing does explain a lot. I wondered why you never really had any other friends. I guess it's not in your nature."

I nodded and yawned. "Can we be done, please?"

Emmett gave a funny little squirm.

"What?" I snapped.

"I . . . may I stay in your bed?"

"Why?" Sleep was dragging me under.

"You're going to think I'm a complete pansy, but . . . I'm scared."

I nodded—I think. With or without my permission, Emmett stayed, and I woke in the morning shivering with only the sheet over me. I yanked the covers back.

"Dang it, Emmett. Stop hogging."

He didn't even open his eyes, but he did yank back on the sheets. I'd been perched on the tiny strip of mattress he'd left me. With no place to get leverage, I lost my balance and went toppling forward onto Emmett's chest. Teasingly he wrapped his arms and legs around me pinning me.

Once upon a time I would have played along as the weaker "girl". But not this morning. Along with the hug came a stiff and unpleasant surprise. I pinched the flesh between his thumb and his first finger at the pressure point. He yelped and let go of me and I scrambled back with a shriek.

"What the hell? I thought you were lying about morning wood! Is today special or does that really happen every morning?"

Emmett sat bolt upright, his face more shades of red than a sunset. To make things worse my parents burst in, looking panicked.

"What is it?" my dad yelled. "Who's attacking?"

"No one," I shrieked back at him. "I had a nightmare."
In all respects. I muttered to myself.

"You're okay then?" my mother asked, breathless as she came down off her adrenaline high.

"What a noisy bunch."

All four of us looked for the unfamiliar voice. My parents openly held weapons. The speaker turned out to be a young man, lounging on the top of the TV cabinet. How he'd gotten in the room past us all and to the top of the tall cabinet was beyond me.

"You won't be harmed if you give up and leave," I challenged.

He barked a sarcastic laugh. "So, you're Olivia Skotadi. Looks like I get double duty." Leaping lightly off his perch, he landed silently.

"Who are you?" I snapped. "Never mind. I don't care. Just go."

He smiled and held a slip of paper out at me. I wanted to slap the smirk off his face. He oozed cocky, his dark brown eyes glittering a challenge. I snatched the paper and unfolded an official message from the Synod matching mine. The Synod had arbitrarily assigned me a partner.

The young man jammed his hands in his pockets and shot me a condescending smile. "Don't worry, sweetheart. I'm talented enough to guard you both."

"This partnership isn't binding, is it?" I thrust the note at my dad. "We can get someone else, right?"

My dad scratched at his head, confused and a little dismayed. "Not really. Not without reasonable grounds."

"How about the fact he's completely aggravating?"

The young man made a mocking pouty face at me. "Sure thing, Catty. 'Cause the Synod has nothing better to do than field hissy fits from moody teenage girls."

Emmett openly glared at the strange man.

But the man ignored his scowl, holding out a hand to shake. "Nice to meet you. I'm Talon Puck. Your bodyguard." He made a face in my direction. "You can finally relax and know you're safe with me."

"What are you?"

Emmett eyed Talon suspiciously as if he might sprout tentacles. Which, in my opinion would fit his personality perfectly.

"Is your hair naturally blue?"

"I'm a toyol. And no, I just happen to like this color."

Emmett stared blankly at Talon so I took the opportunity to fill him in. "No one on the fairy family tree is very altruistic. Fairies are the nicest if you want to call them that. Imps come next and toyol are even worse. Thief and assassin, or at least he's both since he's here." I stuck my tongue out at him.

"This from the kidnapper," Talon threw back. "Don't pretend your hands are clean."

"Kidnapper?" Emmett stared at me with wide eyes. "What's he talking about?"

Talon cackled gleefully. "Are you hiding from him? And I was told you were selected for your merit and the fact he's your childhood friend. Yet he doesn't know something so fundamental to being an imp?"

I lunged for Talon, but he deftly blocked. I skidded past him losing the opportunity to silence him. He focused on Emmett.

"Imps kidnap unwanted children and send them to the Goblin Kingdom. The ones who don't make it back are eaten."

Emmett shook his head. "She wouldn't."

Talon shrugged. "She has to. Kidnapping is how she gains back the magic she uses. If she doesn't, she'll die. I have to steal for the same reason. I owe the Synod an eighty-five percent cut. In return, I'm granted magic rations. Us doing these things doesn't bother you, does it?" He thrust his chin out challengingly at Emmett. "After all, you humans are such a gentle and caring lot."

My dad clapped his hands. "All right children enough bickering. Talon, if you're going to be inflammatory I will petition the Synod. Emmett, I'm sorry we didn't lay details out for you. I figured you'd been through enough. We do kidnap children, but only the ones whose siblings wish them away. And the vast majority return in short order. The sibling who did the wishing simply has to have a change of heart and want them back. None of those kids are harmed."

Emmett gasped. "So, then it really was you who took Poppy?" Betrayal glinted in his eyes.

"I had to," I wailed. "I have to have magic."

Talon stretched and left his hands behind his head. "Actually, given your history together her going out last night surprised me. I thought for sure she'd be drawing from the source."

"He's not *the source*, he's Emmett," I growled at Talon. "He's my friend and my charge. I'm not taking advantage of him."

"Silence." My dad's irritation evident in the slight hiss to his words. "I will *not* tolerate constant bickering."

Talon crossed his arms. "So, leave." His tone with my dad was snarky and my father's eyebrow twitched a warning. "The source . . . Emmett, has two guards. We're good." Talon finished with a smug, superior expression on his face.

My father grabbed the neck of Talon's T-shirt and jerked him close. "Listen up, brat. I know your father, and I know you just reached your majority."

So, Talon was nineteen.

"But to me you're a kid. You *will* be respectful. You will also remember, regardless of her assignment, Olivia's still a minor, as is Emmett. They will stay with parents and they will complete classwork either at home or in a school. This is a working family. You're the guest here. I won't warn you again. Can you behave?"

Talon wiggled free and to my surprise he had turned bright pink with a furious blush. "Yes, sir," he mumbled.

"That's better."

Dad sighed and took the T-shirt my mom held out for him, pulling it on. The fact my dad had been in his boxers the whole time, hit me and I blushed, looking away. Seeing my dad in his underwear seemed wrong. But then again, if our little commotion had been a real emergency what did full clothing really matter?

"There's a continental breakfast in the lobby if you guys are hungry," my mom said. "I'm going to wander over there with your father, since everything is all right." She heaved a sigh. "I desperately need coffee."

My parents disappeared, leaving us alone. Emmett and I were both glaring at Talon, though he didn't act bothered in the least. I stalked over and started rummaging through my bag, looking for clean clothes. I wanted a shower and I needed the private time to think of a reason good enough to get rid of Talon.

Suddenly a hand covered a large portion of my backside. I grabbed the offending arm and threw Talon over my hip and onto his back on the floor. I had meant to give him a blow to knock him out, but he twisted, threw his weight into the roll and sat on top of me. Fury surged through me. He used his knees to keep my hands at my sides, but I managed to get one loose enough to dig my nails into his thigh. When he squirmed, I got the other hand free and took a sucker punch to his goods. I don't usually go so low, but in his case, I'd make an exception. The world would be a better place if he never reproduced.

He flopped off and gave me a grimacing smile. "You pass."

"What's that supposed to mean?"

"I had my doubts, but I think you'll be able to hold your own."

I turned my back on him and stomped into the bathroom. I refused to even hold further conversation with him. I hadn't even been in the shower five minutes when someone knocked at the door.

"Is it too much to ask for a peaceful shower?" I barked.

"Livy? Can I come in a minute or would it be too weird?"

At least the voice belonged to Emmett. I checked the shower curtain. Good enough. "You won't peek, right?"

"After what I've seen you do the last two days? I wouldn't dare." He came in and shut the door behind him. "Did you really? You know . . . last night?"

I dropped my head. So much for peace. "Yeah. I need all the power I can get if I'm gonna keep you safe."

"You don't have to, you know. You . . . uh . . . you could always take magic from me."

"Only if you're really *that* uncomfortable with my living as usual. Your magic won't be around forever. I'm going to have to keep going as I've always done. I'm okay with my role. Can you be okay, too?"

He shifted and sighed. "I guess."

"You're taking this all really well. Are you sure you're okay?"

"I'm sure I don't really have a choice. You know me, I manage."

I scrubbed my scalp. "I know."

I barely had the soap out of my hair when a scuffle broke out in the bathroom followed by a thud and Emmett's yelp. Poking my head out of the shower I scowled. Talon had come in, too, taken a towel and used it to pin Emmett's arms. Then he'd further pinned Emmett to the wall with his weight. At several inches taller, and having far more muscle, Talon had no trouble keeping Emmett there.

"Get out," I yelled at Talon.

"Oh? Am I interrupting?"

"Yes."

"Oh, really?" His voice implied we'd been doing more than having a conversation. He ran his eyes down the shower curtain covering my body. "I can scrub those hard to reach spots for you."

"I'm fine. The dirtiest thing in here is you."

"Then should I get in and you can scrub me?"

"Are you seriously this sleazy?" Talon hadn't covered Emmett's mouth and he let the sarcasm lash.

"No. But I seriously enjoy getting a rise out of you both and you guys make it way too easy." He pulled a gun out of who knows where, since he was wearing a T-shirt with no pockets and basketball shorts with no pockets. "Your dad wants us to teach Squishy here to shoot, and arm him. Oh, and we're bringing lunch back when we come. I vote for Pho."

I rolled my eyes. "I think anything except Wonder Bread and bologna is gonna be hard to get around here. But we can see. Now you boys get out and let me finish in private."

"Sure, kitten. But hurry up. I hate to wait."

"First I'm catty, and now I'm a kitten?"

"Yeah, you're a lot cuter when your claws are in."

I threw the bar of soap at his head and he left taking Emmett with him.

A moment later he came back. "You left these on the bed out there." My clothes were being held aloft, above the curtain rod.

"Thanks. Please leave them by the sink."

"Ah, ah, ah. I really wanted to make you come out into the room in your towel. But I'm taking the high road. What do I get for my kindness?"

"I won't kill you in your sleep."

"That hurts. I was trying to be nice."

"So was I. If I offed you in your sleep, you wouldn't see it coming."

"You know, we're partners for the foreseeable future. You might try being nicer to me."

"Good advice. Try it yourself." I stuck my hand out of the curtain. "Towel, please. And then get out so I can get dressed."

A towel landed in my hand and the door clicked closed. I peeked out. I'd fully expected him to be there, giving me an incentive grin, but the bathroom stood empty. I toweled off, dressed and found the boys watching TV on the foot of one of the beds. I didn't recognize the channel and I nearly fell over when the newscaster folded a set of caramel-colored wings behind himself.

"*Holy Crap.* What are you watching?"

"I brought a connection to Borderland Satellite. This is the morning news." Talon wrinkled his nose at me. "You've really never watched? Have you ever been to the Borderlands?"

"Travel between plains is too difficult and uses a lot of magic. Not to mention humans to kidnap are non-existent there. So, no, going to the Borderlands is not a luxury I've had. I've never toured Europe or anything here either. I'm a normal person."

"Wait. What are the Borderlands?" Emmett asked, confused.

"All magic folk originate from there," Talon explained. "The Borderlands sit outside the Earthly Plain. I can't really explain it any better." He stood and grabbed a bag off the floor. "Are we ready?"

He pointed us out the door. Like most motor inns our room opened straight to the parking lot. I wrinkled my nose as I briefly scanned the lot for trouble and our vehicle. Whichever car smelled the worst probably belonged to Talon.

"Have you been to the Borderlands?" I asked, my curiosity piqued. I shut the hotel room door behind me and made sure the *do not disturb* sign faced out.

"I lived there most of my life. My dad got lucky and it's not really necessary for him—"

"Wait, how does he manage living away from Earth?" I interrupted. "He's a toyol right?"

"Shh . . ." Talon's face had drawn tight.

I fell silent at once and grabbed Emmett's arm pulling him next to me. Talon tensed and leapt into the air. His leap cleared the tops of the cars around him because he wore Hermes shoes, like me. But his were far more expensive than mine. His had been enchanted to look like he had on regular sneakers.

Talon collided with someone midair and they both fell to the ground. I pressed Emmett back into the wall, shielding him with my own body. Talon landed with his knife pressed to the throat of a harpy, her hair and feathers mixed together and her hawk-like eyes flashing.

"You were just passing through, right, pretty bird?" Talon hissed at her.

He'd jumped with incredible grace. I had to admit, at least to myself, he moved with the fluidity and power required of a skilled fighter. He'd also been telling the truth. Everything seemingly mean he'd said had been teasing. His words to this woman were nicer than most of what he said to Emmett and I, but now his voice carried cruelty and deadly intent. This man should never be taken lightly.

Talon gave her a twisted smile. "This is a warning. He's spoken for by the Synod. Pass that around to the rest of the opportunists. I know they're watching you to see how well he's guarded." He pressed the dagger deeper, until a thin pink line appeared, and red drops kissed the edge of the blade. "I'll let you go, but if I see your face around the source again, I'll hack your pretty little head from its perch. Follow?"

The harpy screeched, and Talon let her go. A puff of smoke and a brown hawk took off from the parking lot and soared straight for the horizon. He brushed his knees off and started cleaning his blade.

I stood rooted to my spot. The attack had been beautiful to watch. Talon oozed deadly power. My heart gave a strange throb. And here I thought I'd been attracted to Cory, but I'd been drawn in by a pretty face. Talon on the other hand had decent looks and skills I valued. My heart gave another flutter of a far more real attraction and I squashed it. I'd never met a being outside my family or the Keeler's worthy of acknowledging. Too bad his personality sucked, or I might have had to change my mind.

Talon slipped his knife into its hidden sheath at his back and glanced over at me with a smirk. "Do you two need a few minutes?"

"Huh? Why?"

He raised an eyebrow and I took stock of my position. I'd been so focused on Talon I'd ended up pressed along Emmett's body in a far more provocative than protective manner. I jumped away from him, beyond humiliated. Poor Emmett. I'd have to try and find a private moment to apologize properly.

Chapter 5

Face burning, I followed Talon to a very plain, white sedan. I don't know why but with his personality I expected a speed bike or a sporty roadster or something else flashy. Emmett walked beside me, his face very red, making me feel worse.

Both guys insisted I take the front seat. In Emmett's case the gesture was chivalry. I suspected Talon was only looking for an opportunity to tease me. Strangely he said nothing. He flipped on the stereo and again surprised me. He'd turned on soothing, hypnotic trance music. The road slid by to a soft beat which quickly put me in a relaxed state.

"Do you like the song?" Talon asked.

"Yes. What is it?"

"Borderland Electronica. The frequency has a soporific effect on magic folk which automatically puts you in a happy place. I can load some on your computer if you'd like."

"Sure." I shot him a suspicious glare. "What's the catch?"

He laughed. "No catch. Am I not allowed to be nice?"

"I didn't think you were capable is all."

Talon fell silent and we drove through miles upon empty miles of corn and soy fields before he finally pulled off. "We'll practice here."

I couldn't imagine how anyone would ever know or care. We could probably go at least ten miles in every direction without seeing a human. Talon bustled around setting up a target and Emmett tugged at my sleeve.

"Is this necessary? I really hate guns."

"Shooting is the fastest thing to teach you. As a rule, it's not polite to fight with a gun between magic beings. We tend to use our given talents and blades if necessary. Guns are fighting dirty. Not that we don't cheat when the stakes are high enough. But for those of us who make a living with our fighting skills we've been trained since birth. Close-range fighting would take too long for you to learn.

"Still, we can't leave you unarmed. What if something were to happen to Talon and I, or what if there's too many attackers? What Talon did today will scare off most of the little fish but the big boys won't be scared off yet. Do you really want to be defenseless?"

"Yeah, but guns seem so . . . I don't know, un-storybookish, while everything else seems straight out of legends and fairy tales. Will plain old bullets really kill a monster like Buraee?"

"Uh, yeah, Emmett. When you put a projectile into a living creature it dies."

"Unless I'm a bad shot and I just piss a monster off," he muttered.

"Then you'd better be a good shot."

Talon waved Emmett over. I stayed back and kept a lookout as he showed Emmett how to hold the weapon and to load and fire it. I kept a constant eye around us. I didn't figure on another attack today. Word would get around, thanks to the harpy and the next attack would come after people had a chance to plan better or hire someone nastier. Either way, news would take time to spread. But, whatever came after us the next time would likely be more difficult to fend off.

Suddenly, I realized Emmett stood alone in the field. How had Talon slipped passed me? He wasn't anywhere to be seen. Stupid toyol. He knew how dangerous the situation was, so where had he gone? He must have told

Emmett something because Emmett still practiced, looking unconcerned at being alone.

"Hey, kitten." Talon's voice came from right beside my ear.

His chin jutted over my shoulder and his body hovered very close. I had no idea a single person could be so aggravating. I went to put an elbow in his gut and it met with a very solid wall of muscle.

He chuckled. "So, what had you all hot and bothered earlier? Was it me? Or your little boyfriend?"

I got another of those funny throbs in my chest. Like hell I would tell him he impressed me in any capacity. Building on his ego ought to be a federal crime.

"At least Emmett can hit the target." I tried to change the subject casually. "Even if his shots are all over the map."

Talon chuckled again. "Yes, his budding skill may come in handy as long as you and I aren't on the map." He leaned closer. "Don't think you got out of answering the other question. We'll revisit that soon."

Emmett struggled to remove a spent clip and Talon hurried over to help him. We let Emmett get off a few more shots before our stomachs unanimously agreed we'd practiced long enough. I fell in behind Talon and Emmett and let them chat. Sometime during target practice they'd become comfortable enough with each other to be talking happily about sports.

A soft scratching in the plants to our left caught my attention. I dropped low and crept through the leaves. The sight which met my eyes had me thrilling with the challenge. Two huge, probably thirty-foot, purple snakes were slinking through the soy toward Emmett and Talon.

Unfortunately, they spotted me right after I spotted them and the first drew back and lunged at me, fangs unleashed. I gave a push with my Hermes shoes and pulled the gun free on the way up to head level with the monster. One shot and the snake collapsed, writhing. The second snake took off in the other direction. I let it go. Our orders were only to kill if the creature threatened us.

The wounded snake thrashed on the ground. Man, lamia were tough. I'd given him a point-blank shot to the head. I pulled out my knife and stabbed him a couple times to finish the job. He would have died anyway but this way he couldn't bite me in the back before I got out of there. When the coils finally stopped writhing I left to catch up with Talon and Emmett.

At the car Talon had Emmett tucked behind him protectively. "Who attacked?" he asked.

"A pair of lamia. One left like a good snake, the other wanted a piece of me. He lost, but took his sweet time about dying. Sorry." I reached for the handle of the car.

Talon burst out laughing and stepped between me and the door. "You're not getting in my car."

"Why not?" Now what meanness did he have up his sleeve?

"Have you seen yourself? You look like you've got purple pox. You're completely covered in lamia gore. Not on my tan interior."

I glanced down at myself. He had a point. I looked disgusting.

Emmett pulled off his T-shirt and handed it to me. "Here, you can wear mine."

Talon grabbed the shirt, and before I could react he'd wiped the gore from my face with it. For a second I paid attention to his surprisingly gentle touch then shook my head to clear it; his bedside manner didn't matter. He'd dirtied my only clean option for clothes.

I grabbed the shirt from Talon and scowled at him. "Now what am I supposed to wear? I guess you really do want gore in your car."

"You won't get my car dirty. What do you want to wear? What size are you?"

I puffed out my chest. "None of your business. You don't know much about girls, do you?"

The next thing I knew Talon held a piece of clothing out to me. "Here." He grabbed Emmett. "We'll be around the back of the car. We won't peek. If we do, I'll give you a free shot at us."

I turned my back on them and pulled off my soiled shirt. When I went to pull on the new shirt there wasn't one, only a sundress in deep, jade green. I scowled. The last time I'd worn a dress must have been years ago. Actually, had I ever worn one? They certainly weren't practical, nor did I feel comfortable in one. But I really didn't want to pull my gross shirt back on, so I chose the dress. I'd argue logistics after I'd cleaned up. At least I got my shorts off under the skirt without being exposed. Once I'd finished I deliberately dropped the purple, slimy clothes in the center of the car's white hood.

"Talon, what the hell is this?" I waved my hand over the dress.

"A size eight? A dress? What part don't you get?"

"How am I supposed to fight in this?"

He shrugged. "It looks like you have complete freedom of movement to me."

"Yeah, and complete exposure if I move around too much."

"I think you look nice," Emmett volunteered. "You know, I don't think I've ever seen you in a dress. Or a skirt either."

Talon elbowed him. "You're welcome."

I stalked back to the front of the car. Grabbed my dirty shirt and smeared the words "you suck" in purple gore across the hood and then climbed into the backseat and locked both the doors. I refused to sit next to Talon, and Emmett had irritated me, too. I didn't care if I looked nice. I didn't want either of them to get free viewing of my panties if I got into another fight.

The boys climbed in with matching smirks on their faces. Emmett's eyes sparkled playfully, and I scowled at him. He probably thought something stupid about girls and unnecessary pouting.

Unfortunately for Talon's pho craving, the drive back revealed only three choices for lunch: fast food, BBQ, and a greasy spoon café. We unanimously decided on BBQ. Talon left Emmett and I in the car and went to check out the restaurant. After a couple minutes, he returned and sent Emmett in after the food. Talon climbed back into the driver's seat and closed his door, turning to talk to me over the seats.

"How are you holding up magic wise?" he asked. "After the harpy and making you clothes, I need to go out tonight."

"If I have to take down a lamia every day I should go out, too."

Talon sighed and ran a hand through his blue hair. "Either we're both always going to be tired or we've got to come up with a better way."

I leaned against the back of the front passenger seat. "Are we going to be attacked every day? Can we really keep this up for weeks, or months?"

"Or years," Talon grumbled. "No, I don't think we can. We need to get Emmett a partner. Once he's set up the attacks will stop."

"Yeah, but we don't even know how to pair him off."

"You have to get a unicorn to seal the partnership. Once he's got a partner no other magic being will be able to tap his power."

I scowled at him. "And how would you know? There's almost no information on sources. My parents have been looking into getting him a partner since yesterday, but even they can't find much."

"I know because my mother's a source."

I stopped, unable to say the sarcastic words I'd been ready to spew. Instead I said, "Now I get why they assigned you."

"I didn't want guard duty. Especially not with a brat for a partner. But I guess the assignment could be worse. So far, you're proving capable."

"Then that's why your father can live in the Borderlands. He doesn't have to steal to get his magic rations. Your mom takes care of him."

"Yeah. And a source can extent the bond to care for a child for a while. So, I grew up in the Central Borderlands until I turned twelve. I couldn't share magic with my mother anymore, and I've been living with an uncle on Earth ever since. But I go back a couple times a year to visit."

"How did she get paired with your dad?"

He gave me a sly look. "She ended up with one of her bodyguards. Naturally, when I found you two in bed together, I assumed."

I chose to ignore that. "So, does a source have to marry their partner? I hate to think we're picking a wife for poor Emmett."

Talon laughed. "No. The unicorn creates a direct link between their magic. Being bonded does pose a huge risk, though. To protect the source, the link kills the other partner if one dies. Otherwise hunters would simply kill off a source's partner repeatedly. But the partner can be anyone the source doesn't mind being linked with. Though keep in mind how the power transfer works. The source is getting kissed by their partner daily. I think you can guess why my mother would have been more comfortable with her partner being her husband."

"I'll be Emmett's partner."

"What now?" Emmett opened the door and slid into the

front seat holding enough food for the three of us, plus my parents.

I explained everything Talon had told me. Somehow Emmett took it in stride, as he had with everything else he'd been through.

"I told Talon I could be your partner if you want. You don't have to marry me. And if you died I wouldn't care if I died, too. You know I'd do anything to keep you safe. This way we could skip right to finding a unicorn and fix this."

"Whoa there. You know it's really hard to find a unicorn, right? Especially on Earth. I could probably take you to one in the Borderlands fairly quickly, but taking Emmett there before he's got a partner is like taking a keg to a frat house and telling the boys not to touch. Livy, if you thought our job—"

"It's Olivia."

"But Emmett and your parents—"

"Have known me for years and have the privilege. You don't."

"Fine." He scowled a little. "We'd never have enough magic to protect him in the Borderlands. No shortcut is going to fix this faster. You're going to have to wait."

"Then let's get to finding a unicorn."

"Wait," Emmett protested. "Do I even get a say in this?"

Talon wore open amusement. "What did you need to say?"

"Livy, you don't have to be my partner." He blushed and looked at the floor. "I know you don't love me that way and I don't want you to force yourself."

"Then who would you choose?"

"How about Talon?"

Talon roared with laughter. "I'm not kissing you daily to keep your magic in balance. Sorry. I don't like you that much. I'd rather steal."

"Oh, yeah. I forgot about the kissing." Emmett sighed. "So, who do I pick?"

Talon shrugged. "If you really don't want O . . . liv . . . i . . . a." He over enunciated my full name while shooting me a dirty smirk. "Then I guess you pick another female magic being. Unless of course you want a male partner."

"I'm good with female, but how do I find one? It's not like I know tons of magical people."

"If I knew good, eligible girls our age I wouldn't be single." Talon gave him a derisive look. "Magic folk can get pretty spread out on Earth. There are plenty of types you wouldn't want to be involved with and most are completely ineligible. Ask O . . . liv . . . i . . . a's parents. Maybe they have friends with daughters."

"Ineligible how?" Emmett and I asked together.

"Well, there's a huge bias for magic folk to pair-bond with someone of a compatible type. Mixed breeding isn't done. And on top of that, there's a social ranking just like with humans. Could you walk into New York and get a girl from Park Avenue for the asking?"

Talon arched an eyebrow. "Sorry, Emmett, but the best you can hope for is a girl with a bit of a dark side. I doubt you'd get a high-class, magical girl, even as a source. Not to worry, though. They won't all be as bad as your friend, here." He made a face and pointed at me. "There's only a handful of assassins amongst magic folk and not all the girls are as cranky as O . . . liv . . . i . . . a. You'll find a sweet girl who doesn't kill people for a living."

Emmett fell silent, and I chewed my tongue in irritation. I *so* wanted to rip into Talon over the way he kept saying my name and his digs at me, but I knew Emmett needed time to think. At least this wasn't my choice to make. I got to go back to being myself once we'd gotten Emmett his partner.

A thought hit me like a sandbag. What if whoever he picked didn't let me continue my friendship with him? Some girls were insecure like that. Well, no sense in worrying until he picked. I also knew Emmett wouldn't choose a nasty type of girl anyway.

We dropped my parent's meal at their room and went back to ours. Talon came, churning up my irritation. Couldn't he find anywhere else to go? Or at least stay with my parents and piss them off for a while instead? I offered Emmett the only chair in the room and took it when he refused, crossing my legs and deliberately looking away from Talon.

The day drug on *forever*. My parents were in and out but never told us where our next stop would be or what step to take next with Emmett. Luckily, Talon kept his satellite link plugged in and we watched Borderland television most of the day. I found the news and programs full of magic folk who were openly themselves fascinating. Normally I had to live while hiding so much of myself. Imagine living in the Borderlands and needing to hide nothing. But that would never happen. As a being in a symbiotic relationship with humans I couldn't live somewhere humans didn't go.

I managed to avoid dealing with Talon for the most part until I came back from brushing my teeth and found him in my bed. "Get out," I snapped. I grabbed the extra blanket and pillow off the shelf in the closet and dumped them on the brown Berber carpet. "You can have the floor."

He yawned and lifted the covers. "You can sleep with me if you don't want the floor, kitten."

"I'd rather sleep outside on the concrete."

He rolled away from me. "Suit yourself."

I grit my teeth and glared at the bed. I toyed with the idea of yanking him out and taking my spot back, but he'd probably come right back and join me. I *so* didn't want to be in a bed with him.

"Livy, come here." Emmett patted the bed next to him. "You can sleep with me."

"You hog the covers and you know . . . other stuff . . ." I blushed as I remembered the mortifying morning . . . incident.

Talon laughed. "You'd better take the floor then. You're gonna run into that with either of us."

"Good God, I hope not. I never want to run into *that* again."

"Tell me you feel the same a couple years from now." Talon gave me a cheeky wink.

I ignored him and glanced between Emmett and the floor. Who knew what ickiness hid in the brown of the carpet. I figured I'd be safest with Emmett. Luckily, the room had two double beds, so I managed to take a little space for myself. Emmett gave me a generous portion of the covers this time and we went to sleep.

Chapter 6

At midnight Talon slipped out of bed and into the night. I planned to go when he got back but a hand on my arm stopped me.

"Please don't," Emmett mumbled.

"Emmett, I have to."

"You said you wouldn't if your hunting made me uncomfortable. It does. I can't stop thinking about some poor child being pulled from the bed and . . ." He shuddered.

I patted the hand on my arm. "I don't do anything violent. I send them to the goblins with magic. They never even wake until they're gone. I can't say what it's like, 'cause I've never been to the Goblin Kingdom. But I would imagine it's not so horrible. They seem to come back largely untraumatized."

"And the ones who don't come back?"

Silence stretched between us. I couldn't defend what happened to those kids. I pushed the thought out of my mind for the most part. I also refused to watch nature videos of young animals being eaten by carnivores. Nature was cruel sometimes.

I hated being in one of those food chains. I couldn't help needing magic any more than a lion could help needing dinner. In the case of the lion, dinner always died, but I got magic even when the kids came back fine.

Being too afraid to count it for myself, I once asked my parents how many kids didn't come back. My mother had patted my head and reassured me that I had one hundred percent recovery so far. Some of my targets had even made it back before the first night was over. We'd had that conversation a couple years ago, but I clung to the statistic of all my jobs coming back. My parents would never lie to cover an unpalatable truth.

Emmett scooted closer. "Take as much magic as you need."

My face flamed. "I can't kiss you," I whispered in horror. "Last time I acted on an unconscious reaction to the magic. But you're family. You might as well suggest I kiss my dad."

"I'm mildly insulted by that," Emmett teased.

I poked his ribs. "It's not an insult. It's a compliment."

"I know." He sighed. "I want you to do this. Whatever you feel about kissing me, I doubt it's as uncomfortable as the idea of you sending kids off to be eaten is to me. Don't go. I'll keep still. You kiss me, take what you need, and I promise not to move."

He immediately lay motionless. I hesitated. This had gotten awkward, fast. Then I remembered Talon. He would be back soon. I did *not* need an audience for this. Especially not one with a tongue as sharp as his. I'd never hear the end of it if Talon caught us kissing.

Holding my breath, I leaned toward Emmett. He'd closed his eyes and relaxed his face. Grateful for the illusion of privacy, I brushed my lips to his as lightly as possible and tasted the sweetness of the magic: better than the most refreshing water on a blistering summer day. I couldn't help myself. I pressed my lips harder as I drew power through him, finally managing to break the kiss just before I got tipsy. Too much magic at once had an inebriating effect. I didn't want to be drunk, in bed with Emmett.

"All better?" His voice quavered slightly.

"Yup. Thanks. How about you?"

"I feel a bit wobbly but otherwise fine. Though, I have to say, if that's the way you kiss your family, your husband is going to be a lucky man someday."

I poked his ribs again and he squirmed and chuckled.

"That tickles."

"I know. That's why I do it." I snuggled back into my pillow feeling satisfied. "Thank you."

"Mmm . . ." he mumbled, nearly back to sleep.

I'd entered the comfortable spot before sleep completely takes hold, when someone tapped my shoulder. "O . . . liv . . . i . . . a. Your turn."

"I'm good," I mumbled, swatting Talon away.

He humphed, then crawled into bed.

~ ~ ~

Three days later, I woke to scratching at the door in the middle of the night and pulled a knife from under my pillow, creeping toward the door. Warm breath on my neck revealed Talon behind me.

"You open the door. I'll take out whoever it is." His whisper came so close to my ear his lips brushed the skin.

I nodded, and he moved into position. I could make him out well enough to see him holding up three fingers, two fingers, one finger. I yanked the door open and Talon pounced. From outside came a thud, followed by high pitched shrieking.

"Don't hurt me."

"Why shouldn't I?" Talon growled.

I moved from behind the door. The voice speaking to Talon didn't sound sinister. In between two cars, Talon perched on top of a tiny woman in dark clothing, pinning her to the asphalt.

"Who is she?" I asked, letting my muscles relax. This woman gave off no aura of evil at all. I easily qualified as more malevolent than her.

"She's some random brownie." He gave her neck a squeeze, at the same time he shot her a look to make blood chill. "State your business or beat it. Why would you even come here? You're lucky we're not killing on sight."

Brownies were part of the elven family, like Talon and I were part of the fairy family. Full grown, despite being shy of four feet, she snuck into homes at night and did household tasks to earn her magic. No evil at all. But what on earth did she think she'd accomplish by coming after a source?

"I hate housework," she cried. "I came to ask the source to pair-bond with me. I'll be his partner. I'll take good care of him, so long as I never have to go into a stranger's house again."

I gave a strangled laugh. The idea of her with Emmett tickled my sense of irony. He was probably half her age and almost twice her height.

"What's all this?" Emmett wandered over rubbing his eyes and yawning.

"Okay, here's your chance." Talon let go of the woman and pushed her toward Emmett. "He's the source, Emmett. Ask away."

The light from the street lamps played up the open amusement on Talon's face. I had to work harder to keep a sense of propriety. The situation might have all the hallmarks of a comedy sketch, but this woman really meant her request. At least I could let her get it out without making fun of her.

The brownie barely hit Emmett's waist. A quick duck of her head and she could have run between his legs. But she folded her hands together and looked up, fluttering her eyes at him.

"Emmett," she stammered. "Will you marry me?"

Emmett stared at her in complete disbelief and I turned, snorting with repressed laughter.

Talon clapped a hand over my mouth. "Shh . . . Don't laugh. It's hard work getting up the guts to propose."

"I know," I hissed through his fingers.

I'd hardly finished when his head hit my shoulder and he shook with laughter himself.

I pried his hand off. "As if you've done so much proposing."

I opened my mouth to say more but at this point the brownie had dropped to one knee and taken Emmett's hand. To reach she had her arms straight up over her head and her hands barely covered his fingers.

I buried my face in Talon's hair to keep from giggling out loud. Guilt niggled at me, but the two of them looked so stupid. She told Emmett her reason for wanting him and asked him again if he would pair-bond with her.

At this point Talon had put so much effort into smothering his laughter he squeezed my arm to steady himself. I sucked in a deep breath to replace the air I kept blowing out in silent sniggering. Even through the hilarity I noticed the way Talon's hair smelled—good.

Immediately I felt like I'd been splashed in cold water. Just like during the harpy incident, my head said I should never find anything about this irritating man attractive. I pulled my face back and twisted away, crossing my arms. I needed to put space between us before anymore fuzzy feelings invaded my tummy.

Emmett stammered at the poor, little brownie. "I . . . I'm flattered. But I . . ." He paused, presumably fishing for a nice way to let her down. Emmett had never been the type to hurt people's feelings. "I don't know you at all."

She hopped to her feet and gazed up at him. "That's okay, we'll get to know each other. I'm Brunhilda."

I bit my lip and without thinking stuffed my face into Talon's shoulder against the laughter. Her name literally meant brown. It had the same effect as naming your dog Mutt. What the hell had her parents been thinking? Talon hauled me off behind a car a few spaces away from the door of our room. There he let his laughter out. He plucked me off and deposited me next to him.

"You are not helping," he gasped.

"It's not my fault." I struggled for breath. "Did you catch her name?"

Talon gave a snort. "Yeah." His back hit the car, his body shaking with mirth. "I can't believe she went down on one knee. She must really hate her job."

"Or she's a cougar." I slapped my hand over my mouth, and sputtered, "Maybe she likes little boys."

"Not so little." Talon doubled over. "Can you imagine the wedding night!"

I completely lost my composure and howled. Talon, too, laughed openly. Our amusement completely out of control, I knew Emmett and Brunhilda could hear us. So much for sparing their feelings.

Talon took a steadying breath. "Either you don't see her as competition or you're taking her proposal really well."

"What do you mean?" I took a couple deep breaths myself, suppressing the rest of my giggles.

"She's after your man. You must have changed your mind about him, since you've been getting power from him every night." Talon gave me a sly, sideways glance.

"I didn't want to last night." I leaned against the car and let out a deep sigh as frustration resurfaced. "He's really bothered by the whole kidnapping thing. I tried drawing from him the other night, but kissing has made things awkward. Last night I tried to hunt again, and he got really mad. So I got really mad. I kissed him out of anger and went to sleep on the floor 'cause I couldn't stand to share the bed with him. I meant to make things between us better by going hunting, instead, they're getting worse."

"Oh. I had it all wrong. I thought you were on the floor so you guys wouldn't . . . you know. Since there's three of us in the room and all."

"*Ew. No.* Not with Emmett. Or anyone else for that matter," I added for good measure.

Talon raised an eyebrow. "Not even your boyfriend?"

"I don't have a boyfriend," I snapped. His questions had gotten entirely too personal.

"Hmm . . ." Talon continued staring thoughtfully at me.

"You guys can come back now; she's gone." Emmett's call to us stopped me seconds before I lashed out at Talon. "And stop laughing at me."

I ran from behind the car to get away from Talon. I had all these odd feelings about the last ten minutes. We'd acted like friends. And our little accord didn't bother me like it should have, weird.

"What did you end up telling her?" I asked, as much to distract myself as to get information.

He let his shoulders drop. "She wouldn't take no for an answer. Everything I came up with she found a way around. So, I finally used her age against her." He looked at me with pleading in his eyes. "Livy, I made her cry. I tried so hard. I didn't want to be mean."

I burst out laughing again. Emmett's lip quivered for a moment and then he gave a grudging chuckle, too. Talon glanced nervously around the parking lot and shooed us all back inside. "In case the brownie wasn't the only thing lurking."

~ ~ ~

The fourth day with Talon broke with the promise of continued boredom. We all slept late after the previous night's excitement and I finally drug myself off the floor at ten. Talon still slept, sprawled across the whole double bed, his hair standing on end and his mouth hanging open. I giggled and snapped a picture. I could use the photo as leverage later if needed.

"You wanted a picture because I'm shirtless, right?" he muttered into his pillow. "You know you're gonna set my picture as your wallpaper later. You just want to press my gorgeous muscles against your face every time you make a call."

I grabbed a spare pillow and went to slam it down on his head, but he moved with incredible speed for someone who had supposedly been sound asleep moments before. He snatched the pillow from my hands knocking me backward. I caught myself on the opposite bed and squashed Emmett's magazine in the process.

Before I got to apologize Emmett had launched a pillow at Talon. "Be careful. You crushed my magazine."

"I did not." Talon's eyes were gleaming. "O . . . liv . . . i . . . a did."

"You yanked the pillow out of her hand, setting her off," Emmett countered.

"She shouldn't be trying to assault me with bedding." His grin went straight to wicked and even though he spoke to Emmett, his eyes glittered at me.

I scrambled up and over the bed to the far side. Who knew what he'd try. I crushed the rest of the magazine and Emmett let out a growl and slapped his pillow in my direction.

Talon gave a little snarl as well. I knew that noise, but Emmett wouldn't. My parents made the same noise when they played rough. He'd let out a very playful, impish sound. The next moment Talon leapt from his bed to mine and Emmett's, landing on all fours.

Without meaning to, I snarled back, then clapped a hand over my mouth as Emmett startled. My growl set Talon moving. He tackled me and the two of us flew off the bed landing on the floor. We blocked and grabbed, neither of us hitting hard enough to actually hurt the other, but not going easy either.

We'd rolled into the far wall, my hand on his throat, him tickling me mercilessly when the door between the rooms slammed open and my mother burst in. Her eyes were wide, and she held a slip of paper in her hands.

"I have some bad news." She stared at Emmett. "I . . ." She came over and took his hands, pulling him into a hug. "I'm so sorry, Emmett."

I dropped my hold on Talon and squirmed out from under him, fear squeezing my chest. Had something happened to Emmett's family? Maybe we should have left a guard there. I'd happily send Talon back.

"The Synod has ruled for you," Mom continued. "They're worried about Zaemon getting a hold of you and using you to feed covert forces. So, um . . . new orders have come in for you kids."

"Mom, you're stalling. Spit it out."

"The Lord High Governor's daughter, Elita, will arrive for Emmett shortly. You're to take the two of them to solidify their partnership. Also arriving will be Elita's bodyguard and her personal attendant. You three bodyguards are to protect the other three until the partnership is settled. At which time Elita's people will bring her and Emmett back to the Central Borderlands."

"But . . . I don't . . . why?" Emmett stammered.

My mom ran a hand across his face. "Dear boy, you've been bought by the aristocracy. You're going back as Elita's husband. Arsen and I are leaving. We've been given an assignment as well. We're escorting your parents to the Central Borderlands to await your return and . . ." Mom gave a funny gulp. "Your nuptials."

"I'm only seventeen," he protested. "Not to mention you can't *make* someone get married."

"The people issuing the orders are not from the US, honey," Mom soothed. "It's not even a human society. They can arrange your marriage and they did."

"I'm not going." Emmett crossed his arms. "I'll partner with Livy. Then whoever got picked for me won't matter."

"No," Mom yelped. "You can't. There's a good chance they'd have Livy killed before you lock in the partnership. I'm sorry. I love you Emmett, but I can't let you risk Livy."

"Okay, okay. I won't," Emmett rushed. "Isn't there any way out of this?"

"You have to find someone," Talon pointed out. "At least meet her. Maybe you'll like her."

I kicked his shin.

Mom pulled Emmett into a hug and kissed his forehead. "At the very least you'll never want for anything. You'll be nobility. Look for the silver lining." She let him go and pulled me into a hug. "I love you, Livy. I'll see you when your quest is done. I'm sorry you've been sucked this deep." She kissed each of my cheeks and squeezed me once more.

Mom then took both of Talon's hands in hers. "Young man, your attitude has left something to be desired up to this point." She pulled him close and glared him down. "My daughter is in your care as your partner. Screw off and you could cost her life. Take her life and I'll take yours. Are we clear?" Talon gulped and nodded. Then my mother did something unexpected. She pulled Talon into a hug, as well. "I love both these kids. Protect them for me."

"I . . ." Talon's voice cracked, and he cleared his throat. "I will."

Mom let Talon out of the hug and turned back to the door. "Your father and I are leaving immediately. Elita and her aides will arrive shortly and then you were supposed to start as well. Good luck."

My father came and said goodbye, and before I'd fully grasped our new situation we been left alone to await the new arrivals. For a while a stifling silence settled over the room. Finally, Talon stood and started pulling me toward the door.

"You get to sit and wait outside, O . . . liv . . . i . . . a."

"You sound dumb when you screw up my name. Just say Olivia normally. And why should I sit outside?"

"Emmett is spoken for. I'm gonna give him a quick bachelor party, so unless you're attending as the stripper."

He'd opened the door to push me out. I splayed my arms and legs and refused to go through the door. He shoved me from behind and my arms gave. The two of us tumbled out onto the sidewalk. I closed my eyes, waiting for pain as the pavement came straight for my face. My face hit something soft at the same time Talon crushed me. I cracked my eyes to his palm against my face. He'd caught my head before it hit.

"Are they seriously professionals?" The girly voice sounded sneering and came with a disdainful sniff.

A picture-perfect young woman with vibrant red hair and stunning green eyes stood over me, eyeing me contemptuously. Talon moved even faster than when he attacked, jumping up and pulling me to my feet at the same time. He gave a low bow.

"You must be Lady Elita. It's a pleasure—"

She brushed past Talon as if he didn't exist, pushing inside our room. "Where's Enert?

I swallowed the urge to hit her. "Emmett." I pointed to the bathroom. "He'll only be a minute, I'm sure."

She ignored me as well, and flounced over to the only chair the room contained. "Omri," she whined, turning a two-syllable name into six. "Do something. It's *yucky*." She fluttered her hand in the direction of the chair.

A young man with pale silver hair and over-large ears rushed to lay a cloth over the seat. Elita sat on the edge as if it still might contaminate her. The bathroom door opened and Elita jumped up, rushing over.

"Egbert," she squealed.

I grimaced and tensed. From behind, a hand gripped my shoulder and gave a little squeeze, a subtle reminder from

Talon to keep my mouth shut. Ten minutes ago, I'd thought Talon qualified as the most annoying person I'd ever met. Elita quickly changed my mind.

Emmett's eyes widened as he took Elita in. I didn't blame him. She looked damn near perfect, like a doll. As long as she never opened her mouth he might be happy with her.

"Does he not speak?" she snapped at me.

"Nice to meet you, Rita," Emmett answered.

"It's Elita," she chirped at him.

"It's Emmett," he retorted.

She gave him a swift and dirty look before moving on. "Are we ready to go?"

"If your people know our destination I'd appreciate the information," Talon said.

A tiny woman with black hair and almond eyes stepped forward. "We have a lead on a unicorn in the rainforests of Belize, spotted a week ago. We're headed there."

Talon gave her a quick once over. "Good. And you are?"

She returned him a polite bow of the head. "Yumiko."

I glanced between Yumiko and Omri. How could you tell the bodyguard and the attendant apart? One should never judge magic folk by their appearance but no one in their party volunteered any information.

"Do you have a vehicle for six?" Talon asked Yumiko.

She simply shook her head.

Elita slipped her arm through Emmett's. "The four of us can take one car." She wrinkled her nose at me. "The peasants can find their own way."

My ears got pointy. This girl excelled at getting under my skin.

"But, Mistress," Omri started, "they're part of the guard for you and Master Emmett."

"I don't want them in my car and I don't want to be seen in a minivan." She stomped her foot petulantly.

"I couldn't agree more." I strode over to Emmett, grabbed his face and kissed him deeply, sucking as much magic from him as I could.

When I broke the kiss everyone stared at me, stunned. But I had no desire to explain myself to these *people*. I stalked to the door, kicked it open and hotwired a speed bike in the parking lot. Talon could have gotten a ration for stealing, but I needed extra magic to do something outside my nature. Elita had a sleek little roadster whose backseat simply gave lip service to the word seat. I couldn't imagine where all four of them would sit. Not my problem. At least they'd be able to keep up with my bike.

"Talon, you heard her. Let's go. *Now*." I glared at Yumiko, mostly because I had the gut feeling she'd understand. "I'm obliging your mistress," I told her. "It's now your job to keep up."

I grabbed one of the helmets off the bike, hopped on and kicked it to life. Talon grabbed my arm. "Are you sure you should be driving?"

"Get on or take your own."

He slapped on the other helmet and I barely waited for him to be settled before I peeled out of the parking lot.

"Olivia, you need to stop."

I shook my head at Talon's voice in my helmet.

"You'll be punished if you run off and anything happens to them. Pull over and wait."

Damn it, of all the times for him to go rational on me. I pulled the bike off and against my will something between a snarl and a sob escaped me.

"She's awful. I can't let her have Emmett. I don't care about her birth rank. Emmett's worth a hundred of her. Hell, even you're better than her." I took an impatient backward glance. "What's taking so long?"

His hands squeezed my waist, gently. "They have to return the room key and such." He pulled me toward him, but I resisted. Instead he leaned forward until his chest ran along my back. "You're hurting," he observed. "Is Emmett really so important to you?"

I slumped against Talon. "Yes." The tears started. "I love him. He's my very best friend. The only friend that really matters."

He nodded against my back. "He really has a place of honor in an imp's heart."

"I don't want him romantically. If Elita were a nice person I could handle them being together. Even be happy for him . . . but . . ." I choked off on a sob.

Talon put his arms around me and hugged. "I'm sorry." He climbed off the bike and pushed me gently back. "I'll drive. If you want to talk, I'll listen."

I'd hardly got my arms around him when the others drove past, and Talon joined them. He kept a watchful distance behind their car. Two of us staring at the same spot on the road wouldn't be any extra help, so I let myself go slack. I leaned my head against his back and the tears rolled. I tried to cry silently but every so often a sob escaped and my chest would jerk against his back. Talon remained suspiciously silent. Would I have to pay for this kindness? The Talon I knew couldn't wait to twist this and taunt me.

Chapter 7

Much like the drive from California with my parents, the vehicles slid across the countryside at an alarming pace. At least the magic was in control. In a couple hours we crossed the state lines into Texas. Omri must be taking us to the gulf and a boat. Sailing would certainly be quicker than going all the way by land.

The sky had turned periwinkle, halfway to dark, when Elita's car pulled into a hotel driveway. We stopped in Dallas and she had chosen what had to be one of the most expensive hotels in the city. But hey, her family would be footing the bill for this. In which case, I intended on ordering lots of room service and putting all the toiletries in my bag when we left.

In general, I try not to mope or sulk, so when I pulled off the helmet I gave Talon the brightest smile I could muster. "Thanks."

I assumed we'd have to argue to get a room near Elita, seeing as how we might contaminate her with peasant germs, but she'd gotten us a two-room suite. Elita immediately claimed the only bedroom and told the rest of us to use the pull-out couch. I grit my teeth so hard they might chip when she invited "Elliot" to stay in the room with her. Evidently, he'd had enough of his fiancée because he declined and sat next to me on the couch.

Elita pranced over and perched on his lap. "I need magic," she purred at him.

Emmett shrugged. "Can't. Sorry. My magic is sitting in

the parking lot in the form of a motorcycle. It'll be a day or two probably. I don't seem to get reserves very fast yet."

"Well, what good is that?" Elita pouted. "You're supposed to make enough for me." She rounded on Talon and I. "The peasants can go get enough for the rest of us." She pulled out a jar and shoved it into my hands. "Hurry up. I get cranky when I don't eat."

No need to ask how long she'd gone without "eating". With as bitchy as she came across, she'd probably never eaten.

"Mistress." Omri had stepped forward. "It's not advisable to send out two of the bodyguards. Let me go with Miss Olivia."

"Fine. But hurry up."

I followed Omri out the door and down the hall. I had to work to keep up with his long strides. Once the elevator doors slid closed he held his hand out for the jar.

"You have my apologies, Miss Olivia. I can see my mistress distresses you."

"You think? How do you ever put up with her attitude?"

"I'm a sphinx. By nature, I guard that which I have been asked to guard."

"Holy crap." My eyes bugged out. "You're a sphinx for real? You're elite on your own. Now I'm even more confused as to why you're working for someone as unpleasant as Elita."

Omri shrugged. "My family has served the line of the Lord High Governor for countless generations. It is what it is. But we have no need to discuss my motives in life. I am sorry she's asked you to perform duties you are incapable of. I can gather magic from natural geysers, a simple task for a sphinx. Would you prefer to hunt, or would you like me to gather yours, as well? I assume you used a bit too much on your motorcycle stunt."

"Maybe." I blushed. "I'll let you get my magic if it's truly not too much trouble."

"Not at all." He smiled, and his crystalline aqua eyes twinkled at me. "May I ask a few personal questions?"

"What? You didn't get all the info from the Synod already?"

He ignored my rude tone. "You and Emmett are seventeen?"

"Yes."

"You have been friends for how long?"

"Almost nine years. How old are you?"

I got another of those sculpturesque smiles. If his ears weren't so prominent he'd be stunning. But I already liked his personality, his ears might be overlookable.

"I'm twenty-two. You are an imp?"

"Yes."

He nodded. "You dated Emmett?"

"No. He's too important."

Omri continued nodding but said nothing further. We walked into the city in silence. Him following a trail of magic I couldn't sense, me tagging along behind wondering why he'd taken me. He obviously didn't need my help gathering the magic, nor would a sphinx need a bodyguard.

The geyser turned out to be a fire hydrant of all things. He held one hand over the hydrant and one on the jar. I waited for something amazing to happen, but nothing did. However, Omri screwed the lid back on and held a hand out to me.

"Would you like to drink from the geyser?"

I nodded, and he took my hand. Just like holding the jar, he held mine and put his other back over the hydrant.

"Careful. The magic is quite concentrated like this."

His warning came too late. The raw power had already started filling my body and unlike a ration, the geyser offered nearly endless reserves. I opened myself up and let the power fill every nook and cranny of my being. The flood of magic hit my system like a drug, swift and potent. I felt capable of busting through a brick wall. Something close by issued a growling purr. Strangely the noise came from me.

"I think you've had enough." Omri broke my link to the magic.

"No. Don't stop. The magic's awesome." Were my words really slurred? They'd barely sounded English. I giggled and a tugging sensation at my back made me turn my head. "Hey, lookee. I've gotta tail." I tried to step forward but ended up going sideways.

Omri sighed and put a strong arm around my waist. He pulled me off into an alley. "Olivia, you need to center yourself. You look very inhuman right now. We can't walk back with you looking this way."

I giggled and put a hand on his chest. "You actually sound like you care." I sighed and plucked at his shirt. "Talon doesn't. He just likes pissing me off. And that bitch you work for hates me and she's taking Emmett from me." I gave a very gross sob/hiccup. "I'm risking my life and the only one who would miss me isn't going to be allowed to. You tell me Elita-Rita's gonna let me stay friends with Emmett."

I pulled Omri's face closer. "Would you miss me?"

He patted my head. "Of course, I would. I don't think you're giving—"

Shoving him sideways, I launched a dagger at the figure in the shadows. I staggered over to the blubbering man on the ground with my dagger in his thigh.

"I'm sorry," he sobbed. "I wanted to see if I could have you when he finished. I've never seen a cosplay hooker with a tail before. You're my kind of kinky."

Omri stood stiffly beside me. His face had grown cold, deadly, and sinister. "You lie," he hissed. Without warning Omri had sprouted a set of wings. "Filth. You will plague this city no more."

With a flick of his wings Omri sent razor sharp feathers into the body of the man until he bristled like a pin cushion. He turned his back on the man before the agonized groans stopped and held an arm out to me.

"Come. We're going back the easy way."

I let him hold me and we lifted off. "You killed a human."

"He harbored more evil than most of us classified as malevolent. Power is given to the sphinx to see and judge the heart. He wasn't worthy, either of life or mercy. I gave him only a fraction of what he deserved."

"I'm curious as to why." I still slurred a bit but the wind in my face helped.

Omri shook his head. "You don't want to know. But I will say he intended on killing me. And you, well, eventually he'd kill you." He left the words hang heavy.

"I can handle myself," I protested. Then something occurred to me. "Oh, wait. I thought you said two of the bodyguards shouldn't go together."

"I'm not a bodyguard. Yumiko is a kamaitachi, and quite ruthless. I wouldn't underestimate her."

Yumiko's breed perked my interest immediately. Unlike Buraee, Yumiko wouldn't be very flashy. Kamaitachi were essentially humanoid weasels. But they were renowned for their skill with blades.

"Is she really? I would never underestimate her, but now I'd really love to see her work."

He gave a chuckle. "After seeing you work in your completely inebriated state I wouldn't underestimate you either. I can only imagine what you are capable of when sober."

We landed on the roof of the hotel and he went straight toward an access door. Suddenly, he stopped and took my face in his hands, tipping it up.

"By nature, you will be hit hard by the events which are taking place. Please ask me if you need space to center yourself. As a fairy, my mistress is greedy and selfish, however her father wields more power than you can imagine. Do not get on the wrong side of her family."

I caught his sleeve. "Wait. Will . . . will she treat Emmett well?"

Omri sighed and took my hand, patting it. "As long as he provides the promised power and doesn't rock the boat. She'll probably treat him like a beloved pet. When she gets displeased she tends to act childish. Irritating, yes. But will she hurt him, no."

"There's more than one way to hurt a person. He's being doomed to a loveless life. Why does she even want him for his magic if she has you? You can get it from any geyser."

"She's worried I'm leaving."

"Are you?"

Omri shrugged. "They had a fortune teller at a party about a month ago. Her services were supposed to be offered in good fun. However, she read my fortune as finding a true and undying love soon, and this teller has an impeccable reading record. Elita took this to mean she'd lose me, even if it's only my attention. She heard about Emmett and decided she wanted someone who could never leave her."

"But Talon said the source doesn't have to marry."

"We tried arguing logically with her, but she refused to see reason. From her father's point of view, bonding them gets rid of the headache of an unpartnered source, so he issued the orders for her."

"Have you fallen in love?" I asked Omri. "All this seems stupid for her . . . I mean, she could marry you and keep you, right?"

"No. I haven't fallen in love. I suppose I could ask to pair-bond with her, but she wouldn't believe any offer on my part. We've been together too long. I don't claim she knows me well. But she knows everything about everyone if the information pertains to her. Though I serve her loyally she would know I don't love her in the manner she desires. Besides, her father wouldn't allow a union between us with my being a sphinx. If you want lessons in choosing appropriate mates according to Borderland tradition, we can go over options another time." He reached out and ruffled my hair. "Your tail is gone. Are you in a state to handle business?"

I nodded. "Thank you. For understanding."

~ ~ ~

We walked in on Elita, mid-tantrum, trying to destroy the room. Yumiko and Talon played a bizarre game of catch, keeping the things she sent flying from smashing into anything else. Emmett stared blankly at the TV, ignoring the ruckus, or trying to. I went over to the couch and sat next to him.

"How are you holding up?" I whispered.

"I'm not. She's so shallow and self-absorbed. Don't bother guarding me. I don't care who takes me now because I don't see how anyone could get much worse."

I took his hand and patted it. "I asked Omri about the reality of life with Elita for you. He promised she's never been cruel. Just childish."

Emmett rolled his eyes. "He's her man. Why believe him?"

"I *feel* we can believe him. I trust my gut and my gut trusts him."

He gave a grim nod. "Talon already agreed to this. You and I are sneaking off for a bit. Wait for our cue."

The next lamp Elita threw Talon dodged, and it exploded on the wall, busting a huge mirror. In the ensuing chaos Emmett pulled me out the front door and ran for the staircase. We stopped on the seventeenth floor and made our way behind some palms in the pool atrium. Omri would be quick enough to figure things out and cover for me. With Talon backing us up too, we could be sure of some privacy.

"There's some things . . . I wanted to say them, you know, before I can't anymore." He blushed and looked at the floor." I wanted you to know you're my best friend."

"I know and you're mine, too."

"Stop. Just listen for a minute. Everything I want to say I'm sure you already know. But I don't want to assume you do since I'm getting hauled off as some evil princess's boytoy never to see you again."

He expounded on our friendship and thanked me for little things I'd forgotten I'd even done for him. The tears came easy. Though by the end I wanted to cover my ears and run. I wasn't ready to hear "goodbye" from him.

"Have you said what needs to be said?"

I looked up through my tears. Omri stood on the other side of the palms. I shook my head and he turned without a word, taking a few steps away. I gave Emmett a huge hug.

"I love you," I told him. "I would do anything for you. I wish I could do better for you this time. No matter where you go or who keeps us apart, you'll always be family to me." Letting go, I walked quickly to Omri's side. I received a gentle pat on the head.

Emmett and I were guided back to the suite but the closer we got the harder I cried. Omri steered me beside the door and pressed me against the wall.

"Stay here," he whispered.

He led Emmett back inside, eyes dry but otherwise looking completely miserable. I slumped against the wall and put my face on my knees. Goodbye had been said and I needed tonight to process this. Tomorrow I would be ready to work.

The door clicked, and soft hands pulled me away from the wall. I caught the blue smear of Talon's hair through my tears. He wiped one cheek then the other.

"You scare me, you know? Toyol aren't so different from imps. If this is the state opening your heart leaves you in . . ." He sat down in front of me. "Just so you know, I suck at stuff like this."

"Then feel free to go away." I sniffled.

"I can't. I tried to ignore you, but you sounded so freakin' pathetic. I mean, what kind of assassin sobs in the hallway? I—"

I swung at his face. What the hell? Did he really need to make my misery worse? I would never understand how his twisted mind worked. He caught my arm and held it, but I didn't have the will to fight.

"Geez, O . . . liv . . . i . . . a. You're even punching weak. How are you—"

I tackled him, landing on his chest and threw another punch. He slid sideways taking the blow on the shoulder. We repeated the sequence on the other side. He wasn't even fighting back. And he accused me of being weak?

I threw another at his face out of frustration and he caught my arm, pulling on it until we were nose to nose. He'd made me lay on him in the middle of the hall. Who knew you could be so embarrassed and livid at the same time.

"At least you've stopped crying," he said in a soft voice.

"Huh?"

"Letting you fight instead of cry. I meant to distract you. Like I said, I'm bad at talking and touchy-feely stuff."

Why was his face so close still? I tried to sit up, but he held me there. Confusion tangled his words in my brain.

"You were distracting me?"

"You looked so miserable. I had to do something."

"So, you decided to piss me off?"

"I know I could probably find a better way." He was turning red. "I suck at these things . . . you know, with girls." He was redder still. "But . . ." He closed the distance between our faces and I stared wide-eyed at him as he kissed me. "Anything seemed better than tears. Please don't be so sad."

"You kissed me."

"You said you didn't like me pissing you off."

"You kissed me."

"I know."

"Why?"

"Because I like you."

I fell off the side of him. I tried to scramble away but he caught and held me.

"Stop it. Stop teasing. This isn't funny. Not even remotely."

"I wasn't trying to be funny. I don't date much. I hate girls who are weepy and weak and foolish. And then I meet you and you're feisty and strong, a near match for me, and smart. Then this hurt you. I don't know what I'm supposed to say. I'm not stupid. No words will fix this for you. I . . ." He tugged at his hair making it stand on end in two-inch blue spikes. "I'm completely lost. I'm helpless against you, as a girl. I'm helpless against this problem that's hurting you. I'm never helpless. I fix things, solve problems."

He crossed his arms and gave me a challenging stare. "Go on. Get mad at me. Tell me how much you despise me. You've made your feelings for me abundantly clear. You're going to laugh at me."

"You like me? For real?"

He relaxed a little, but still had a wary look on his face. "Well, yeah. I meant what I said. You're not like other girls, you're . . . really . . . cool."

I shook my head. "But . . . no guys like me. I've never been asked out, or even to a dance."

"Guys aren't gonna ask if you only hang out with one guy. They probably thought you were together with Emmett. I did. Besides, you're not like most girls. You can tell you're tough. They might have been scared of you. Most guys don't want a girl who can kick their ass. Personally, I'd like to spar for real and see who would actually win."

"If you like me then why have you been so mean? I seriously wanted to pull a knife on you."

Talon's face turned a shade of scarlet which clashed with his hair. "I . . . at first I meant the things I said, I didn't think a little girl like you would be a capable guard. Then I got flustered and I didn't know how to talk to you and—"

"Oh my God. You've been trying to flirt with me this whole time?"

His face and neck went a darker shade and purple mixed with the red. "Hurry up and tell me you hate me, so we can both move on. I shouldn't have said anything in the first place. Stupid me."

"You're not stupid. I just didn't . . . expect this." I sat up and crouched next to him.

His gaze turned pathetic. "How do you feel? I mean, are you interested at all?"

"Can I be honest?"

"Are you asking for permission to be rude?"

"Not this time." I heaved a breath. "For a minute, when you took down the harpy our first day, I thought I could like you if you weren't such an insufferable asshole."

"Yeah, nothing rude there."

"Shut up and wait for the good part." I glared at him but for a change, a smile tickled the corner of my mouth. "As for how I feel about you, I have no idea. I might be able to like you if you didn't spend all your time pissing me off. So, try this, chill for a bit and let's see what happens. I'm not saying yes or no. Let me see the not so mean Talon for a while so I can think without seeing red."

He pulled his knees up to his chest. "I can live with that."

"Well if it's not something you can live with, then you'll have to curl up and die. I'm not giving any more. But you won't have to wait too long to die." I grinned. "Just let the next critter to come after us have you."

He bumped his shoulder against mine. "I'm not the only one who flirts mean."

I gasped and then laughed. "I don't date, so maybe I'm wrong, but isn't the guy is supposed to be Prince Charming? You know, sweep the girl off her feet."

Talon stood and held out a hand for me. "I'll take that to mean you're not interested, because Prince Charming I am not."

"No kidding." I took his hand and let him help me up, sidestepping the extra pull toward his arms.

He jerked harder and I stumbled into his chest. "You say you want the fairytale, but I doubt you'd be satisfied if you got your prince. You'd be so bored with the poor sap you'd probably put a pillow over his face in the middle of the night."

"Why wait for night with you?" I pressed my knuckle into his sternum making him gasp and squirm. When he let go I jumped back to avoid getting caught again and shot him a teasing look. "I'll give . . . it could be interesting."

He blinked at me. "What, killing me?"

"No." I laughed. "Dating you." I let myself back into the hotel room feeling pleased at the stunned and happy look I'd left on Talon's face as the door shut behind me.

Chapter 8

I woke to find myself staring into crystalline blue eyes.

"Good morning." Omri smiled at me. "Mistress would like to start early. I hoped I might ride with you today. I'd like to lay out our plan of tracking the unicorn, and I assume you are not interested in riding with Elita and Emmett." Omri grinned as I stiffened. "I thought not."

"Sure. We can ride together."

A crash and a shriek from the bedroom sent me flying off the floor followed closely by Omri and Talon. Yumiko stood outside the bedroom door, holding a finger to her lips. Inside Emmett screamed at Elita.

"I don't know what the hell you want from me."

"I want you to love me. You're going to be my partner and my husband. You have to." Something crashed again.

"I don't, and I won't."

"You love the stupid imp, don't you? That's why you ran off with her last night. Well you can't have her, and she can't have you."

"She's like my sister. And yeah, I love her. More than anyone could possibly love a selfish bitch like you. She's hands down a better woman. You should strive to be like her."

"She's an imp. I'm fairy aristocracy. I've been better than her since birth."

"I don't give a rat's ass about your bloodline. I'm talking about actions. She's risked her life for me repeatedly. I bet you've never even lifted a pinky for yourself, let alone anyone else."

"That's what my servants are for. I shouldn't have to."

"Your servants are paid to do things for you. They're not paid to like you and I promise you, they don't. You're a job, not a friend. Our magic will be tied, but I'll be just like your servants: stuck with you. I'll never love you, because you're completely unlovable."

The door slammed open and Yumiko barely jumped out of the way in time. Emmett, red-faced and furious stomped across the common room. Elita wore an equally angry scowl and reached the bedroom door before we could all scramble away.

"What are you four doing?" she shrieked at us.

"We heard a crash—" Omri started.

Elita slapped him leaving a hand print across his face. I gasped. I'd never dare strike a sphinx so casually.

"You were all eavesdropping. How *dare* you."

She rounded on me and I backed off. They weren't paying me enough to take physical abuse. At least not from her. But Emmett moved between us blocking me.

"Don't you dare. They're hired to check on anything suspicious. You throwing things around the room certainly would have sounded fishy. Besides, it's not like they had to listen hard to hear. Your shrill voice could pierce concrete." She moved to slap him, and he caught her hand. "I won't live like this. Find a way to be a better person or I'll let the next creature that comes for me eat me."

"You wouldn't dare. I can have your little girlfriend punished in your place if you let yourself die."

Emmett narrowed his eyes and squeezed her wrist. "If I ever seriously think you'll harm Olivia I'll wait until the unicorn seals the partnership and I'll kill myself and take you with me. I know if I die you go, too."

Elita gave a hard laugh. "Why die for her? She's not worth your own life."

"She's saved me several times. I owe her and to protect her you'll find I'll do whatever I have to."

Elita went pale for a moment and wheeled around on Yumiko. "Pack my stuff I want to go. And tell the rest of them to stay out of my sight."

I scurried over to the table near the TV and grabbed the ice bucket. Filling a hand towel with ice cubes, I brought them back to Omri. "Here. For your face."

He gave me a dead smile. "Thank you."

I glanced back at the closed bedroom door and decided Elita didn't care what a peasant had to say. "You executed the guy last night for sins weighing on his heart. How is hers possibly good enough for you to take this treatment?"

Omri cast a look at the door with his aqua eyes, then pulled me so close his lips nearly touched my ear to whisper, "I should not discuss this with you. But seeing as how you're turning Emmett over I'll grant you knowledge that is not yours to know. Please don't repeat what I say."

I nodded solemnly.

"Her heart is tarnished like silver," Omri explained. "Given a polish she will shine as brightly as the precious metal. But if the correct solution is never applied she will grow blacker and blacker. I don't see the future, only hearts. I simply know what her potential is. She could be beautiful."

I snorted. "I'm not seeing the beauty."

He winced as he smiled, the ice still on his cheek. "It's hard to see the butterfly in the worm."

"Whatever. Cleaning her up is going to take one hell of a polish. All I see is a twisted lump of black metal." I paused for a second. "What do you see in me?"

He dropped his chin so it rested on my shoulder. "Beauty, danger, loyalty, courage, love, heartache, and so many other things."

I shrugged him off. "You're teasing me. You don't need to be a sphinx to pick up on those things, though the beauty, I'm not sure how you figure."

He chuckled and pressed a finger to the tip of my nose. "If you were meant to know these things you would have been born a sphinx. And you *are* a beauty. So many factors play into being lovely beside the physical. You would judge yourself harshly against Elita. But ask any man in this room who he would pick."

He turned and walked away leaving my head spinning. I'd never really thought of myself in such terms. I looked in the mirror. My reflection glared back, painfully plain and a little worn. What other factors could possibly improve the view? Besides, the three men in the room would probably have taken a spider over Elita if forced to choose.

I was out of time to ponder anymore. We needed to move, yet again. I went to grab my bag, but Talon already had it, so I trotted after him.

"I can carry my own bag."

Talon shot me a gleaming smile. "I thought you wanted Prince Charming? Besides whatever Omri said to you sent you into la la land. I figured this would get you moving faster."

"You know he's a sphinx, right?"

"No. But I do now. So?"

"I asked him what my heart looked like. He said I'm beautiful and maybe more attractive than Elita. But I can't see how. She's gorgeous. It's her personality which sucks."

"Omri's right. Any guy would happily screw her once just to see her pretty face under him. But seriously what would you do with her afterward? The only time she's pretty is when she's silent and still. You could use duct tape but too much ruins the effect." He dropped the bags and in a flash had me pinned against the wall. "You on the other hand, your looks aren't as flashy but . . . *grrr*."

I tried to wiggle out. I didn't like how my heartrate had ramped up. "Yeah. *Grrr*. That's what a girl wants to hear. *Hey, baby. You're not pretty, but grrr.*"

He dropped his face very close to mine. "Yes, you'd rather be *grrr*. *Grrr*, means you make guys wanna . . . well, if you don't know how guys think then I won't destroy your illusions yet. Let's explain it like this. The same way lots of girls like a *bad boy*, you're a bad girl. You're dangerous and that's its own thrill. You know, taming the untamable."

I struggled again. "We're falling behind. They're gonna think . . . things."

"So, let's not leave them disappointed." He leaned in and I dodged and gave his head a push so he knocked his forehead into the wall.

"I said we'd see. Don't make me maim you."

He grinned at me and picked up our bags. "Whips and chains, Livy. Whips and chains. The harder you fight the more interested I get."

I sighed and followed him down the hall. Omri stood waiting at the bike with my helmet in his hands. He shot me a grin and tossed the helmet to me.

"Wait," Talon protested. "I thought Livy and I rode together."

Omri waved him toward the car. "We have business to discuss."

Talon gave me a little scowl and I rolled my eyes at him to remind him not to count his chickens before they were hatched. Popping the helmet on I climbed on the bike and started it up. Once we'd gotten out on the open road I prodded the silent Omri.

"What did you need to talk to me about? I thought Yumiko said we were headed to a unicorn in Belize? Sounds pretty straightforward to me."

"The chase is a lie to placate Elita's father. A unicorn had been spotted in the rainforest, but we have no hope of catching up with a unicorn on Earth. However, the alignment with the supposed sighting was providential. Hidden in a temple in the forests of Belize is a gateway to the Borderlands. We'll simply go to the gateway and return to the Borderlands. A unicorn will be much easier to find, since most have their permanent residence there."

"Wait, the Borderlands? Talon thought protecting Emmett and his partner would be nearly impossible there."

"Yes, protecting him there would have been impossible for the two of you, but in this case, you have two additional guards. I might not be an official bodyguard, but I don't think I'm helpless."

I laughed. "Not hardly. You didn't even break a sweat the other night. I think I'd be hard pressed to win a fight against you. But do you really think this plan is safe?"

"It's absolutely *not* safe. But I'm focused on the outcome. Realistically, we'll likely face the same number of adversaries on Earth. The encounters will simply take place over a longer period. Why make everyone suffer? We'll finish this and get you back to normal faster."

"You really have a loose definition of normal."

Omri squeezed my waist. "You will thrive. Change hurts but it's not in you to give up."

"It's creepy you know me, when you don't know me." I squirmed and changed the subject. "So, what exactly are the Borderlands like?"

"Much like Earth, but the sun is red. You'll find this changes colors. Human's don't exist there. In the Borderlands, they're nearly as fabled as we are on Earth. And since there are no humans, there are no human transformations. You will look like an imp the whole time."

"That's not sounding much like Earth."

"The two locales boast a short list of differences. Would you prefer I expound upon the sameness?"

"No. We're good."

He spent the rest of the ride, which wasn't very long, asking me about growing up on Earth. Since sphinx were powerful creatures, he would have needed a reason and permission from his lord to visit. Naturally, he'd never been to Earth until now.

We reached a wharf where a luxurious yacht awaited us. I had to admit Elita traveled in style. Not that she appreciated it and immediately retreated to the main cabin, still sulking.

Omri explained since water is denser than air the boat couldn't handle being pushed by magic like the cars. We would have to go at normal speed, meaning several days at sea before we would reach the rainforest. Elita sulked for the ride and the words said by Yumiko tallied on two hands. I got stuck alone with the three guys.

Our first night at sea mermaids accosted the boat. They don't really attack, being rather prissy as a rule. But they slowed the ship to a stop, using seaweed to clog the propellers and then mobbing the vessel.

Trying to count in the dark left me unsure of the number fifteen I came up with. Each one lived up to the reputation of the intoxicatingly beautiful siren. I doubted we'd be able to talk reasonably with them, but I also hated to attack them.

Omri went to the edge of the boat and gave a sort of screech. A moment later the mermaids were gone. I stared openly at him, wondering what Talon and I were needed for. We seemed rather superfluous given Omri's set of talents.

I tagged after him as he walked the outside of the boat making sure the mermaids were really gone. "How did you get them to go? What did you say?"

He chuckled. "Not telling. Enjoy a little mystery in life."

"You're mystery enough for a couple lives. Why do you even need us? Or Yumiko? You seem more than capable of protecting Elita and maybe even Emmett, too."

"You're here because despite your flattering admiration of me, I'm not capable of guarding everyone by myself. But I'm glad you hold me in esteem. Thank you." He turned and leaned against the rail of the boat. "I think we're good, and I'll be very surprised if we're bothered by merfolk again."

I leaned next to him. "Can I be honest with you? Will you give me an honest answer?"

"Of course."

"I'm really worried guarding Emmett has been so easy up to this point. Zaemon is hardly going to give up after one try and we haven't seen anything from him since the day I found out Emmett carried magic." An involuntary shiver ran through my body.

Omri put an arm around me giving a one-armed hug. "I agree. Something will happen. I just don't know when or where."

I leaned my head on his chest. "Is being a bodyguard always so hard? As an assassin, I'd take a job, which might be terrifying for a bit but then it's over. This never seems to end and being on high alert twenty-four hours a day is exhausting."

"Guarding is not always this hard. Usually it's boring. I would assume life as an assassin is far more interesting than life as a bodyguard, under normal circumstances. This job is special."

"Lucky me." I snorted. I stood and started back toward the cabins. "Thanks for listening."

"I wish I could do something to alleviate your tension."

I gave him a smile. "Don't go anywhere. I can't imagine trying to do this job without you."

We arrived in Belize the evening of the third day. Foreboding had settled over me, stronger than ever and I couldn't rest. Talon caught me pacing the stern of the boat.

"Want to fill me in on what's got your panties in a knot?"

"I can't really say. I have this nagging feeling something isn't right."

"Pick a number off the list. There's dozens of things wrong."

"No. I feel like we're sitting on the edge of a precipice. Something bad is at our feet and I can't see what. I told Omri I felt uneasy after the mermaid attack but today it's stronger."

"Don't tell Omri." Talon crossed his arms. "Tell me. Remember who has the training. He may be a tough breed but he's the domestic help. If you don't trust me tell Yumiko."

"I didn't tell Omri because I trust him more, Omri is . . . calmer. Or maybe more worldly is a better way to explain." I didn't want to admit I was avoiding being alone with Talon, too.

He started to reach for my face and let his hand fall before it got there. "We can do shifts tonight. If we put Omri and Yumiko in the rounds no one has to do more than two and half hours of lookout during the sleeping time. Then we'll all be rested for tomorrow. Speaking of which." He gripped my arm. "What do you know? Omri didn't take you on the bike for a date. If we're going to be partners, you need to fill me in."

"Partners?" The word came out in a gasp.

He heaved a sigh. "Not for good. For this mission. But seriously, would having me for a partner be so bad? We both need one. If we get through this mission, we could team up. We'll already know each other's style." He gave me an exasperated look, probably because I'd begun backing away. "Never mind. Just fill me in."

I told Talon what Omri had told me. Omri's silence raised suspicion. Why wasn't he filling Talon in? I'd have to figure that out later. For now, I'd be the bridge between Talon and Omri. When I finished explaining, Talon didn't look as surprised as I'd been at being told we were going back to the Borderlands.

"Are you sure you're ready for this?" He looked me in the eye. "You and Emmett are the only ones who've never been to the Borderlands. Nothing will prepare a human for it, but you . . . never having been there makes you basically human mentally. Are you going to be all right?"

"I'm always all right. Omri told me the Borderlands aren't so different. Aside from the fact I'll look like an imp all the time."

"Omri's a little blasé about this. The differences aren't just in the way we'll look. Things smell different. The food's different. The government is different. No one will look human and no one will hold back on their true nature. No one's trying to assimilate there. So, you have to know how to tread or how to hold your own, or both."

"Oh."

"Oh, is right. Have you even been in a fully released imp form?"

"A couple times I've lost control and sprouted my tail."

He sighed and ran a hand through his blue hair. "That's a big no. On Earth, your magic is set up to keep you as close to a human as possible. Think of it like a default setting. If you let go of the default, all sorts of things change. For example: I have green skin and white hair. I have cat eyes which see perfectly at night as well as the day. I prefer my meat raw and I have a tail, too. Exactly what you get depends a little on you personally, but your looks are going to be way different than what you're used to." He leaned back against the boat rail, crossing his legs and arms. "There's really not time to run you through the finer points of not pissing magic folk off, so let Omri or I do the talking and follow my lead."

"But—"

He raised a hand, cutting me off. "I know you're a take charge kinda girl, but you're gonna have to let go of the reins on this one."

"I'll try."

"Good girl."

I stuck my tongue out at him.

Chapter 9

Nothing happened that night, despite our vigilance. Nothing happened the next morning when our guide took us into the jungle and downriver to the ruins. Monkeys howled at us from somewhere deep within the vegetation. Humidity hung so heavy in the forest we might as well have been breathing underwater. And from the moment I set foot in the jungle mosquitoes buzzed at my ears.

I slapped one against my neck and Talon made a face at me. "Gross. The bug popped and now you have a blood spatter on your neck."

"Hah. Better a little blood then the way you look. They bit all over your face and you look like you've got zits."

Omri used a magic geyser to shrink Elita's stack of luggage into something pockct sized while the rest of us lounged and waited. Except Elita. She buzzed around us making a constant and irritating whining, like a giant mosquito. Though I doubted I'd get away with slapping her.

Once Omri had packed Elita's bags in his pockets, we headed off into the jungle in the direction of the unicorn. Omri kept checking a compass and a map which no doubt led straight to the gateway rather than a unicorn.

The further into the jungle we went the worse the heat got since the trees blocked any breeze. The air stood completely still and almost vibrated with life. I would have given anything to be back on the boat with a breeze.

I'd nearly reached needing to scream at someone about the atmosphere when we finally emerged into a partial clearing. In the center, a huge stone step pyramid reached above the tops of the trees. Moss covered the sides of the ruin and dirt had built up around the base. The temple remains oozed creepiness. In fact, the whole clearing made my skin crawl. I sidled up to Talon and gave his arm a poke.

"Do you feel that?"

He nodded and the tight expression he wore let me know we were on the same page. Yumiko as well, for though she never said a word she stood tense and ready. I smelled them before they came into view. The stench almost made me lose my lunch: dead things.

When the first one lurched into the clearing I gulped down rising bile. The creature resembled a body which had been completely charred, black with flesh hanging from exposed bones in strips. Random clumps of stiff hair clung to his head and he stared at us with empty eye sockets. I would have screamed for Omri, but Elita beat me to it.

Omri turned from studying the temple and let out a hiss. "Draugr."

My lack of understanding must have shown on my face.

"Zombies," Talon explained as he pulled blades from beneath his clothes.

"Zaemon must be practicing necromancy," Omri added, tossing a wicked looking sword to me. "Hack the heads off and cut out the heart and brain. If those are destroyed they'll die again."

"This is against all laws," Yumiko said, herding Emmett and Elita into the loose circle we'd formed. "We need to report to the Lord. Action must be taken."

At this point I counted ten of the draugr in the clearing.

Talon grunted. "Let's save ourselves first."

Omri held two short swords and attacked first. He dashed out bringing both blades across the neck of one of the draugr, hacking the head off with a scissor slice. As the skull hit the ground a dark purple gas issued from the still standing body.

Omri's face swiftly turned a strange shade of orange. "Poison," he gasped out. "Don't cut. Burn."

Omri crumpled to the ground as Elita screamed and clung to Emmett who swayed, ready to pass out. Yumiko had switched out her blades for a torch. I assumed she made the weapon with magic, but she took a huge risk since we still had nine draugr and the guts of one to deal with. Evidently a weapon would be a worthwhile expenditure of power because Talon had done the same. Yumiko ignited the first of the remaining draugr. The creature went up like dry grass. His mouth gaped in a silent scream, rotten teeth hanging from his jaw.

Talon took down a second as I switched my blade for a torch, too. I took out the third. The draugr were hanging back, obviously unwilling to come near but unable to go against their orders. Yumiko went for one of the remaining six and screamed. As soon as she lit the draugr on fire, the mouth opened, and the same poison gas billowed out.

Talon and I were alone now. We backed Elita and Emmett against the wall of the temple in the hopes of protecting them, but I doubted we stood much chance.

"Now what?" I asked Talon.

"Try these." He tossed me a handgun.

"What are they?"

"Something nasty my dad concocted. They lodge in the body scattering shrapnel and poison. Head shots, let's scramble some draugr brains."

I gave a quick nod and took a shot. The draugr fell to the ground with a sick thud.

"They work."

"Don't get cocky," he gritted out, taking a shot of his own. "There's three more of them and only two of us and they're adapting."

The body of the draugr he'd shot leaked gas from the bullet hole. He aimed at the draugr who stood furthest from us and shot him through the center of the forehead. This time the head exploded, and the fallen corpse disappeared, shrouded in a cloud of gas.

"What about the last two?" At least the adrenaline kept my voice steady.

"Do you trust me?"

Ready to trust or not I had no choice. "Yes."

"Were going to have to move quick. I'll hold, you drive your dagger through his ear. Make the smallest hole possible."

I nodded, ignoring a whimper from Emmett. A point-blank attack left no margin of error. If this didn't work, I would be mauled or worse.

Talon started his count. On three we leapt. Talon slammed the draugr to the ground and pinned his body. I rammed a dagger through his ear and twisted for good measure. When the draugr stopped moving we both jumped clear as I jerked my blade free. The blade came out covered in thick, black sludge.

Elita screamed. The last draugr had a hand on her arm. Talon ran, tackling the creature and knocking it to the ground. Before I got to him the draugr had raked dirty nails, like claws, across his neck and back. The skin around the wound started to turn a sickly green even before the blood welled up.

"*Talon.*"

I ran for him, driving the dagger into the skull of the draugr. At least Talon had kept him pinned. The last things I remember were the bang, like the popping of a balloon, and a stench which stung my nose, sweet and deadly at the same time.

Then blackness.

~ ~ ~

Somewhere a monkey shrieked and light flashed in blotches. Why was I so hot?

Zombies.

I sat bolt upright and blinked in confusion. At the same time, Emmett tackled me. He sobbed joyfully over my head, smoothing my hair and hugging me by turns.

"You're alive. Can you talk? Are you all right?"

"I can talk if you'd stop strangling me."

Emmett immediately backed off, bouncing happily on his heels beside me.

I rubbed my temples. My head throbbed. "What happened? Are the draugr gone? Is Elita safe, too?" Not that I really cared.

"You guys were amazing. You got all the draugr. I thought you were all going to die. You probably would have but Elita . . . Well, Talon made her a gas mask just before he collapsed. I never had a problem with the gas. Elita said the draugr were supposed to collect me so the demon lord must have made the gas nontoxic to humans. But seeing you all on the ground, dying, Elita snapped. She sent all the fallen draugr up in a blaze at once and then healed all of you. She's been fretting over Omri and Yumiko since yesterday. She's been sobbing about them being her only real family."

"You're kidding? The snooty ice queen?"

"Yesterday I would have agreed. But she's pretty capable if forced, and I guess fairies are talented at healing. She took care of you, too. I didn't even have to say anything. She said she didn't want to owe you for saving her life . . ." He paused a moment. "But I'm not sure that's the only reason. She treated you very gently. I don't think she's really a bad person. I think maybe she's just never needed to be good. If that makes any sense."

I nodded. After what Omri had told me Emmett's theory made perfect sense. "What about the others? How are they?" Emmett frowned, and my stomach clenched.

"Omri and Yumiko are both up. Omri is all right. Yumiko fell with her face in the jet of poison. The purple gas seems to have damaged her voice. She can't speak."

"How can you tell?" I muttered.

"She tried to thank Elita, no words. Elita isn't sure she can fix the damage."

"Talon?" My heart gave a funny lurch as I said his name.

"Still asleep. How about you? Anything we can fix?"

"My headache?"

"You need magic." Omri stood over me. "Drink." He handed me a cup.

The stuff inside tasted like the magic from the fire hydrant. Omri must have had time to find another geyser. A few sips and I felt like myself again.

"Thanks."

He shooed Emmett away and crouched in front of me. "Without your friend near. Are you truly okay? No need to hold back. Zaemon has pulled off his gloves, you'll need to be working at 100 percent to fend off his minions."

I gave myself a thorough assessment. "Really. I'm fine. I'll let you know if I find anything once we're up and moving."

"Good. You worried me, you slept so long. Can you—"

Talon let out a groan and I went hurrying over. "Talon, Talon. Are you okay?"

He held his head. "I'm so drained I could kiss the source." His voice came out so deep and raw, talking must have been painful.

Omri handed him the cup. "No need for kissing. Drink. Olivia saved plenty for you."

He wrinkled his nose at the cup and looked up at me. "Maybe I should go with Emmett. I'll get less spit. You backwashed, didn't you?"

I stood with a huff. "He's fine. He's far too feisty for a little poison gas to do him in."

Turning to go, I nearly bumped noses with Elita. I blushed and tried to run off. I didn't care what Emmett said. I couldn't promise to be nice, so I'd be better off leaving. She stepped back in front of me and I worked to bite my tongue.

"Th . . ." She was turning pink with the effort of trying to speak with a peasant, evidently. "Thank you. Even if you kept going just for Emmett, you saved me, too."

Huh? I froze in place. After being one step shy of a snake all week, now she wanted to be nice? My head started spinning again. Hands steadied me from behind.

"Acknowledge her," Omri hissed in my ear.

"You're welcome." I gaped, goldfish style. Before I said another word, she'd flounced away. "Wha—"

"She's moving toward the polish we talked about." Omri kept his voice low and right in my ear. "Her new behaviors should be encouraged. The transformation won't happen all at once but if you encourage the change she will blossom, and life will become easier for everyone."

"Hey, doctor," Talon croaked. "Stop examining Olivia. She's fine. I've got these scratches the draugr left. They're throbbing like a mother—"

"I'm not the doctor," Omri snapped cutting across Talon's language. "Elita fixed us all up. If you need something further, you'll have to ask her."

Omri finally let go of my arms from where he'd steadied me. For some reason, I wished he'd stay. Omri called Elita over and she started tending to Talon's wounds. I watched, fascinated. Omri was right. She treated him quite kindly.

"You're gonna have to do something about them." Emmett stood next to me speaking quietly.

"About what?"

Emmett sighed. "You we're this oblivious at home, too. You may have super cool skills in other things, but you never noticed boys. Talon and Omri both like you. It's gonna get weird trying to work together if their crushes get out of hand."

"No," I said slowly. "Talon likes me. Omri, well, I kinda feel about him the way I felt about you when we met."

"I'm not completely sold he feels the same way in return." He stared after Omri. "Maybe I got the idea because Elita seems to think Omri has his eye on you. She ought to know."

"Weird." I shook my head. "You talk about her like she's normal. Even Talon's a picnic compared to her," I griped.

Emmett shrugged.

"Oh, dear Lord. What happened while I was asleep? You're crossing over to the dark side, aren't you?"

"We'll see. I'm clinging to the silver lining that maybe she's not all bad." He gave me a nudge with his elbow. "I'm not going to harp since I can't be sure. Just be aware and don't let things get uncomfortable."

I nodded, looking away. This conversation made me want to squirm and it couldn't be over fast enough for my taste. Thankfully, Omri and Elita worked fast. Talon was already up, flexing his arm and thanking Elita. She pranced around, pleased as a cat who's left a mouse on its owner's doorstep. Whether she was basking in her own accomplishments or soaking in the genuine thanks I couldn't tell.

Omri began arrangements for going through the gateway. We'd lost a full day after the attack, and until we got moving we were sitting ducks. Packing and planning weren't my job, so I tried applying Emmett's theory of attraction to Talon and Omri while I waited.

Talon scooted closer when I joined the group, but made no further moves. He didn't even strike up a conversation. And Omri seemed indifferent as usual.

I heaved a sigh, letting relief run through me. The idea Omri had a crush on me was as ridiculous as saying Emmett did. Talon's interest stemmed from our compatibility professionally, which didn't strike me as romantic at all. But my guesses didn't matter. Sex appeal and I were oil and water. I *couldn't* be attractive to two guys. Emmett was wrong.

Yumiko's whole body drooped sadly as she packed up the cookware. I understood and could handle her emotions. She'd been left all alone, so I got up and went over. Helping her would give me something productive to focus on. Grabbing some plates from what must have been breakfast, I magicked them clean and brought them to her.

"Here." Yumiko looked up and I smiled at her. "I heard about your voice. I'm sorry."

She shrugged and looked away.

"I know you never said much but it must suck not being able to speak at all."

She stuffed a few more things in her bag and took a quick swipe at the tears on her face.

"Um, look. I know we don't know each other very well. I don't know you well enough to know what to say, but can I give you a hug?"

She looked up at me, surprise in her eyes.

I blushed and looked away this time. "I just feel . . . without everyone, we'd all be dead. I'm grateful for your being here. I wanted to . . . I don't know . . . do something."

She stood stock still, and I gave her a tentative hug. To my surprise she tucked her face against my shoulder and silent sobs shook her body. I wasn't prepared for this. I hadn't expected to open flood gates. But I understood. The poor girl never said anything but that didn't mean she didn't feel anything. I can't have been the only one to find her unapproachable. She must have been lonely.

I wrapped my arms around her and tried not to cry myself. Her injury would only isolate her further, assuming she got to continue guarding. How can you effectively warn anyone of danger without a voice? Magic folk were deeply tied to our roles as being a part of our individual identity. The thought of losing her job must be terrifying for her.

"I understand," I soothed. "You'll find somewhere to go when this is over. Until then we'll make sure nothing happens to you."

Yumiko sniffed and nodded into my shoulder and I patted her back.

A voice cleared beside us. Elita stood there with a strange look on her face. "She doesn't need to worry. If she can't be my bodyguard she can work with Omri. I won't cast her out." Elita wrinkled her nose. "Maybe I'll hire someone like the imp or the toyol to act as bodyguard." She turned on her heel and stalked off.

I couldn't help bursting out laughing. I laughed so hard everyone stopped packing and stared at me. I gave Yumiko a squeeze and pushed her away. "There, you see. Sourpuss can't come out and say it, but she loves you. She won't get rid of you no matter what's happened. Your place in your bizarre little family is secure. Now she's even admitted she's learning to like the peasants."

"I think maybe I could like you, too," I called after Elita. "Assuming you act more like you have the last two days."

Yumiko glanced between the two of us and gave us a huge smile.

I took her hand and squeezed it. "That's what made you sad, wasn't it?"

She nodded.

Elita flipped her hand over and created a spiral notebook, tossing it to Yumiko. "If something's bothering you say so. My job as your mistress is to listen and meet your needs."

Yumiko hurried off after Elita who'd evidently reached the limit of her newly found kindness. I started to go help Talon with the pile of weapons we'd be wearing but two strong hands gripped my shoulders.

"You did well. Bridging the gap between them," Omri whispered, his lips on my ear again.

This time I blushed as Emmett's words rung in my head. He wasn't telling me secrets. He didn't need to be so close. But the proximity didn't mean anything, right? This must be Omri's way of speaking privately. Even as I explained the proximity away, I knew I'd never seen him talk to Elita or Yumiko this way.

"Too . . . too close," I muttered and moved away.

"My apologies." His voice was as smooth as his step in the other direction. "Would you assist me searching the temple for the entrance?"

I followed his directions but didn't help at all. The whole ruin looked like a moldering pile of rocks and vines to me. But Omri, in his usual capable fashion, found a hidden passage into the interior. In less than half an hour we stood inside the temple, staring at the open gateway. Its shimmering surface reminded me of looking through leaded glass, the other side waving and unclear but visible. The gateway led out into a busy street, though the people bustling past didn't give it a second glance.

"We go in pairs," Omri ordered.

Talon immediately took my hand. "I've got Olivia. She's never been to the Borderlands. No need to let her cause a ruckus."

Omri snorted and shrugged. "I'll take Emmett. Elita can go with Yumiko." He sighed and rubbed the back of his head. "Talon, understand you're traveling with a princess and a source. Yumiko be ready for the usual welcome."

He gestured Talon and I toward the gateway. Feeling my hands grow clammy I followed Talon through. As my feet landed on pavement, the noise of a city assaulted my ears, even more shocking after the silent interior of the temple one second before. I got shoved out of the way as Elita and Yumiko stepped through. The next moment Omri and Emmett came out of thin air, appearing with a pop. I stared at the spot they'd come from. The gateway was invisible from this side.

Chapter 10

A variety of creatures I barely recognized immediately accosted us. Flashbulbs went off in our faces and recording devices were being shoved up our noses. Elita flipped her hair over her shoulder. It now hung in luxurious waves down to the middle of her back, all in a soft lavender. Delicate butterfly wings quivered on her back and wire thin antennae stuck up from her hair. She was exquisite.

"I will answer five questions," she announced to the paparazzi.

"Did you really go to Earth after a source?" a man with blue skin and goat horns asked.

Elita gave a cruel laugh. "Like I'd waste my time on marrying a human. In order to better rule beside my father I've been spending time on Earth learning to blend in."

"Then why do you have a human with you?" asked a cat-woman.

Elita shot Emmett a cold look. "He's a pet. He's here to answer any questions I might have about humans. You should all know better than to pester me about this. The source is a myth."

"Why do you have so much security with you?" a small, half-bird woman asked with narrowed eyes.

"Earth is primitive and uncivilized. I would never risk the trip without a proper security detail."

"Since you've returned home, will you be attending the gala at the dragon symposium?"

"You'd have to ask my father. I don't arrange the guest list."

"What brings you to the city? Are you shopping today? Who will you be wearing?" an overzealous satyr asked.

"Well, there you have it." Elita gave them a derisive look. "I said five questions and goat-boy's gone and ruined your chance. He asked seven, so we're done."

She snapped her fingers at us. I swallowed my pride and followed. I had to admit I'd have been at a loss for dealing with them. She answered the questions and got us out of there without undue attention.

Elita took off down the street. I stared around curiously as I followed. The street and sidewalk looked exactly like Earth except the material used to pave. The pavement shone with a slight gloss and resembled stone, in brown with cream marbling. The red sun hung lower in the sky to our right. On Earth, having the sun there would have meant late afternoon, but I doubted the sun had the exact same alignment here. The red light made all the colors around us pop with vibrancy, giving the otherwise human-looking cityscape an animated quality.

Completely at ease here, Elita pranced us to a nearby hotel and stopped at the door. "Omri, Yumiko will escort me to the spa. I expect my usual suite ready when I get done." She eyed me head to toe. "The imp, uh, Olivia comes with me, as well."

Confused as to what she could possibly need me for, I followed her into the spa. She was moving at a slower pace inside the building and I snatched the moment to admire our surroundings and catch my breath. I'd been so focused on keeping up with Elita, I'd paid no attention to Yumiko. Now the slinky tail swishing behind her caught my attention. She had short, glossy black fur all over her body and two pandaish rounded ears peeked out of the long black hair on her head. On our way past a large gilded mirror I paused to see myself and gasped at the reflection.

"I know." Elita had joined me in front of the mirror. "You're a complete travesty. Don't worry. When we leave the spa, you'll be fit to be seen with me."

I couldn't tell if she was promising me something good, or insulting me. So, I nodded and followed as she led on. In the spa she ordered me a list of services I'd never heard of. Of course, I hadn't been to a spa on Earth either, so I had no idea if the services were exclusive to the Borderlands. Maybe I simply lacked all basic spa knowledge.

After the three of us changed into light cotton robes, a willowy looking dryad whisked me away. She took me to a room filled with the smell of incense and flickering with candlelight. A fountain played at the back breaking the silence with the soothing patter of water.

The dryad laid me out on a table, a sheet spread across me and the masseuse entered. I gasped and quickly clapped a hand over my mouth. Without meaning to I stared at the centaur who had come tapping in. His horse half shone rich mahogany bay, the coat glossy and well groomed. From the waist up his skin was the same handsome brown but completely hairless and taut over muscle. A head of thick, wavy black hair and a diamond smile met my eyes.

I had never seen a man so beautiful. I would have been happy to lay there gazing at him, but he gently pushed my head down and started massaging my shoulders. A moan escaped me before I caught it. I'd underestimated how tense I'd gotten. He had magic in his hands. Whether he truly used magic or whether I imagined it, I suppose doesn't matter. I only cared that he not stop.

Three hours of being massaged, rubbed with oils and hot rocks, smeared in mud, and rinsed in herbal water later I'd gone jellyfish in the best possible way. I wanted to ask the centaur to marry me, but he'd vanished before the herbal bath. I flopped into a lounge chair poolside. Elita and Yumiko were already there.

"How was your session?" Elita asked.

"Aahhh . . ." The noise came out with a quaver and sounded slightly naughty.

"Good. I figured you hadn't been to a spa before." She made a trip to the spa sound like some employee training I lacked. "Enjoy today as my treat."

I stifled a laugh. Her efforts were genuine and with my social prowess, poking fun at her might be a bit hypocritical. "That's good," I said, "because I could never afford this. You're lucky."

She gave a little sniff. "We still have to get you to the salon. Your looks are disgraceful."

I considered the imp from the mirror when we first came in. In the Borderlands, my skin was pale-yellow in a buttercup sort of way, not a sickly way. My hair had more of a golden quality to the brown, though it still hung rather limp. My ears pointed, my teeth pointed, and my tail swished. I had a fairy tale tail, buttercup yellow to match the rest of me. And complete with a little heart shaped point at the tip. So, I wasn't a beauty like Elita, but "disgraceful" seemed a bit harsh.

Another hour and a half later and I emerged from the salon a new imp. Elita had dressed me up in a shimmery skirt, two-inch metallic heels, and a ruffly tank top. The bra made me look a full size larger than before I put it on. The stylist left my hair in dozens of curls and glossy, honey highlights, something impossible to recreate on Earth. With a smirk, Elita sent me back to the room saying she and Yumiko had a massage with the centaur. Secretly I was jealous. I wanted another round with the centaur, but I obeyed.

I'd forgotten to ask Elita for a key and Talon opened the door when I knocked. He gave me a quick glance.

"Lady Elita isn't in. You can find her in the spa if you'd like."

I thumped the door into his face. "Just let me in, Talon."

His eyes widened. He slipped out of the door letting it close behind him. "Holy Shit. Is that you, Livy?"

I crossed my arms and glared. "I never said you could call me Livy."

"You haven't corrected me for days. I assumed we were good." He let out a sigh. "You look . . . incredible."

"I'd better. Elita probably spent a fortune playing dress up with me." I started toward the door but he blocked me. "And what about you?" I gave him a quick scan. "It's a good thing you told me what you were going to look like. I hardly recognized you."

Talon had vibrant spring green skin, and silvery-colored hair, though the blue dye stuck to the tips and made him look frosted. His ears pointed like mine, his teeth matched mine, and his tail matched mine. But his eyes were now cat like, with slits, though still the same dark brown they had been on Earth. The hallmarks of being a part of the fairy family tree were obvious.

"Livy?" His voice got all husky. Boys are so predictable.

I rolled my eyes at him. "Talon?"

He scanned my body head to toe, slowly, letting his eyes linger on my scowl. He heaved a sigh. "I left my key in the room."

"Huh?"

"Have you got fluff in those pointy ears? I don't have my key."

My cheeks grew hot. Maybe I couldn't read boys like I thought. That's not what I had expected at all. I shook my head. I must be going crazy. Why would anything else even cross my mind? Talon scanned my body again and I blushed deeper. Must he be so unsettling?

"Can you even fight in those clothes?" he asked. "It's not really a good outfit given your job."

"Yeah, Elita seems like a girl who thinks about the practicality of her clothes. Since she gave directions on everything I'm wearing—"

"Everything?" He stared at me curiously.

"Yeah, why?"

Like lightning he had the edge of my skirt in his hands. "I've seen the granny panties you've been packing. I'm curious what the princess likes."

I snatched my skirt back and in the same movement grabbed his wrist and twisted it behind his back. "No one is looking at my panties, pervert. I can't believe you went through my stuff."

He laughed at me. "I didn't go through your stuff. I packed it. Hey, can you blame a guy for helping out?"

I swiped his feet out from under him and landed with a knee in the center of his chest. "That sounds like the reasoning of the guilty to me."

"Come here for a sec." Talon jerked his head, nodding me toward him and like a fool I leaned over. "Thanks." He gave me an incentive grin. "The princess has good taste in bras."

I clamped a hand across the top of my ruffly tank top and took a swipe at him with the other. He laughed and grabbed my hand. A quick push and he'd flipped our positions.

"See," he mock scolded. "I think you've mixed up what you want. You wanted me to play nice, be the kinda guy who sweeps you off your feet. But I think you really need a guy who can knock you off your feet. Anyone less is gonna get trampled by you."

He leaned in for a kiss and I took the momentum and tossed him over and behind my head. "Looks like I need to trample you. I didn't say we'd do that kinda stuff."

He gave a little flip and landed on his feet like a cat. He held a hand out to help me, at the same time giving me a wicked grin. "I'd enjoy the challenge and thanks for wrestling in a skirt. The gold lace panties are hot."

I slapped his hand away and got to my feet myself. Not with my usual grace, being both unaccustomed to moving in a skirt and heels, and being extra careful to keep my undergarments hidden. Once up, I did my best to flounce past him to the door. But I knew, even without his chuckle, I couldn't act prissy like Elita. Not to mention the getup she'd put me in marred any attitude I had as a fighter.

I knocked on the door again, pushing past Omri as he opened it. He sucked in a little breath when I went past. Talon came in the room behind me, hot on my heels and still chuckling.

I rounded on him, about to give him a piece of my mind and stopped. Omri stood beside Talon and I couldn't help but gasp at his appearance. He even blew away the centaur in terms of wild looks. His lower half resembled a lion, the way a satyr is half goat. His waist, haunches, paws and tail were covered in pale silver fur. His torso was naked, probably because it would be hard to pull a shirt on over the wings. Like Talon, Omri's aqua eyes now had leonine slits. But with his pail skin, pale hair, and pale lion fur he looked like a moon child.

"Omri? Is that really you?"

"I was going to ask the same thing." He chuckled. "My compliments to Elita and the staff. You look remarkable. And compliments to you as well for putting up with her scheme."

Emmett hung back, looking uncomfortable.

"What's wrong?" I asked.

A fat tear dripped down his cheek. "I thought I could handle coming to the Borderlands. Even though everyone looks like they popped straight out of a movie. But even you . . . Livy." He burst into tears.

I rushed over and hugged him. "I'm still me, Emmett."

"But you've looked like this your whole life and I never knew. You've hidden so much from me."

"If it helps any, I didn't know I'm really the color of a buttercup," I said, trying to lighten things up.

He gave a watery chuckle, dried his face in his T-shirt, and heaved a sigh. "Sorry. You know I'm not usually so overemotional."

I snuggled into his chest, still hugging him. "I know. My looks are shocking enough for me. I've never been here either, but at least I knew I was a part of this world. I can't imagine what you're going through."

The door opened and Elita came in followed by Yumiko. Elita looked at Emmett and I and made a slightly irritated noise.

"He's having trouble adjusting to leaving Earth." I gave her a stern look.

She mellowed and nodded. "Emmett, is there anything you need, to help?"

Emmett patted my back and I let go. He went over and took one of Elita's hands. "Just time. Be patient with me."

A lot must have happened between those two when the rest of us were unconscious. They appeared to have come out this side in a state of tentative friendship. For the first time, I felt a different sort of pang. When Emmett and I had both hated her, we had an extra bond. Now that we were giving her a chance he'd gotten way closer to her. I wasn't ready to let go.

Talon suddenly appeared at my side. He slipped his fingers through mine and gave me a sympathetic look. How could he flip-flop so fast? From the pervert, teasing me in the hall a few minutes ago, to this. His grip was soft, and when had his presence become reassuring?

Now that he had everyone in the same room, Omri explained a plan, utilizing a labyrinth of tunnels from centuries past which ran below the hotel. We'd use these to sneak out as soon as he finished talking. No one would notice us missing until we were long gone. Thankfully, we hadn't even unpacked. All the magically shrunken bags were in a backpack Talon offered to carry, since Omri's wings were in the way.

Talon and I were the forerunners. We left the room and slunk down the hall first. When we'd made sure the way was clear, Talon made a chirping noise with his teeth. The rest followed. We caught the service elevator down to the basement. We'd left late enough in the day we missed the dinner rush and only a few staff remained to clean. Light from the rooms they occupied cut bright rectangles across the otherwise dark hallway. We tiptoed past those doors down the cement hall to the service shafts.

According to Omri the shafts were simply part of an old tunnel system which had been repurposed for hotel storage. I blinked against the harsh orange fluorescent lighting as I stepped into the first passage. Our group stayed silent, following Omri along the tiled length of the shaft.

After walking *forever*, Omri opened an access door. He pointed us through, holding a finger to his lips. On the other side, the tunnel changed significantly and reminded me of pictures I'd seen of the London underground. These tunnels were made of a dark gray brick and the floor was slick with dampness. The air smelled musty and old. I shivered. I didn't like this place.

Once we all went through the door Omri let out a sigh and whispered, "We should be safe from here on out if you need to speak. Though prepare yourself, it's going to get very dark."

Before I could ask what he was talking about, the door closed with a bang and total darkness engulfed us. "Why?" I squeaked.

Omri ignored my whining. "I know some of you are unable to see. Talon, Yumiko, I assume you can see well enough?"

"Yes." Talon's voice rang hollow in the darkness.

Yumiko must have touched Omri to affirm, because he moved on. "Each of us will take one of the others and lead them out. We have a little over two miles of tunnel, but the bright side is this tunnel dumps us out at the edge of Setmyth Forest. From there I know at least one unicorn calls the far side home. With no hiccups, we're about a three-day journey from there."

"Omri." Elita whimpered.

"Yes, Mistress. You may come with me."

Feet shuffled in the dark as they found each other. A warm hand grabbed mine.

"I've got Livy," Talon announced.

"Yumiko's got me," Emmett added.

We began moving slowly down the tunnel. Talon put his hands on my waist, guiding me. "Stay in the center. There's low pipes along the outsides."

For some reason, my hips grew hot under his hands. He'd also left very little space between us.

"I'm gonna trip over you like this."

He pressed along my body. "I won't let you fall."

His whisper came so close to my ear his breath moved my hair. Why was it so hot in this tunnel? Something brushed along my ear. Were those his lips? *Oh my God.* I couldn't do anything to escape. He was my eyes right now. And why the hell did I have a fluttery feeling under my ribs? *So* unfair.

What I assumed were lips began to slide down my neck. I stopped walking. This was getting ridiculous. I swear, he only took my hand for the chance to take advantage of me. His arms were halfway around me when he froze. I went rigid, too. The hair on the back of my neck stood on end. An evil aura had filled the tunnel.

Chapter 11

"We're not alone." Talon's voice held sharp fear.

"Yumiko, take the others," Omri ordered. "Talon and I will fight them."

"Them?" My voice came out slightly hysterical.

"You wouldn't know the aura," Omri explained, "since they never leave the Borderlands. They're sigbin and they hunt children. Unfortunately, we're probably all young enough for them to attack. They're evil enough for us to feel even if they're way back at the start of the hotel's tunnel. But even if they're way back we don't have long. They travel fast."

Ice invaded my blood. "I'll fight."

"You can't," Talon snapped. "You're blind."

"You two can't take on these things by yourselves. If I fight, you have extra hands and Yumiko only has two to worry about."

I got caught in strong arms and a firm hand tipped my face up. I could smell Talon, close to my face. Now what?

"You're putting your life in my hands to fight blind with me. Are you ready to trust me?"

"Yes."

"Livy, I'm serious." His voice trilled with fear. "You have to trust me completely and you have to do what I tell you."

"Okay," I whispered.

"You're not going into the thick. Hang back at my left shoulder and do exactly as you're told."

"Yes."

He let me go and shifted his stance. I felt around in the darkness until I got his shoulder and took my place beside him. Suddenly I remembered something. I fumbled in my ponytail and pulled a vial of poison out of its usual hiding spot. I ran my hand along his arm until I found his hand.

"Here, take this."

"What is it?" His hand closed around the small vial, and I slid my hand back up to his shoulder to keep track of him.

"Concentrated naga venom."

"Ah, the more you hang around the more I like you. That's perfect."

"Got any more?" Omri asked.

"Just the one vial."

"Talon, let me have the poison," Omri said.

Talon gave a little purr and leaned away from me, throwing me off balance. He helped steady me as he took an upright stance once more.

"Omri made himself a bow." He filled me in. "He's poisoning his arrows."

I drew my knife in my free hand and Talon armed himself with his blades as well. Then we waited. I wanted to scream as the dark and oppressive atmosphere engulfed me. The tapping of hooves ricocheted off the walls. At the same time the tunnel filled with an overwhelming stench.

A moment later Talon tensed. "They're coming."

A twang of bow string, followed by a yelp, a thud. Omri must have fired an arrow. Judging by Talon's calm, the thud had been one of theirs.

"I count eight." Omri's yell coincided with another twang.

I counted three more twangs and thuds, before Talon moved.

"Knife under my left hip," he barked at me.

Keeping my free hand on his body for a guide, I did as I was told. Something with short, wiry fur jerked the knife from my hand and screamed. Talon twisted too fast for me to keep up with and I got knocked to the side by the beast as Talon fought with it. The sigbin landed against me. I slid my other dagger off my hip and rammed it between the creature's ribs, twisting as I went. The beast screamed again and shuddered, but fell. I managed to keep my blade.

"Thanks." Talon helped me back to my spot beside him in time for the next attack.

Breath, hot and stinking washed over my neck as teeth snapped inches from my face.

"*No*," Talon screamed, and bodies collided.

Everything went crazy from there. Omri let out a blood-curdling scream. Followed by a gunshot and whimpering which didn't come from a sigbin. This couldn't be happening.

"*Talon*?" I got no answer.

I used my reserves of magic and threw them into creating light. Focusing the power in my blade, the scene in the tunnel blazed to horrifying life. I took in the goat-like sigbin with his jaws around Talon's neck and blind fury drove me forward. Using my Hermes shoes, I launched myself at the beast. I went fast enough to startle the creature and the tunnel went dark as I sunk the blade into its eye socket. I felt the beast fall and realized it landed on top of Talon.

"*No, no, no*." I pushed at the beast to get it off. "Talon? Talon?"

The world spun, and my legs faltered. Small hands were pulling me back.

"*Talon*," I screamed, but my voice echoed strangely in my ears.

Suddenly I was being kissed. My body filled with Emmett's irresistible scent of fresh magic. I drank in desperation, trying to fill a void in myself. Though lack of power wasn't really the cause.

Emmett broke the kiss. "Save some for the others."

"Talon? Omri?" I shook my head but the blackness in my eyes stayed.

The small hands which had pulled me away from Talon were now smoothing my cheeks.

"Yumiko?"

Gentle pressure followed my question.

"Are you helping them?"

Again, came the gentle pressure. She took me and led me a few steps, placing my hand in a familiar one. I jammed my face into Emmett's chest and sobbed. He cried, too.

"Yumiko." Elita's voice echoed through the dark tunnel. "Take me to Talon."

I gulped. Why were they only getting to Talon now? He'd had one of those goat-fiends on his neck. Once again silence settled over the tunnel like a black woolen blanket. I was going to suffocate. My panic got worse when Emmett left me for a moment. Yumiko must have taken him to give Omri magic. When he came back I clenched his hand, not wanting to be left alone, desperately waiting for any word on Talon.

After an excruciating delay, Elita sighed. "Emmett?" Her voice was hoarse.

Emmett left again. I waited anxiously in the darkness, but didn't try to keep him with me. I couldn't be selfish when everyone needed him.

Elita finally spoke, her voice hollow in the darkness. "Yumiko wants to know if we can move away from the gore. Omri and Talon are still unconscious, so we'll have to carry them."

"I'll take one," I offered. "But I want out of here. We must have gone most of the way before the attack. Can we finish?"

"Can you carry someone that far?" Elita asked from the darkness.

"I'd like to try."

"Emmett?" Elita asked. "I know you're drained but can you carry the other?"

Emmett sighed. "I'll take Talon. He's lighter. I'm sorry, Livy. I can't manage any more after powering four people."

"I'll take Omri then." I stood. "Yumiko, put him on my back, please."

I got a heavy, furry body draped over my shoulders and my knees wanted to buckle. I clenched my teeth and forced myself to stand. I couldn't give up. If the others could manage, so could I. The others scuffled, presumably loading Talon onto Emmett's shoulders. Emmett grunted but said nothing. Yumiko scooted past us in order to take the lead. Elita called out where the kamaitachi directed her to go.

We moved through the tunnel in inch long increments. Omri's lion fur baked my back and every muscle in my body screamed for me to quit. But I swore the air had gotten lighter, so I pushed on clinging to slivers of hope. Emmett staggered behind me. I knew he would push himself to keep up with me. Hopefully I didn't hurt him in the process but we'd all do better outside where we could see. At least then I wouldn't be so helpless.

A scream echoed through the tunnel and my heart nearly stopped. My stomach dropped. We couldn't handle another problem, being completely defenseless at this point. But instead of trouble, another wild shriek followed. As did a rectangle of purple light and a rush of cool air. We'd gotten out.

I made my way to the grass and dropped to my knees, Omri rolling off to the side. Tears streamed down my face. I'd never seen anything as beautiful as the night sky. Emmett and Talon tumbled to the ground beside me. The next thing I saw was the indigo grass on its way to meet my face.

~ ~ ~

Horrifying dreams of beasts and darkness plagued my sleep. I couldn't stand another second. I bolted upright with a scream. Immediately a cool cloth pressed against my head and my eyes met the kind, almond eyes of Yumiko. Her furry ears twitched with obvious irritation. Holding up one finger she scrambled off and came back with her writing pad.

The others are sleeping. You are the first to wake today. How do you feel?

"Like hell." I rubbed my head. "I don't think I have anything which doesn't hurt."

That's not surprising. You were scratched by one of the sigbin. Why did you not tell us you were wounded before you carried Omri back? You lost a good deal of blood. Much more and you would have been past what Lady Elita could fix.

I chuckled. "I've never heard you say so much, Yumiko."

She looked at the pad and rocked with silent laughter.

I took her hand. "Seriously, though, how are the others?"

Everyone will live.

"I couldn't see the fight. What exactly happened?"

Be glad you couldn't see. Emmett has been plagued with nightmares. He wasn't fighting when you lit your blade and had time to see all the carnage. You saved us all. Lady Elita is anxious to repay you in some way.

"I didn't do much. I couldn't see a thing. Besides, it sounds like nearly everyone needed everyone else. If anyone hadn't been there we'd have been screwed. Who knew such an odd little band would make such perfect partners."

I got a genuine smile and a hug from her. *Yes. That's true. But I was referring to your quick thinking with the poison. Without your poison on those arrows and your willingness to fight despite not being able to see, Omri and Talon could not have won. We would all be dead.*

I blushed and focused on my sleeping bag for a diversion. "Thanks. But you're dodging the question I want answered the most. What happened to Omri and Talon?"

Her eyes filled with tears. *Omri has a punctured lung. One of the sigbin got a bite around his chest.*

"They must have been far bigger than I thought."

About the size of a large buck, minus the antlers. But thanks to your parents for giving Emmett the gun. He gave it to me and I took the shot. I hesitated. You guys were moving so much, and I had no way to warn you. I waited too long, and people got hurt. I also meant to shoot the beast who had Talon, but you flipped out and did the job for me. She smiled at me.

"Yumiko, what happened to Talon?" My worry had come roaring back to the front of my mind.

He . . . he was badly ravaged. Elita didn't go to him right away because . . . Because I told her he'd gone. He looked dead. Fairy magic is wonderful, but it can only do so much. He's got scars on his neck and he lost half an ear. But he'll live. And unlike me he'll be able to fight as long as his hearing wasn't damaged.

The tears started to slide. "If only I'd been able to see. Why don't imps get night vision? We hunt at night, right?"

On Earth. But this is not Earth. You are not the same here. And please stop. This is not your fault.

I shrugged off her friendly hand on my shoulder. "Where is he?"

Yumiko pointed to a pile of blankets near a fire. I went over and sat beside him. He looked younger asleep than he did awake. The dark purple of night which had hidden us when we'd staggered out of the tunnel still blanketed the sky and in this light his skin shone pale and an almost glow-in-the-dark green. The scars where his neck had been ripped apart tore darkly across the lighter, healthy skin. And sure enough, the top half of his ear, with the point which identified him as my kind, was gone.

I curled beside him and took a limp hand in my own. "I'm sorry." My voice caught on a sob. "I let you down. I wasn't enough for backup and look where it got you. You took on the beast who tried to eat me." I smoothed my fingers across the scars. "Those were meant to be mine." I pulled his hand up and kissed the palm. "I promise things will be different when you wake up. I trust you now. No holding back. I will try my best to be a partner worthy of your sacrifice, assuming you still want me after what I did."

Rubbing the tears away, I went back to Yumiko. "How about Emmett? He wasn't anything more than drained, right?"

She took out the writing pad again. *Emmett and Elita are fine. They've been tending to you for almost four days.*

"Four days?" I yelped and clapped a hand over my mouth as Elita stirred. "Sorry."

Yumiko nodded. *Recovering from injuries as severe as yours takes a good deal of time, even with fairy magic.*

Talon and Omri didn't wake until the next afternoon. I spent the day poking around the woods curiously. Having a red sun intensified all colors into jewel tones. But otherwise Setmyth forest could have passed as earthly woods, filled with trees like oaks and firs. Birds and squirrels darted around about their business. The setting would have been pretty if I hadn't been so worried.

Without Omri's particular talent of finding magic geysers, Emmett had taken to giving everyone power. I wanted to laugh when he kissed the passed-out Omri and Talon. But my stomach felt tight and slightly sick when he fed Elita. He took her face in his hands and gave her a gentle kiss which was uncomfortable to watch.

Elita had changed the most through the aftermath of the attack. I had thanked her for saving me and the others and for caring for us for days. I figured she'd blow my gratitude off but instead she blushed and tentatively reached for me. The next moment lavender hair tickled my nose as Elita hugged me.

"I didn't like you when we met," Elita started.

I tried to keep from rolling my eyes. Obviously, she still needed a bit of practice.

"But you're a good person like Omri and Yumiko," she continued. "And you carried Omri all the way out even when you were hurt, just for me." She squeezed me again. "Thank you. If you decide you want to stay in the Central Borderlands, I'll give you a job and see your magic rations are taken care of."

I gaped at her. "Are you kidding? That's a huge offer. I don't even know what to say. Thank you."

She smiled. "I'm happy to be in a position to reward my friends."

Feeling gushy and impulsive I squeezed her hand. "Friends, for sure."

I worried I might have over stepped but Elita turned pink and giggled. "I've never really had friends before. I'm so excited."

"Me too."

Omri really knew his stuff. She was taking one hell of a polish. All the challenges were certainly getting the job done and each time she conquered one she shone a little brighter. Her feelings made me bubbly inside, too. I had my first female friend.

My ears perked after we'd settled in for the night. Talon, laying in his sleeping bag beside mine, moaned. I reached over and grabbed his hand. "You're okay, Talon. I'm here."

"Livy?"

"Yeah. Do you need anything. Do you hurt? Can I—"

"Slow down? That would be great, because my head is spinning."

He rubbed his temples and let his fingers drag down his face. They paused on his neck. He gave me a startled look and tears crept into my eyes.

"I'm so sorry," I burst out. "I couldn't see and because of me you have scars all over your neck. I'm a failure as a partner. I'll understand if you want to break off our working together."

He stared at me. "Is that what you think?" he croaked. "I'm alive because of you. What part of saving me is failing? You fought blind against a herd of sigbin to help me. I don't want to break off our work relationship. Just the opposite. I don't want to work with anyone but you." His blush even showed in the firelight. "I mean, if you want to work with me. I know you don't think I'm ideal."

I put a finger to his lips. "I trust you, implicitly. I'll work with you and I won't give you crap anymore."

He'd scooched very close to my face. "I can't make the same promise." His lips were so close they were almost touching mine. "I like giving you crap too much to stop."

"I meant about work." I wasn't backing away. Strange. "I'll never stop giving you crap about your crappy personality."

"Partners, then?" he whispered.

"Yesss . . ." Heat flared in my chest. "But being partners doesn't mean we're more." Though for some reason I still didn't back away. He slipped a hand behind my head. I closed my eyes and tipped my head back into his hand. "It's just business," I whispered.

"Of course," he murmured, his lips brushing mine.

Fire rippled through me at his touch and I leaned toward him, cementing the kiss. He gave a low moan and pulled me tighter. Firelight flickered and in the forest, crickets trilled, like a scene from a movie.

I slapped down the voice in my head asking if I really wanted to be doing this with a man who, two weeks ago had me wanting to throttle him. I wasn't going to listen to my head. I was going to listen to my heart. Without my head's permission my picky, impish heart had found space for Talon. At least I knew toyols were wired similarly. He wouldn't be taking this lightly, reducing the risk of my being hurt. My head could handle that logic, and I gave myself up to being well kissed.

Chapter 12

I woke in Talon's arms and stretched, jumping slightly at the touch of a body next to mine first thing in the morning. And a bit wary to tell the truth. I got a firm kiss to the back of my neck.

"Out of my sleeping bag," he ordered. "I've gotta go, unless you like waterbeds."

I rolled my eyes. What a Talonish way to ruin a moment. I scrambled out of the bed and blushed to find the others staring openly. "I . . . Nothing happened. We just . . ."

"Whatever." Emmett shrugged. "You two are weird enough you might work together."

Omri winced and grabbed his chest as he sat up. "Now that everyone is up we need to get moving. Sitting around only gives Zaemon time to arrange something worse."

I pointed around at our weary and injured ranks. "Are we even still up to this?"

"We don't have a choice. We can't keep taking on legions of evil ourselves. We've got to find the unicorn and get them partnered. Bonding them is the only way to stop the attacks."

I crossed my arms. "Do we really have to do this by ourselves? Isn't Elita's father the next thing to king? Can't he fight the demon lord's forces for her?"

Omri shook his head. "You would have her father take the entire region to war over this?"

"Well, no. I thought—"

"No," Omri snapped. "If you value Emmett, don't even bring such a plan up. My Lord would easily have him killed to ensure peace. He wouldn't flinch at the loss of one man to save thousands."

"Omri's right," Elita added. "Father indulged me with this in the first place. He won't give more help than he already has. If we make ourselves a nuisance he'll be rid of the whole issue." She glanced meaningfully at Emmett.

"Okay. Then what's the plan?" I asked.

We set off in the direction Omri indicated, but we moved tediously slow. Omri labored to breathe and Talon frequently winced as he turned his head. In less than an hour even my scars had begun to burn. I scurried forward and grabbed one of Omri's wings which were now dragging behind him.

"This isn't going to work. We're in no shape to fight and we're going way too slowly."

He shot me a sharp look and dropped to the ground, head, tail, and wings hanging. "What would you suggest?" His tone held a definite bite.

"Isn't there somewhere we can hide until we've had a chance to heal?"

Omri shook his head. "After Zaemon finds his sigbin wiped out, his minions will track us down. Every time we defeat something he gets a better idea of our strength. Which of course we no longer have. The only hope I can see is to try and stay ahead of him."

I crossed my arms and shook my head. "Then we're not thinking hard enough. Because we're not going to win when he shows up. At this rate, we might as well set up a comfortable camp and at least enjoy ourselves as we wait for the inevitable. Or we can use our brains and come up with something else."

Talon patted my head and flopped down next to Omri. "As much as I hate to admit my own weaknesses, Livy's right."

My tail lashed behind me in frustration. "Is there some

way to send a message to the unicorn and get him to come to us?"

"We could try." Omri frowned. "But they're very elusive and not particularly accommodating. Usually they grant requests like ours to get visitors to clear off."

"Good." I'd started pacing little circles. "You work on a message. I'm going to think. I'm not going to sit around and let a demon lord toy with me."

I was still pacing when the forest around us fell silent. I glanced over at Talon and Omri, but they were staring past me, their mouths hanging open. I spun, reaching for my blade. The sight which met my eyes left me nearly wetting my pants. A pair of dragons grinned wickedly at our group.

They were smaller than I would have expected, their serpentine bodies ran about fifteen feet from snout to tail. Each had four equally sized legs, with clawed toes. They sported horns which glittered as viciously as the gleaming tips of daggered teeth peeping from their lips. The right-hand dragon had purple scales so dark they almost shone black. The other was an equally dark blue.

We all backed in around Elita and Emmett out of reflex rather than reality. Even in top form the four of us fighters wouldn't have stood a chance against a pair of dragons. The purple dragon stepped forward and gave us a frightening smile.

"Put down your weapons and come with us peacefully. Lord Zaemon wishes to speak with you. *All* of you. If you do this, you will remain unharmed."

I blinked in surprise. Her voice rolled through the air, carrying power and intimidation, but there was no mistaking the femininity. I'm not sure why it never occurred to me female dragons existed, but the reality shocked me.

Elita pushed past us and stood between us and the dragon. "You understand who I am, right? Taking me or harming me is tantamount to a declaration of war."

The blue dragon gave a chuckle, which churned my stomach with vibration. "Yes, little fairy. We're aware of who you are. Lord Zaemon has taken this into consideration. You'll need to come with us. You'll be hard for your father to rescue in pieces." He inclined his head toward all of us. "My sister did not properly introduce us. I am Farak, and this is my sister, Ferika. If you agree to come peacefully, you are to be escorted as guests. Lord Zaemon has business with you."

Omri stood. "And if we refuse to do business with a demon lord?"

"Then we'll be staying to lunch." Farak tightened his claws on the dirt, running a tongue across his teeth.

Ferika snickered. "Don't worry, we're quick eaters. We don't play with our food."

Omri sighed. "We will come."

"Zaemon has a really loose definition of guest, doesn't he?" I snorted. I caught flashing dragon eyes at my impertinence as well as a painful grip from Talon.

"Don't piss them off," he hissed at me.

Farak gave us a grin exposing his impressive set of teeth. "You will ride three apiece on us."

He flattened his back to where we could climb up and I scowled at the glistening scales incredulously. How was I supposed to hang on to a back as slick as polished metal? Talon pushed me up on Farak's back and then helped pull Yumiko up. Emmett, Elita, and Omri climbed aboard Ferika. A moment later both dragons took off and the forest fell away beneath us.

Talon's nose jammed in my ear as we clung to the dragon's back. "Whatever happens, I'm glad we met."

"Why does it sound like you're saying goodbye?" I tried to swallow my heart which had somehow ended up in my throat.

"Oh, Livy." His voice was tight and sad. "Dragons are unforgiving, cunning, and excellent liars." He choked on the rest. "I . . . can't believe how deeply I care about you. I wish we could have had longer."

He ran the tip of his nose along my ear, and despair choked me.

"Oh God, Talon. Please, don't do this. If you're waiting for me to say the same, I won't. Because I just chose a partner. That's a huge decision for an imp. I'm going to work with my partner for years yet. And I can hardly believe he's saying things which sound like he's given up."

I pressed my back into Talon's chest. "Seriously," I whispered. "My partner is one of the most infuriatingly stubborn and feisty people I know. He pisses me off and still somehow demands I like him at the same time. He's brave, to the point of foolish. And I'm wondering where he went to right now."

"That's not fair, Livy." Talon gave my waist a squeeze so hard it hurt. "The Talon you're describing didn't have a partner. He only had to watch his own back. Now I need to watch out for you, too. Do you not understand how much I care? You have to. These feelings are not much different for a toyol than an imp. If you got hurt, I'd be crushed. And . . . and I can't see this ending well. I'm not quitting. I will stand between you and the dragons if necessary, but I wanted you to know how I feel just in case. I want this partnership to go on for years, as well. I want to make you say out loud that you want more than a partner from me. I . . ."

His voice fell away as we began to descend toward what I assumed to be Zaemon's palace. The whole building, nearly a city, shone in the sunlight. The palace looked like a three-dimensional scene from a stained-glass window. Nothing like what I would have expected from a demon. I'd been imagining cruel spires of black stone and green slime and toadstools.

We landed on a large terrace, overlooking the glittering sea. I slid from Farak's back. Talon slipped his hand in mine, his slick with sweat. He must know more than I did, not being from the Borderlands and all. Though, in this case I couldn't say I wanted to know what had him so worked up. The old saying ignorance is bliss might have held a point.

Once Ferika's passengers were on the mosaic pathway she led the way down a glimmering hall. Farak herded us from behind. Colored shafts of light cut through the hall. Under other circumstances the palace would have been breathtaking. My breath was certainly being taken away. Unfortunately, not by beauty. Apprehension had wrapped bands around my chest and the squeezing hurt.

We'd taken so many turns I'd completely lost track of where in the labyrinth of a palace we were. I got so lost it almost came as a relief when we entered what was clearly a throne room. Almost, because in the throne at the center, sat Zaemon.

The figure on the chair blew my expectations out of the water. His looks were as incongruous to the term *demon lord* as the glass palace was to the *demon lord's castle*. Maybe because I'd been raised on Earth, but when anyone mentioned the demon lord I expected some sort of CGI monster: horns, bat wings, fire issuing from the mouth. Or the other portrayal of the sleek, sexy villain. This man was neither. Okay, so he had wine-red skin, but otherwise he was a pudgy man, dressed in khaki slacks and a Hawaiian shirt. Two small horns peeped from canary yellow hair which exactly matched his eyes and he had dragon-like claws for feet.

His evil aura nearly brought up lunch. And black scorch marks dotted the glass floors around his throne. The remains of his victims. Only a fool would underestimate this man. He sat up causing his buttons to pull against his paunch.

"Welcome. Welcome." His voice was nasal and oily in a suave gangster sort of way. He rubbed his hands together gleefully. "I'm so glad you decided to accept my invitation."

Farak and Ferika stood with their bodies curved in a U-shape nesting the six of us inside, leaving no way to run. Zaemon ambled toward us, slowly looking each of us over. When he reached our group he held his hands out in front of us like warming them over a campfire. As he did I felt a wash of alien magic probe at my own. He gave us a sleek smile.

"Now that I know who is who, let's separate you." He went to Emmett first, running a hand lightly across his cheek and tipping Emmett's face up. "My beautiful source. So nice to finally meet you. And they've prepped you so much better than I could have hoped. You've been keeping your companions alive, haven't you?"

Emmett didn't move.

"Powering so many has forced your connection to widen. You are now pouring fourth so much magic. How truly delightful. You will be such an asset to me." He pushed Emmett to the side of the main group.

"Dear child of my rival." Zaemon took Elita's hand and kissed it. "You are lovelier than I expected. How pleased I am." He pulled her off to the opposite side from Emmett. Then he caught the rest of us in his stare.

His yellow eyes were mesmerizing, and I found I couldn't look away. "You four must be the guards then. And what exceptional guards you are. To have gotten past all I've sent for you." He took a deep breath as if smelling us and gave a satisfied sigh. "And all so young as well. Still plenty of time to develop your talents properly."

He stepped back and addressed the group. "I've been impressed by your feats and it takes much to impress me. Especially after you wiped out an entire company of my personal guards. Originally, I had plans for only the source. And while those have not changed, I have readjusted my other plans."

He folded his hands behind his back and stared at me. The power in his eyes pressed down on me. "You took out the diablita I was grooming for a wife. I'm now without a partner. But I will forgive this since your little band has brought me such a divine replacement."

I shuddered and hoped he wasn't referring to me. But instead he turned his gaze on Elita, who went pale.

"I will take the daughter of my rival as my wife. Then when the rest of my plans come to fruition I will rule the Central Borderlands from both sides. No one will oppose me with you as my bride.

"As for you four, such strong fighters would be a shame to waste. You will be allowed to join my ranks in return for your lives." He held up a hand as Omri opened his mouth. "Ah, ah, ah. Let's not jump to noble, yet wasteful decisions. To help make the choice easier I'll add an extra stipulation. If any one of you chooses to decline, I'll kill all four. You have one day to choose." He ran a hand through his yellow hair and gave Elita a lascivious look. "Farak, take the source to his new quarters and Elita to my own. See they're properly cared for. They're our special guests."

The dragon bowed his scaly head and herded the two off down a glass hall. Zaemon then turned a grimace of a smile on us. "Ferika, take them to their quarters, as well. If they make the proper decision they will be replacing the herd as palace guards. Care for them accordingly."

She inclined her head to him and used her tail to move us down a different hall than Farak had taken. To my surprise Omri moved to her head and spoke to her.

"I wish to see my companions properly cared for. Would you be so kind as to escort me to my room last?"

"Whatever."

She forced Yumiko into the first room. The accommodations looked normal enough on the inside. I caught a glimpse of a bed, a table, and shelves as Ferika slammed the door, locking it from the outside. Yumiko was a prisoner.

I clung to Talon as we continued down the hallway. Ferika pushed me into another room and Talon's look grew increasingly desperate as the door slammed between us. Then the lock snapped outside my door.

I pitched myself face first on the bed, rolling quickly to my back. The brown quilt reeked of sigbin and evil. These rooms must have belonged to members of the herd we'd killed. Zaemon hadn't joked, we were going to replace his fallen soldiers. I shuddered. The idea of serving a demon lord repulsed me. On the other hand, I knew I could never refuse and thereby sign the death warrant for all three of my friends.

Chapter 13

Time moved so slowly Zaemon's palace seemed to exist in some sci-fi void. Life had gotten weird enough that such a concept could be plausible. I lay staring at the ceiling, waiting for anything to happen or to fall asleep. A soft noise at my door brought me back and I braced myself for the unknown. Who knew what wandered the halls in the palace of a demon lord. The door cracked open and a familiar green figure slipped inside.

"Talon?"

He gave me a wide grin and a wink. "You can't keep a thief in with the locks they used." He gave a push with his Hermes shoes and in a blur he tackled me, kissing my face all over. "There, you stupid girl. Do you understand my worry, now?"

I elbowed him. "Who's the stupid one? I knew you wouldn't give up and here you sit, the first to have broken out."

He caught my arm and pressed me back into the pillows. "Who knows what service to Zaemon really means. We might not be allowed to be with each other. Since we only have one day as normal, let's make good use of it, shall we?" He kissed my neck and my collarbone.

"Gross, Talon." I flipped him off me and dumped him on the floor. "First off, can't you smell this bed? The whole thing reeks of sigbin. I'm not fooling around on it. Second, if you really want to put this time to good use, let's go get the others and get the hell out of here."

He gave me a huge smile and let his eyes sparkle. "Too bad about the bed, but I guess rescuing everyone will be almost as much fun."

I rolled off the bed and onto his lap. Grabbing his face, I planted a wild kiss on his lips. "What are we waiting for? Let's do something completely insane." I paused. "But they took all my weapons."

Talon sighed and shook his head at me. "You didn't even look around your room, did you? These belonged to palace guards. Evidently, they assume their defenses are strong enough inside the palace. They haven't even bothered to empty the rooms, or at least mine." He flipped up his shirt flashing two daggers and a sword he'd strapped to himself. "I also found magic rations. I've got one in every pocket. Let's see what your room has."

We poked around and found the quarters were similarly equipped. I armed myself with the same weapons Talon had chosen and slung a bow over my shoulder in case we found Omri or Yumiko without weapons. I poked through a drawer in the dresser and gasped. Pulling out the little jar I held it up for Talon to see.

"Jackpot."

"Is that what I think it is?"

"Come here, I'll put some on for you."

Talon hurried to obey.

I opened the jar which was filled with a specialized healing cream. I doubted the cream would do anything for the already formed scars or the missing chunk of his ear, but for the internal damage which hadn't fully healed, the cream would finish the job. Talon tipped his head so I could get at his neck, completely vulnerable and trusting. I swallowed hard both on my guilt and the fluttery feeling in my stomach.

"Let me know if I hurt you. I'll try to be gentle."

I took a glob on my fingers and smoothed the cream across the damaged skin. I made sure to get up onto his chin and down his shoulder and chest where all those muscles connected. I wanted him to be fully healed. Then I went back and started to rub the cream in. Talon leaned into me, making me stumble back.

"Geez, Talon. Stay upright."

"You have no idea how good that feels." His voice came out in a purr. "Everything is feeling right again. And to have you touching me at the same time." He sighed. "Do you think the others would mind waiting an hour or so?"

I made a little growl at him and tried to hurry rubbing the rest in. When I'd finished he took the jar and pulled out a glob.

"You're next. Where were your injuries?"

I blushed and shook my head. "I'm fine. Let's go."

He caught my arm with his clean hand. "I could see you working to look fine on our walk this morning. You still hurt. Where?"

My face flamed as I lifted the back of my shirt. I hadn't checked out my injuries in a mirror, but I felt the angry scar which started on my left shoulder blade and wrapped around my chest. The wound went all the way under my left breast and ended over my ribs. He was right. I did still hurt. But letting him spread the cream along the scar's full length made me want to squirm.

"Livy." His eyes were full of pity. "Why didn't you tell me you were hurt this badly?"

"Mine's nothing compared to yours and Omri's."

"Yumiko said you pushed yourself to carry Omri despite this"—he gently touched the scar—" and you nearly bled out. Hold still, I'll fix it for you."

I trembled as his hand started on my back. I was afraid the rubbing might hurt but he hadn't been exaggerating. My torso felt heavenly as the damaged tissues repaired themselves. He massaged in the cream, starting at my shoulder and followed the scar along my side. I blushed when his hand grazed close to my breast but surprisingly he focused on healing. I wasn't sure how he managed, I certainly couldn't. I lost track of the healing sensation, devoting my whole focus to the touch of his fingers on my skin. By the time he finished my ears were so hot they might actually catch fire. I also wished we could start over.

Talon screwed the lid on and tucked the jar in a pocket inside the chest of his shirt. "All better?" His voice cracked a little, and he blushed as he cleared his throat.

I nodded and straightened my shirt, following as he slipped out into the hall. We tiptoed along the corridor in silence. The fact we both had Hermes shoes playing in our favor. We found Yumiko's room without finding trouble and Talon made short work of the lock. She sat on the bed, armed and waiting as if she'd had no doubts we'd be along for her. I flashed her a smile as she took a spot behind me.

Talon led us to Omri's quarters. I was curious how he knew exactly where to look for the others, but didn't want to speak in the hall. He placed his hand on Omri's lock and in a second his specialized magic had silently disabled the lock and we let ourselves in. Or at least we started to.

Talon got about halfway in the door before stopping short and giving a small choking noise. I had to stand on tiptoes to see over his shoulder. The sight in the room sent me falling forward into Talon. Knocking into his back, we both tumbled into the room. Yumiko backed into the wall with a thud. Talon moved like lightning, shutting the outside door and drawing his sword.

"What the hell?" he growled at Omri.

Omri sat on the bed, Ferika curled around him and . . . they were . . . *kissing*. Or at least they had been when Talon had stepped in. Now they were staring at us, Omri turning very red against his natural pale coloring.

"*You can trust her*," Omri blurted.

"Yeah, but can we trust you?" Talon had his sword pointed at them both.

Behind me Yumiko started gasping for breath. I pulled her into a hug. She'd worked with Omri far longer. This must have come as a complete shock to her. She buried her face in my shoulder and refused to look at Omri.

Omri scrambled out of the dragoness' coils. "Yumiko. Do you remember the fortune teller at Elita's party before we left to find the source? Remember, she said I would find love in an unexpected place?"

Yumiko gripped me with her hands until I yelped. "I think she remembers. But I don't think she's very happy about your 'unexpected place'."

Omri gave me a piercing look with those aqua eyes. "Ferika's heart is in better shape than most. She simply serves here because her family does. Without them she has nowhere to go. She can't live on Earth, obviously. I saw her heart at the beginning and took the opportunity to get her alone." He turned an even deeper red. "I had meant to try getting her to help us escape, since her heart is so good. But . . . she wants freedom from Zaemon. And, um, after discovering we have much in common. I, uh, I said she could have a place in Elita's household if she could get us out of here."

Yumiko scribbled frantically on her note pad. She handed the note to me to read aloud.

"The Lord won't have her. You should know that."

Now Omri's neck and upper chest turned red, too. "I think he will if she's my wife."

"How, but, you only met her this morning?" I sputtered.

"I know her heart. What more do I need?"

His logic stopped me. He had a point. After all, isn't that why people spent time dating? To learn about their significant other? To see if they would make an acceptable spouse or partner? If Omri already had the knowledge . . .

"But what about her? She can't see your heart. And she's a dragon, what if she's lying? Or using you?" Talon protested.

"The heart can't lie about its true nature. I would know if she were an evil dragoness," Omri said, completely sure of himself. "And of course, she's using me. She's using me to get out of here and have a different life. The same way I'm using her to get out and get back to my life."

Yumiko tapped me, handing me her paper.

"Yumiko doubts the Lord High Governor is going to overlook the fact that you're a sphinx and she's a dragon." I wrinkled my nose at the paper. "It really matters that much?"

Omri's confidence visibly wavered. "Well, normally pairings stay between members of magic family trees. We will face bias, but I think the Lord High Governor will see the benefits in this case."

Talon snapped his mouth shut and lowered his sword. "All righty then. I'm not going to argue the finer points. Obviously, she'll be useful getting out of here."

Yumiko tapped my shoulder and handed me the pad.

"Yumiko wants to know if you're sure. She's worried you're sacrificing yourself for the rest of us."

Omri turned and took a surprisingly gentle claw in his hand. "I'm happy with this."

Talon had started talking in low swift voices with Ferika and Omri.

"We still need to get Emmett and Elita," I interrupted. "How are we supposed to do that?"

Ferika stretched her body out and slunk off the bed, twining between the four of us. "You can't. Nor can you get out of here alive. All reasons you need me." She narrowed her eyes at us. "I'll relock your doors on my way to go get the others. Having them locked will take some heat off initially. Once we move we're going to have to go fast."

She coiled herself around Omri and tickled her snakeish tongue in his ear. "We're pretty sure where your unicorn is. But this won't be over once they're bonded anymore. Zaemon doesn't lose. He'll see you're punished for defying him. Believe it or not we'll all be safest on Earth until Elita's father can take the heat off us. Remember, the worst of Zaemon's minions can't be sent to Earth without retribution from the Lord High Governor. Even Zaemon won't go so far. He's not prepared for an all-out war."

She'd uncoiled herself and moved to the door. "I have the power to create a gateway. But understand I'll be feeding when we return to Earth. If I get your butts out I don't want any complaints."

We all shook our heads. I wasn't a sparkly clean creature myself. Who was I to judge? Ferika slipped out the door and the room fell silent. A little over a half an hour later the door opened and Elita came in looking confused, followed by Emmett. A moment later Ferika slunk in.

"We have less than ten minutes to get outside the palace," Ferika warned. "Any longer and someone is bound to notice the source and the princess are missing. Once we're out I'll take four of you. Omri will fly with Talon, since he's the largest, to spare me a bit of the load. We're running straight for the unicorn. He'll bind you and we'll get our butts to Earth as fast as possible. Use lethal force on anything after us. You aren't going to want any of these bastards to have a grudge against you."

"How are we getting out?" I looked nervously at the door.

"The sewer." Ferika hawked out a ball of fire and the window melted. "Out we go."

We followed Ferika out dropping about eight feet to a rooftop below. She opened an access port and pointed us down a metal ladder. Every nerve in my body buzzed. I wanted to do almost anything rather than go back in the dark.

I landed in slimy, ankle-deep water and hoped the sludge wouldn't negatively affect my Hermes shoes. I blocked out every other thought of the water. Instead, I focused on the flickering orange glow which glinted off the curving walls of the shaft. Ferika had left her mouth open and the light shone up from deep inside her. I was more grateful than I could put in words to her for illuminating our way. Being blind sucked and I kept getting stuck in situations where I couldn't see.

The tunnel disappeared into blackness above our heads, leaving a creepy feeling of the unknown hanging over me. Worse, the walls were made of something like smoke-colored glass and were nearly as slick. The idea of what the slime might have come from made me shudder.

For as short as her legs were Ferika moved astoundingly fast. I had to rush to keep up. Not that I wanted to linger. A faint twittering or squeaking bounced off the walls of the tunnel, reverberating until I had no idea which direction the noise came from.

"Blood bats," Ferika hissed at us. "They're going to go crazy at the first bloodshed. Our blood or theirs, doesn't matter. One drop is enough to start a frenzy. But you'll have to kill them, or they'll drain you."

The twittering got progressively louder and something dark brushed past my head. A growl from Ferika rang off the walls and made my stomach clench. I had the impression many of those dark things hid in the shadows overhead. Not until the first made a try for Elita did I get a good look. I wished I hadn't.

The blood bat had thick, shaggy brown fur, crusted in clumps from whatever it had previously fed on. The bat's eyes shown an eerie red-orange when they caught the light and its fangs had to be at least three inches long. The creature came swooping in at Elita. She screamed and ducked at the same time Yumiko skewered the animal. She dislodged its body, which fell in the water with a splash. Then the tunnel erupted in total chaos, like watching videos of shark feeding frenzies on TV.

"Get behind me," Ferika yelled. "I'm barbequing bat."

We all ran, covering our heads. Pain shot up my arm, but I didn't want to get roasted, so I ignored my wound and kept going. Ferika reared back and let out a stream of fire which singed me though I stood behind her. The bats shrieked for a moment before they burned in the inferno.

Suddenly, brown fur blocked my vision. I slashed with my blade, getting lucky and cutting straight across the creature's face. The beast fell but not before the throbbing started.

"Get the healing cream on her."

Maybe Ferika screamed, or maybe the horrible noise came from me. My skin was stretching. I almost wished it would rupture. Surely the pain of my skin splitting would be less than the pain of it trying to hold my swelling body in.

There might have been several sets of hands rubbing cream on me. I couldn't really tell because every inch of me burned like I'd caught fire. The flames would burst forth when my skin finally split. As they got the cream rubbed in, the searing heat gave way and my body began to return to normal.

Strong hands were helping me sit and a long reptilian face pointed into mine.

"Congratulations, you're one of the few who are allergic to blood bat saliva. A fairly rare allergy but for those who have it, it's deadly. You're going to feel off for a bit, which is unfortunate. But you'll live."

Ferika held a claw out for me and I pulled myself to my feet.

"Can you move?" she asked.

"Let's go." My voice echoed strangely. "I hate tunnels."

She nodded and started back down the sewer tunnel. I wobbled and got a painful grip on my shoulder from Talon, who even in the orange glow from Ferika's fire, was pale.

"Are you really okay?" he asked as we walked on.

"I have to be. I'd love to rest, but that's not really an option right now, is it?"

"Ferika," Talon called out. "Wait a minute. I'm going to carry Livy."

I wanted to protest but Omri had already loaded me onto Talon's back. Then we were moving again. I couldn't help but blush, in part because of the embarrassment of having to be helped along like this. And partly because the proximity and the feel of his muscles thrilled me far too much.

"Okay, we've hit the end of the tunnel." Ferika pulled up and examined a hatch above her. "They have to know we're gone by now. Zaemon's forces won't take long to be on our tails. Omri, you've got Talon. The rest of you hop on as fast as you can. Our two biggest advantages are surprise and speed."

I got deposited from Talon's back onto Ferika's. Then Omri and Talon lined up to exit, Omri's hand on the latch. Fortunately, the walk had given the healing cream a full chance to work. I felt pretty much like myself again.

Omri threw the hatch and he and Talon scrambled out and into the air. Ferika went next with me clinging to her back. Emmett, Elita, and Yumiko rushed out and I helped them onto her back. I barely had them on when she took off.

Chapter 14

Elita grabbed my arm and helped steady me as Ferika rose above the glass palace. Dragons evidently flew incredibly fast because the palace already sat behind us, dollhouse sized.

"Thanks." I groped at purple scales, trying to find a grip.

Elita nodded.

Something in the air off Ferika's flank caught my eye. "We've got company."

"Stymphalian birds," she yelled over the rushing wind. "I can smell them. Watch the beaks and feathers."

I glanced down at the ground rushing past. *Big* mistake. Trees like bushes blurred below me and my head whirled with the height. How were we going to take on the approaching birds without falling? Ferika's scales were so slippery they made holding on hard enough, even without fighting. We'd have to divide the work.

"Yumiko, keep everyone on Ferika," I ordered. "I'll take out the birds."

Yumiko nodded. As I readied my bow, Yumiko pulled out rope she'd gotten from who knows where and secured Emmett and Elita. Ferika snapped her teeth at the rope as it slipped around her body.

"Sorry, Ferika. You're too slick to fight on," I apologized for Yumiko. "Can you get closer and warn Omri?"

Ferika stretched out her neck to make up speed but the effort came too late. The first of the Stymphalian birds shot past us in a dive toward Omri and Talon. I let off an arrow and the bird went down in a puff of feathers. I hit the bird before it could touch Omri.

"How is Omri bleeding?" I asked.

"The feathers," Ferika explained. "They're razor sharp."

Damn. I'd have to take them out before they got close enough to shed on anyone. The birds were huge, on top of being well armed. The one I'd shot near Omri had been almost half his size. Three more circled off our left and two on the right. I really hoped none of the birds hid behind us where I couldn't see. I pulled back another arrow and took out another of the left three.

One of the remaining birds took a dive at the guys. My hands grew slick as Omri clutched Talon and rolled so Talon could hack the head off the bird with his sword. This incensed the rest of the birds and they dove in unison. Omri did a fantastic spin, covering both him and Talon with his wings. As he opened them out, his own feathers flew off and the birds fell, dead.

Ferika heaved a huge breath of fire and the feathers which should have hit us melted, falling to the ground in molten rain. The blazing heat must have disrupted the airflow because Omri was buffeted by something invisible. As he fought to right himself Talon slipped from his arms.

Time came nearly to a standstill. I screamed and Ferika's back slipped away, my outstretched hands reaching for Talon's. Then mine stopped moving but his did not. As tears took my vision, Omri dove for him. I had a fiery pain in my backside and another in my heart as the world spun below me.

"I've got him," Omri called out. "Can you get her back up?"

"No. We're nearly there. You can fix her tail later."

I rubbed at my face, drying the tears. Omri flapped back to our side with a very pale Talon in his arms. I then registered why I still hurt, even though Talon was safe. I dangled from Ferika's claw by my tail. Suddenly, my stomach lurched, and nausea set in. The world really was spinning below me as I hung upside down. Now that I'd regained my senses, the pain in my backside became nearly unbearable. I reached up, frantically trying to get a hold of her claws to take the pressure off my tail.

The world grew closer as we began descending. Ninety feet above the forest floor thick conifers closed around us shielding us from unwanted gazes. I found Ferika's claws and held on to lessen the pain. She descended slowly now and dropped me into Talon's waiting arms. He nearly crushed me in the hug.

"You really are a stupid girl! Why would you jump?"

"I didn't mean to. I didn't think. I just reached for you."

He crushed me again and set me on my feet. The rest of the group had already moved off into the woods, Elita in front calling softly, "Lumarian."

"Ferika, are there more of those birds?" Talon asked.

"Probably not. Zaemon keeps them as messengers. Those would have been a scouting parting. We killed six, which ought to be all of them. Hopefully they didn't send anyone back before taking us on."

"Lumarian?" Elita still called.

Something shifted in the undergrowth and I grabbed the hilt of my sword. Whatever stepped out of the bushes, blinded me. I blinked desperately and when my vision finally cleared, I gasped. A unicorn, so white its coat hurt the eyes, stood next to Elita.

"Why do you call me, young fairy?" he asked.

Elita quivered, but whether excitement or fear caused the trembling was indiscernible. Her voice, when she spoke, betrayed neither. "I beg of you to please bind me to this source, Emmett."

"Does Emmett desire this as well?" Lumarian asked.

Emmett paled. "I want the bond." His voice came out weak, but his answer satisfied Lumarian.

The unicorn tipped his head and sparkles of light from his pearly horn glinted off the trees. "You ask a favor of this magnitude after dragging danger to my door? You have mere minutes before your enemy's attack."

Elita dropped her head. "Yes. I want to stop the attacks on all my friends. I want to keep him safe from those who would use him."

Lumarian tipped his head further, resting his horn on her shoulder. "You are a maiden of pure heart. I believe these are your intentions and I will grant your request." He looked her in the eye. "Nothing in life is easy. You will pay in pain for your bond to the free magic."

Elita shifted uneasily. "The pain will go away?"

"Eventually. This will not hurt the source. He is but a vessel for the magic. Yours is a part of you. Are you prepared to bear this pain alone?"

"Yes." She tipped her head up and met his eye with a firm gaze. "I will do what I need to."

"Then place your back against his and face your pain."

Elita put her back against Emmett's. He rubbed his palms against his pants out of nerves. Lumarian took a few steps back and directly faced Elita. Emmett would be blind to whatever the unicorn did. A moment later I wished I hadn't seen either. Lumarian lowered his nearly three-foot pearl horn and charged.

I'll give Elita credit. She never screamed as the horn pierced the center of her chest, going out her back and spearing Emmett as well. Emmett never made a move. I had to assume he couldn't feel the piercing. Tears ran thick down Elita's face and she groaned as Lumarian pulled his horn free. Shockingly, it stayed as clean as before the charge. Somehow, the unicorn used his horn to pierce only magic.

"Use nothing to heal her," Lumarian warned Omri. He'd started toward her with the healing cream. "Their magic must heal together to finish the bond, though it is already undoable. Your enemies are too late for their own ends. The speed at which your mistress will heal all depends on her. If her heart wavers healing will take longer. But she will be on her feet in a day or two and well inside a week. Now go, before you bring a demon lord down on my head." Lumarian left as swiftly as he'd appeared.

"Come on. Through the gateway. Now." Ferika had reared back and started growling. Crashing came through the trees behind us, snapping limbs and horrible animalistic calls, closing in swiftly.

Emmett grabbed Elita's limp body, helped by Omri, and rushed through. Yumiko went next. Rough hands shoved me and I fell through.

I landed in a pile of random limbs. A heavy object landed on my legs and I bit back a cry. The whole pile bounced a foot into the air as Ferika landed. On the other side fur and teeth blurred as her gateway snapped shut. What if she hadn't had the foresight to make the gateway while Lumarian was at work? I shook the thought off, letting gratitude replace it. We owed her our lives.

The limbs belonged to our whole group. Somehow, we'd become tangled into a human knot. We struggled on the ground, wrapped up like a Twister game gone very wrong. As we extricated ourselves I had a chance to survey our surroundings. We appeared to be in a parking lot, surrounded on two sides by a grimy chain-link fence. The lot belonged to a run-down gas station and convenience store. We'd arrived at twilight and the air was cool to the point of almost being cold. I gave a shiver.

"Where are we?" I asked Ferika. As I took her in my mouth hung open. "*Holy shit.*"

She'd taken human form and gorgeous didn't even begin to describe her. Talon whistled. "Well done, Omri. Straight up jail bait, and hot as f—"

"Stop." I covered my ears. "Please don't drop that kind of language so casually. Especially not to describe a friend's looks."

Talon scowled at me. "You said 'shit' and I get in trouble?"

"Cussing's like earthquakes." I tipped my nose up at him. "What I said is like a 7.0. What you were going to say is like a 9.0. You'd think they're close, but they're worlds apart."

Ferika had glossy black hair, dark eyes with impossible lashes, skin like polished teak and what had to be double D's. Oh, and don't forget the perfect hourglass figure. I bit back the urge to snarl at her. The feeling might have been petty, but I reveled in the fact even Elita looked plain next to Ferika.

On second thought, maybe Elita's downgrading wasn't such a good thing. The pair of them must make me look like a complete hag. No, I had no reason to worry. Elita and Ferika were both spoken for. Talon would . . . wait . . . I'd been so caught up in feeling sorry for my looks I'd missed the start of the conversation concerning where we would be staying on Earth.

"Hold up guys," I cut in. "Since Emmett, Talon, and I are the only ones with experience living on Earth all ideas are to go through one of us. And I'll tell you right now, the over the top princess parade we made on the way to the Borderlands isn't low profile enough. No luxury suites, fancy cars, etc. Not to mention someone has to pay for that crap. Even if Elita's father offered to foot the bill, who wants to go back and get the money?"

Thankfully, everyone nodded in agreement. "Good." I continued. "For tonight, I'm calling my parents. Not only do we need money but we're going to need help getting everyone to blend. We also need someone who can move between here and the Lord High Governor's palace for us."

Ferika gave what was supposed to be a growl and looked startled at how squeaky the noise came out of her human body.

"Yes, Ferika?" I asked, trying not to snicker.

"I need to hunt or I'm gonna pass out. Do you know how much magic making a gateway uses?"

"What do you need?" I asked.

"Human flesh."

I tried not to flinch, after all her gateway had saved us.

"Maidens are best, but I'll make do with anyone right now."

I took in the graffiti covered wall of the convenience store. "There's got to be some punks around here. Eat a couple of them. Less people will miss them anyway. Not to mention, we don't know if we'll be staying in the area. Human police will blame the disappearance of punks on other punks. Less questions asked."

She nodded and focused on transforming back. Luckily for her evening had turned to night. A broken street lamp left the parking lot in darkness. She slunk off unseen, the ultimate predator. I took my necklace and used it to send a message to my parents. Hopefully, even if they were still in the Borderlands, my message would reach them.

"While we wait for my parents, does anyone else need to feed?"

Unsurprisingly everyone except Elita raised their hand. She was still passed out. I waved a hand to shoo them off.

"You guys go now. I'll stay to guard Emmett and Elita and meet my parents."

Omri put a hand on my shoulder. "I'll find a geyser and bring you some."

"Thanks. But hurry, I'm sure my parents will be here soon."

Once the three of us were alone, Emmett sat on the sidewalk and put Elita's head in his lap.

"Are you okay?" I asked, standing next to him. "You're basically married."

"She and I can worry about our relationship later. For now, I'm relieved we only have to dodge retribution until her father can quell everything."

"Emmett, you're talking about retribution from a demon lord. This isn't a little case of revenge."

"I know, but somehow things seem to be getting better. Like maybe there's a light at the end of the tunnel."

I sighed and rubbed my head. "You're crazier than I am."

"I doubt that."

"As long as you're happy." I set my hand on top of his head.

He took my hand and snuggled it. "Someday I'll think of a good way to thank you for everything."

I squeezed his hand back. "Just don't let Elita spoil our friendship and we'll be good."

The small click of a gun cocking made my stomach sink. How had I missed the evil aura? I was so tuned into dark magic right now.

"I want all your money."

I rolled my eyes. You had to be kidding. A human mugger? Really?

"I'm getting it," I said as I turned toward him.

The man had a ski mask on. I could tell he stood a good six inches taller than me and probably weighed twice what I did. At least his extra padding didn't hide more muscle than I could deal with, as long as he didn't get a hold of me. Though catching me would be impossible for a human, since I still had my Hermes shoes on. Not that they made me faster than a bullet, so I'd still have to play carefully.

I reached behind me, pretending to get my wallet. Instead I grabbed the hilt of my dagger. I spun and drove the blade through the hand holding the gun. The weapon fell and fired, making an echoing bang as the bullet hit the dumpster and put a hole in the side. I'd already kicked the man to the ground and had my other dagger to his throat.

"You picked the wrong girl to mess with, jerk-off."

I crossed my fingers and hoped I could scare the thug off. I really didn't want to start my time back at home by having to kill a guy. I trained to assassinate other magic folk. Turning my skill on a human seemed about as fair as killing squirrels in the backyard. Then again, this squirrel had a gun. He used his size to free a hand and I knew I'd have to finish him. I leaned as he made a grab for my neck.

"Oh, good. You saved me desert."

I got pushed away by a dark purple claw with gleaming black talons. Knowing what was coming, I launched myself at Emmett and curled around his head, so he couldn't see. At the same time, I ducked and hid my own face. Screams echoed around the parking lot, followed by horrific crunching noises, and then eerie silence.

"You can look up. I'm done."

When I peeked, Ferika had turned back into a human and was tiptoeing away from a stain on the pavement.

"So you know, I'm usually more merciful to my victims. But seeing as how he'd pulled a gun on you . . ." She held up her hands and shrugged, then covered a burp and giggled. "Sorry. Thugs give me heartburn."

I squinted around at the yuck on the sidewalk. "What happened to his gun?"

She patted her tiny stomach. "Ate that, too."

Emmett turned a little green. "Do you digest metal or does it—"

"Don't answer, Ferika. He's in shock, he doesn't really want to know."

"No, actually, I kinda do." Emmett opened his mouth like he might continue to pry but a gateway appeared, and my parents hopped to the ground.

Chapter 15

Strong, familiar arms closed around me. My dad held me tight, his face pressed into my hair. I tried to hug him back, but my mom was prying me away to hug me herself. She nearly crushed me in her distress.

"Whose blood is that? Are you all right? Where are Talon and the others? Who's the young girl?" She fired questions off faster than I could answer.

"We're okay, Mom. Everyone's in one piece. The blood's all that's left of a thug who tried to rob us."

My mom set me down, grabbed my shoulders and gave me a stern look. "Explain."

"Okay, but this is the fast version. The girl is Ferika. She ate the thug. She's a dragoness."

My parents gasped but I shushed them.

"We've been under attack from Zaemon from the start. He wanted Emmett. He finally captured us in the Borderlands. Ferika got us out of his castle and to a unicorn. He bonded Emmett and Elita, but Zaemon's bound to be pissed. He planned to use Emmett and marry Elita to try and take over the Central Borderlands. So, we're kinda on the run. We need help. We need—"

Mom put a finger on my lips and my father was already gone. "We wondered if something like this might happen. We were prepared for trouble. Your father's gone back to the Lord High Governor. We'll get this sorted out. Until then I'll get you guys into hiding."

"Where are we going to go?"

"Home," Mom said. "Right now, it'll be the safest place."

"How's that gonna work?" I couldn't believe she'd even suggest going back. "I killed a diablita in front of the staff and half the student body."

"The arrangements were already in place for when you got done with your mission. We pleaded your case with Lord Feéroi and he helped you out. You and Emmett are all set to go back. We even made arrangements so Elita could join you for your senior year."

"That still doesn't explain how it's okay to go back."

Mom sighed. "Your father and I did the Lord High Governor a favor in return for making your indiscretion go away."

"Do I even want to know what you did?"

"No, you don't. But those are the sorts of details you can let your dad and I worry about. Be thankful our preparations are working in your favor now."

"How did he make my 'indiscretion' disappear?"

"Honey, you can make anything go away if you wield the right magic."

"Oh."

Talon greeted my mom. "Hi, Mrs. Skotadi."

Mom turned and gasped. "Talon. Your neck. Your ear."

He reached up and fingered the ragged edge of his ear. "Oh, you can see the scars in human form, too? No worries, they're no big deal. Nothing hurts anymore."

"It is, too, a big deal." I crossed my arms and gave him a dirty look. "Don't let him play those injuries down. 'Specially not to you, Mom. We were fighting in complete blackness. A sigbin tried to kill me and Talon jumped in the middle." I ran my fingers across the scars. "I'm so sorry he ended up like this because of me."

Mom gave me a funny look. "Is there something you'd like to tell me?"

"I suppose there's all sorts of things you ought to know. They can probably wait for the car ride home. Besides, then everyone will be there. They can help make sure I don't leave anything out."

"I meant about Talon. Is there anything you'd like to tell me about Talon?"

I scratched my head. "He's a pain in the butt?"

Talon poked my ribs and smiled at my mom. "We're partners now. I wouldn't want to work with anyone else and luckily, she agreed."

My mom gave us both another funny look, then took Talon and hugged him tightly. She kissed one cheek, then the other. "Talon, dear. Thank you. I asked you to watch them and you did." She swallowed hard. "I . . . I'm so grateful. You'll never understand until you're a parent. Her safety is something I'll never be able to repay you for."

Talon turned faintly red and patted my mom on the back, uncomfortably. "You're welcome. I wouldn't want to see her hurt either."

Mom cupped his cheek with a hand and looked at him with sparkling eyes. "And you're partners, now. You're practically family. Are you and Livy . . .?" She let the question hang.

I had to be as red as Talon. But I kinda wanted to hear his take on us, too. So, I hoped he wouldn't chicken out of answering.

Talon squirmed out of her hug and scuffed his foot a little. "There, uh, hasn't really been time for things like that. But yeah. When this is over I'd like to date her for real. I know partner pairs get married a lot, like you and Mr. Skotadi. Maybe . . ."

Mom stared at me. I nodded and let my eyes fall to the ground. Our relationship was still too new and unfamiliar for me to put into words. What Talon had said pretty much summed my feelings up. We would date and then we'd see.

But sometime when we weren't fighting for our lives at least once a day. Mom nodded and focused on Ferika.

"Talon. While I ask our new friend a few questions, would you please procure a vehicle with space for everyone?"

Talon nodded and disappeared.

Mom gave Ferika a shrewd look. "What's in this for you? What did you make these kids promise to pay for your help?"

She shrugged, looking like she didn't care whether or not my mom approved. "I'm marrying Omri. He's gotten Elita to agree to my living in the Lord High Governor's palace. I won't have to feed like this." She waved her hand at the mess on the sidewalk. "I didn't want to serve Zaemon, but I had no one on the outside. Nowhere to hide once I got out. Their freedom for my own seemed like a fair trade. Elita promised the Lord won't cast out her body servant's wife and Omri seems happy enough with the deal." She flipped her hair over her shoulder and met my mom's eyes.

Her look of defiance turned to one of shock when my mom hugged her, too. "Thank you, Ferika. That's gold coming from a dragon. How old are you, dear?"

"Who's this?" Omri had returned and immediately took a defensive stance.

"Omri, this is my mom, Dyna. Dad's already gone back to Elita's dad for help. Mom's going to get us settled."

As mom ran her eyes over our group, she gasped and covered her mouth, her eyes over-bright. "You're all children."

Omri gave a half-laugh. "Yumiko and I are twenty-three and twenty-two respectively. The only other children are Elita who's eighteen and Ferika's sixteen. Though in her case, 'child' only applies on Earth. She is a dragoness, after all."

I was confused. "Why?"

"Dragon's only rarely live on Earth, because of their appetites," Omri explained. "They need special permission to even be here. In dragon form they're pretty much self-sufficient at about three. Dragons aren't particularly maternal, so most dragons leave the nest about then and fully settle into adult life in the second half of their first decade."

"You left home at three?" I asked horrified.

"No." Ferika took on a fierceness. "Farak and I were hatched in the same brood. We left the nest at two. Our mother is a particularly brutal dragoness. Oh, she would have savaged anyone who tried to mess with us. Probably still would. But at home . . ." Ferika shivered. "Let's just say dragons aren't above eating their own young. Best not to misbehave and when in doubt, leave."

She looked seriously at my mother. "You'd better hope the Lord High Governor scares Farak enough to keep him in the Borderlands. He inherited my mother's savagery. Her brutal streak is why Zaemon kept us in the first place. Mother is completely unmanageable, but Zaemon gave us a home when we were very small and thought he'd finish raising us. He's always given us plenty of opportunity to indulge those baser instincts. Farak loves to be cruel. I don't, so here I am. But Farak's going to feel nearly as betrayed by my leaving as Zaemon."

My mother shook her head. "Wow, you kids . . . I don't know what to say. You've come up with several lifetimes worth of trouble and crammed it into less than a month."

A black van with a dragon decal sprayed on the sides pulled up next to us. Talon poked his head out and gave my mom a cheeky smile. "Will this work?"

I rolled my eyes. "Sure, if you're aiming to be listed as a sex offender." I shoved his face toward one of the backseats. "Ferika and I are underage. I think it's illegal to give us a ride in this. Not to mention, do I really want to sit in the seats?"

Talon laughed outright. "I took the van from the lot at a detail shop. The paint's not quite finished, so everything ought to be new. Some poor guy is going to find his mid-life crisis gone tomorrow. But I thought the paint made a perfect joke." He shot a look in Ferika's direction.

She stuck out a very snake-like tongue at him.

My mother sighed and rubbed her head. "Excellent. Suddenly I'm the mother of seven. Okay, everyone in. I'll drive. I'm sure you could all use a break, but don't doze off. I'll be giving you the plan until my husband gets back."

She climbed in the driver's seat and the rest of us clamored in. In the back, bench seats ran the edges facing an open center. Omri helped Emmett get Elita into one of the seats. Emmett took his place as her pillow again. Ferika gave Omri a look nearly as hot as her breath and he stumbled dumbly into the seat next her. I'd shoved Talon onto one of the seats so he was laying down and buckled all three belts across him.

Yumiko took one look at us, shook her head and climbed into the front with Mom. I stuck my head between the front seats.

"Mom. Yumiko lost her voice to poison on this mission. She can't talk to you."

Mom gave Yumiko a sad look. "I'm sorry to hear that."

Yumiko turned and stared out the window.

"Everyone's in," I told Mom. "You can go."

"Okay, then here's what we have set up so far. Measures had already been taken to bring Elita, Livy, and Emmett back to their old lives. I'm taking you guys back to Redding. You have school waiting and enough protection around the town for Elita's status. You'll go back to school and we'll all wait for orders from the Lord High Governor.

"Ferika, you're a minor on Earth so you might as well go to school with the others. Going will give you something to do and give me some piece of mind. Not much would dare mess with a dragon. Omri, Yumiko, and Talon can do as they wish. If you're willing I'd like you three to assume some duties for me. Livy's father, Arsen, and I will be in and out and we'll need reliable eyes on things."

"Sure."

"Of course."

Yumiko nodded silently.

"Good. Yumiko, I'm so sorry to ask this, but given your condition could you maintain security on the house? Talon, would you and Omri keep a perimeter around our part of town?"

"Sure," Talon agreed.

"Hey, Mom. Where were we and how long until we get home? Oh, are we going back to our old house?"

"Yes, we're going to our old house. You were in Detroit. And we ought to be home in about two hours. Evidently Talon knows his way around a vehicle. The magical modifications were already done. And thanks for being preemptive, Talon."

"Anything for you. I got a bit of a bonus for stealing a car. So, the modifications were no problem."

"Ah yes, you're a toyol." Mom sniffed the air. "Elita's obviously the fairy. I'm going to assume Yumiko is the kamaitachi. So, you're a sphinx, Omri?"

"Yes, ma'am."

"Ma'am makes me feel old."

"As you wish, Dyna."

I yawned and leaned back to find Talon waiting. I cuddled in for the ride, letting the exhaustion of our narrow escape and the warmth of his chest put me to sleep.

Chapter 16

The first day back at school had been surreal, walking through the doors to have people blankly ask how I'd enjoyed my vacation. No one remembered anything about Buraee. Not a single person thought anything out of the ordinary had happened at all.

Elita and Ferika blended seamlessly. To my discomfort they picked up a veritable entourage of fans. They were new and pretty, I could understand the fascination. Not that understanding made the extra bodies around me any more comfortable. The worst afternoon came after Elita requested to see a human mall. Word had gotten out and instead of grabbing a peaceful snack in the food court, sitting around us I counted at least three other groups of students.

I debated urging Talon and Omri to get our group on the move. I hate shopping but if we wandered around the other kids would have a harder time following us. But no, Elita had to have human pizza and Emmett happily sat down with a giant plate of fries covered in cheese and bacon. Talon picked at those, too. No one was going to leave.

Mom had picked up an electronic scribble pad and I sat writing notes to Yumiko. Her nature left her as withdrawn as I tended to be, and she had been my biggest sympathizer the last two weeks. She'd clearly only come along as a babysitter.

One thing did have me laughing. One of the groups which had followed us to the mall was Ferika's fan club. Those poor boys looked ready to cry as Ferika sat on Omri's lap sharing a sucker with him. PDA is disgusting, especially when it involves fluids, but watching the exchange of spit was worth seeing the boys' reactions. Maybe we'd get some peace and quiet now they'd seen her "boyfriend".

One of the other groups, comprised largely of Elita's new devotees and their boyfriends, had sat at a couple tables next to us. Emmett and Elita were in the middle of a conversation with them but I wanted to escape. Lord only knew how long this torturous afternoon would last.

"Hello, sister dear."

My blood froze, and the color drained from Ferika's face. I had no idea how he'd managed to suppress his aura so well, but the voice had to belong to Farak. I whirled around in panic. Behind me stood the most stunning young man I'd ever laid eyes on. His deep blue eyes gave him away. They were the same color his dragon hide had been in the Borderlands. He gave us an evil smile, his arm slung over the shoulders of a female student named Cassy.

"I was wandering around, a little lost, your aura is hard to track with the blockers in place. Luckily, I happened across this most helpful girl."

Here Farak gave Cassy's neck a squeeze and I cringed. She acted like she enjoyed the attention, but she was a hostage.

"She helped me find you." He narrowed his eyes, open disgust on his face. "Please tell me you're not seriously considering mating with *that*." Farak pointed at Omri.

Ferika finally found her voice. "What are you doing here, Farak? This is forbidden. You will be executed if you misbehave."

"The same applies to you," he hissed.

"I got myself a place in the household of the Lord High Governor. My rations are now of no consequence to humanity."

Farak gave a cruel laugh. "So, you've turned yourself into a fluffy bunny? Some household pet? How shameful to turn your back on your true nature."

He was now squeezing Cassy hard enough she squirmed and whimpered. I caught Ferika's eye for a moment and let my own eyes slide to Cassy. Dragon nature doesn't really involve saving humans seeing as how they're a dragon's natural food and source of magic. Nor has saving the helpless ever really been my job, but we had to do something. Farak would pop Cassy's head off if he squeezed much harder. Literally. We certainly didn't need the other kids in a panic before we even got a chance to move.

I didn't have my Hermes shoes. I cursed not being allowed to wear them to school. Talon caught my eye. He looked down at his feet. He had on the right footwear. I also knew he and I were on the same page. He really had turned out to be an awesome partner.

Farak stood to my left with Cassy between me and his body. Talon sat at the table next to me, about three feet of space between us. To our right at another table sat Omri.

Farak and Ferika were still squaring off. I had to get Cassy out of his arms before anything escalated. I formed an "okay" with my fingers under the table and Ferika, Talon, and I all moved at the same time.

Talon leapt out of his chair and over me, grabbing Farak's arm and twisting it back. I dodged below him, knocking Cassy backward and away from Farak. At the same time Ferika lunged, taking Farak by the neck.

"Get out of here, Farak. Before I have to watch them execute you."

Cassy started to speak but I shook my head. I needed to hear in order to be prepared.

"Get out of here," I whispered to her, before listening in.

Farak laughed coldly. "I wouldn't worry about me, sis. Zaemon is coming for you and I've never seen him so pissed. Now, I'll tell you what. Since you're my sister, I'll give you one chance to come home like a good girl and return the captives. Zaemon, will never forgive you, but I might be able to get him to take you back. See, there's a dragoness I've had my eye on. But to buy her, I need something her older brother considers of value. If I give you to Velor, he said I could have Vixaria. Zaemon will spare you for your first clutch and Velor's a typical dragon. He doesn't care what happens to one clutch as long as he gets to make another."

Ferika turned red with rage. "You bargained on me and my eggs!"

I flinched. The heat on her breath singed even from the ground behind Farak. Unbelievably, Cassy still sat next to me. I pushed on her to go.

"I'm *never* going back to Zaemon. I've never liked what we do, as you know full well. I saw my chance out. The choice is mine, not yours."

"And screwed all these people over in the process." Farak gave a slow clap. "How very dragonish of you. Too bad, really. They could have lived quite pleasantly under Zaemon." Farak shrugged. "Never say I'm as cruel as our mother. I gave you a chance. She'd have gone straight to ripping you into pieces. Not that she'll get the chance, since I'll do it for her. I'm done talking."

His body had begun to ripple. Shit. I couldn't believe he'd change in the middle of all these people.

"Get out of here," I screamed at Cassy and the other kids, who'd stayed to watch the sibling fight.

They all sat rooted to their spots and I scrambled back, dragging Cassy by the arm. In seconds, our spot on the floor was taken over by Farak's long, twisting body.

Ferika had also turned. The snap of her jaws made my stomach clench. She tried to drive him back as Talon, Omri, and I attempted to herd the students away from the fight. I had hoped they would do the natural thing when faced with a formidable predator and run. Instead, they kept asking about special effects and cosplay. This must have been the backlash of fixing what they'd seen me do. They were now convinced this was a game.

Farak and Ferika were swaying like snakes in a standoff. Farak moved first, lunging in with open jaws and Ferika met him head on. The squeal of teeth on teeth made me cringe. They might have been evenly matched until Farak twisted and managed to clamp his jaws around Ferika's head. A sickening snap reverberated through the room like a gunshot and Ferika slumped. Farak turned on us, licking blood off his lips.

"The guard spells you people have set up are a huge drain on me. I don't feel like fighting anyone skilled until I recharge." He held up a talon. "Pardon me for a moment."

In a blur, he'd snatched up one of the girls who'd been trying to figure out the secret to the special effects. Screaming filled the room, but didn't block out the tearing and crunching noises. I squeezed my eyes on the scene but couldn't escape the sound.

"Maiden is so good." Farak sighed. "Maybe one more."

I peeked out. Farak made a much larger mess when he ate than Ferika had. At the sight of the pieces I ran for the nearest trashcan and puked. I've got a fairly hard stomach. You have to, to be an assassin. But watching a classmate be devoured was beyond what I could handle.

The other students sat where Farak had left them, entranced and immobilized. No one could get them out of there now. I looked helplessly at Talon. What were the four of us going to do against a monster who had downed Ferika in one bite? I'm an assassin, not a dragon slayer. My job involved stealth and cunning and a silent hit, not a white steed and a blessed blade.

Talon appeared at my back, as if thinking the same thought. "I have a plan. But we're going to need to be sneaky."

Farak was slowly sorting his options.

"Omri and I will distract him. Yumiko will take Emmett and Elita and run."

"What about me?" I whispered.

"I'm sorry. You have to do the most dangerous job. I hate sending you in but you're the only one small enough to slide under his belly without bumping him." He pressed the flat of a sword along the length of my back. "My sword's been blessed. It should do the job. Thrust it between the belly scales, one foot shy of his forelegs. His heart should be right there."

"How long will I have?"

"Seconds at best." He pressed a kiss at my temple. "Be safe. I have all these mushy things I want to do with you someday." Talon slipped away to Omri's side and took all the air in the room with him.

His goodbye made my heart hurt. "Assuming we even got a later."

I had no more time. Farak had selected his victim and no one wanted another kid to get eaten. Omri and Talon said something to get Farak's attention. I wasn't paying attention to their words. I was watching the dragon. I needed those brief moments between when he first focused on them and when he acted against them.

Now.

I dove like Farak was home plate, sliding the few feet of tile under his belly. Grabbing Talon's sword, I rammed it up between his stomach scales. At the initial prick, Farak ducked his head and caught me in his glare. An overwhelming fear threatened to freeze my body. Closing my eyes on the sight of a dragon in a killer rage, I shoved my body weight against the sword. Farak's scream shook ceiling tiles loose. Four points of fiery pain seared my body as Farak's talons pierced me. Then I flew in an arc above Farak's writhing body, all the wind shoved from my body as I slammed into the ground. The world started to go black, screaming echoed from the void. A thud which made the room shake jerked the talons still lodged in my body. Now I screamed.

~ ~ ~

I was floating. The shirring of waves running across sand surrounded me. I smelled cinnamon and cookies. The darkness smelled like Christmas.

~ ~ ~

The murmuring of water sounded more like voices, but still I floated. Only now I felt pain, too, throbbing from deep within me. I wanted to groan, but something got in the way.

Did the voices come from robots? Why did they beep? I wanted to float again. My pain had gotten more acute. I liked the beach better. I wanted to go back there.

"She has to fight her way back to us."

Wait. The speaker wasn't a robot. That was my mom's voice. Why did she sound so sad? I tried to open my eyes and find her, but I couldn't.

"Have the doctors said how long they think it will take?" This voice belonged to my dad.

"They told me any time." Oh, Talon was there, too. He sounded miserable. "Several internal organs were pierced. I guess deep injuries like hers can take a while to heal." Talon made a strange noise and when he spoke his voice came out thick. "I shouldn't have made her go. I thought she'd fit best underneath, but I underestimated the danger. I should have been the one to go under him."

"Talon, you've got to quit blaming yourself. You made a call, and it was the right one." My dad's voice strained as if those words hurt him. "If you or Omri had gone, you probably would have met the same or worse before you accomplished your goal. At least . . . at least no one else got hurt. Livy did what had to be done. We understand the job all too well."

I wanted to call out to them, but I couldn't. I needed to know if I'd killed Farak. I needed to know if Ferika had lived. I needed to tell Talon . . . I needed to tell him so many things. I needed to tell him I was still here, and that I didn't blame him.

Chapter 17

Pain. But this time in my throat. I gagged and fought. Somewhere an alarm screamed. People yelled. Running footsteps pounded closer. I opened my eyes at more pain and tried to paw at the tube they were pulling from my throat. As soon as the tube was out, much of the pain disappeared. I gasped air in. My lungs filled in a way I was sure they hadn't in a long time.

"Mom," I tried to say, but not much came out.

With a mother's instincts, she seemed to know. She took me in her arms and held me gently.

"Ferika?" I asked.

"She'll live, sweetie. Don't worry about that. You worry about getting better."

"Dad." Each croak came out more like English, but my voice still grated terribly.

He came over and traded places with my mom. He gave me a gentle hug, his eyes over bright. We must have come back to the Borderlands because they were both yellow and sported tails. Dad brushed my hair back and kissed the top of my head.

"My daughter, the dragon slayer, who knew."

"I did it?"

"Yup." He gave me a small smile. "But we'll talk more later. Your mother's right. You focus on healing. Do you need anything?"

"Talon?"

"I'm here." He moved in beside my father. He looked

like hell. His face shone a pale rendition of its usual green and he had purple circles under his eyes.

My father gave a sigh and let go of me. "I have to get back." He gave my mom a look.

"Yes, and I need to check on Ferika and the others. They'll want to see you. Can they visit?"

I nodded. The movement made my head spin. Mom and Dad snuck out. I was alone with Talon. Laying back in the pillows I caught his hand.

"I want to know. What happened?"

"Shh . . . They just pulled the breathing tube out. You'll hurt your throat."

I scowled at him.

He sighed. "All right. I'll tell, but only if you promise to keep quiet. If you have questions you can write them down, Yumiko style."

I made a zipping motion over my mouth and waited expectantly.

"You slaying the dragon was incredible, really." He gave me a wan smile. "You're kind of my hero now."

I search the table beside me for paper and a pen. Talon got up and came back with some.

Don't talk like that. I don't know if I should be grossed out or waiting for the sarcasm.

"Geez, you don't trust me at all. I'm being serious. I felt like two different people watching you work. On the one hand, I was scared shitless. For the time I thought you were dead or were dying . . . Well, I never want to feel that way again in my life.

"Then I had a more detached part which was like *my girlfriend is a total badass*. And you were, too. You slid under Farak, speared him with the sword, ramming it in while he gave you a look which would have made most men piss their pants. Then . . ." He shuddered, and his eyes filled. "It was so awful, Livy. He impaled you with all four talons on one of his claws. And you were stuck there like a ragdoll while he did his death throws. We couldn't get to you because he thrashed so much. I . . ."

He hitched a sob. "I thought you were dead for sure. I was a coward. I made Omri go get your body. I didn't want to . . . if you were really . . ."

I took his hand and squeezed. "I'm here. I'm okay."

"You promised not to talk."

Frustrated, I grabbed the paper. *Fine. Please don't cry. I'll be all right. Actually, I can't remember anything after I felt his talons go in. Sounds like that's probably a good thing. What about Ferika?*

"Your mom told the truth. She's a couple doors down, recovering. Farak fractured her skull. But ultimately, she'll be fine. Like you. You both have a long recovery in front of you."

Where exactly are we?

"You're in a hospital in the Lord High Governor's palace. I guess the shields they set up had alarms on them. If anything with too powerful an evil aura showed up, Lord Feéroi's secret service would know. Omri had just gotten you free when your parents and a team of law enforcement arrived. They helped get you guys back. Good thing, too. Without magical intervention, I don't know if either of you would have lived. Human care can fix the holes and replace the blood lost, but only magic can replace the magic you lost."

Emmett? Elita? Omri? Yumiko? The human kids?

"I have no idea about the humans. The secret service took care of the details. Everyone else is back in the palace now. Lord Feéroi took Farak's warning about Zaemon moving against us seriously. We're all confined to the palace. I'm not complaining. We've lived fear free for almost two weeks. We get magic rations, so no need to steal and—"

I shoved the paper at him. *Two weeks?*

He ran a hand across my head more gently than he'd ever touched me. "You've been in a coma. Livy, I don't think you get it. You had a punctured lung. One talon pierced your liver and a kidney. One fully impaled your shoulder. And the fourth nicked your intestines. They said we're lucky you didn't go into septic shock and die before they got a magic healer to stabilize you. Four healers took the better part of a day to repair all the holes. Since then they've been using spells to get your body to regrow nerves and tissue. But there was no guarantee your body wouldn't give up. Magic can't give you the will to live. We've all been waiting."

A tear ran down his face and hit my blanket.

I waved him close and gave him a soft kiss. "Thank you for staying with me."

He cleared his throat and gave me a very Talonish look. "Enough about what happened. You know all the details. I don't want to relive the attack anymore. So, if you're done asking questions, I never want to discuss it again. From here on out go torture someone else if you want more."

I nodded, and he gave me the first unadulterated smile since I'd woken up.

~ ~ ~

I woke to bickering. Talon tried to shush the anxious-looking Omri, Elita, Yumiko and Emmett at my door.

"Hi," I croaked, sitting myself up slowly. The stupid breathing tube had left my throat feeling like the worst sore throat ever.

Elita shoved Talon off to the side and rushed over, throwing her arms around me and gleefully hugging me. "Olivia, I was so worried about you," she gushed. "You'll never guess! Daddy has named Talon, Omri, and you heroes for saving me." She plopped next to me and I winced as she jarred the bed. "You and Talon have been appointed my new bodyguards, permanently! You never have to go back to Earth and you never have to prey on humans again."

Elita gleamed at me and I tried to wrap my head around this huge development. "But what about Omri and Yumiko?"

She waved a dismissive hand at me. "Yumiko is taking over Omri's duties as my body servant. Daddy wanted Omri and Ferika as his personal bodyguards. I mean, a dragon and sphinx pair? Really, Daddy couldn't get much better. His current detail has been put in charge of the special guard unit. They're keeping the entire capitol safe from anything Zaemon might send this way. But from what Ferika has told us, she and Farak were his main lieutenants. He'll be scrambling to reorganize and find new power. The chaos gives Daddy time to be ready. Talon's already taken up his post. The brat makes me stay here with him, so he can be with you."

Elita had barely paused for breath in all of this, but still managed to blaze on. "I'd rather be at home, but Emmett didn't want to leave you either." She took my hand and patted it. "No offense, but the hospital sucks and it's boring. You need to hurry up and get out of here. Then we can go back and shower you properly." She wrinkled her nose at me. "And your hospital gown absolutely has to go. I brought you proper clothing weeks ago, but the nurse said no."

I giggled. Elita managed to sound so put upon by my situation. "Thanks for trying. I don't want to be here either. I'll do my best to get out. And thank you for the job. I'm honored." I squeezed her hand.

She leaned close and gave me a soft smile. "Now you don't have to leave Emmett either."

This time I hugged her. "I know. Thank you."

Yumiko had wandered over and handed me a tablet. *I'm glad to see you up. I'm so glad you're staying with us. Heal up quick.* She ran her hand across my hair and gave a sort of hiccup as she fled from the room.

Emmett came next. He sat carefully on the other side of me and pulled me into a gentle hug. He buried his face near my ear and whispered, "I've never been so scared. Livy, I can't lose you. I'd rather lose a leg. I love you." He squeezed a little tighter and heaved a huge sigh. "I can't even tell you how good it is to see you up."

I squeezed him back. "Now we get to stay close. We have a lot of help and hopefully we won't be forced into any more dire situations."

Omri cleared his throat. "Might I have a word with Olivia? Alone?"

I got lots of pats and smiles as everyone cleared out. Omri stood beside my bed with his hands tucked behind his back until only the two of us remained. I patted the bed beside me and Omri sat, giving me a strange look.

"Spit it out, Omri." I put my hand on top of his. "I saw the glare Talon shot you on his way out and I can read you better than this by now. You have bad news." I straightened up. "Whatever you have to say, I can handle it."

"I've been fully immersed in the latest intelligence since I took up my new post. Elita lied. I will be the Lord High Governor's bodyguard once Zaemon has been brought to justice. For now, Ferika and I have been assigned to you. You have indeed been declared a hero, as have Talon and I. But you were the sword bearer. Zaemon is holding you personally responsible for the loss of Farak. You have an enormous price on your head."

I gasped, and my eyes filled.

Omri reached out and stroked my hair reassuringly. "Everything is being done to secure your safety and the safety of the rest of us. There's no doubt once you have been killed, Zaemon will seek out the rest of us involved. But he intends to make an example of you first. Talon is serving as Elita's bodyguard, but you are compromised for the time being. He's been given a temporary partner."

My heart stopped. "A new partner?" Partnerships were such a personal thing.

Omri's hand ran across my cheek and tipped my face up to meet his gaze. Even the blur of tears couldn't blot out the pity in his eyes. "I know what you must be thinking, but this is a single assignment and business—"

"So was guarding Elita." I lashed out at him. "Talon got arbitrarily assigned to me and look where that went." Something inside me started crumbling. Without thinking, I grabbed and mashed the call button.

The nurse's voice answered immediately. "Yes, Miss Skotadi?"

"Get Omri out of my room. *Now.*"

Omri gave me a horrified look. "No. Olivia. It's not—"

I covered my ears and shook my head. "Life's never going to go right for me, is it? Ever since this mess started my world has slowly and completely crumbled and every time I think it's about to get better something new is dumped in my lap."

Omri reached to touch my arm and I slapped his hand away. "I know I needed to know, but you've given me the bad news. You're done. Get out."

The door burst open and two nurses with scowls on their faces took Omri's arms, escorting him from the room.

Omri grabbed at Talon. "You need to talk to her. She wouldn't listen to me."

Talon shot Omri a look of loathing, but stepped inside my room. I couldn't even focus on him without hurt overwhelming me.

"You took a new partner."

"I was assigned a new partner," he corrected.

"How you got one doesn't matter. You agreed."

"I had to. Who else is going to protect Emmett and Elita? I assume you want him guarded properly?" His voice had an irritated snap and I hoped it wasn't directed at me.

Another stab of pain ran through my heart and I let my head droop. "Just go. I hope you're happy with your new partner. Good luck to you both."

Talon crossed his arms and glared at me. "No. I'm not leaving. I refuse to let you victimize yourself and villainize me in the same breath. If by wishing us good luck together you're implying I'm going to be in a relationship with my new partner you're wrong—"

"Am I? Look what happened with us."

"Shut up, Livy."

I blinked up at him and kept my mouth shut. He'd never been so angry with me.

"That's better. Things won't happen like they did between us. I insisted on a male partner."

I blinked again. "But that's never done, unless it's siblings."

"When your partner saved the princess from the dragon, you can pretty much get what you want. I pulled strings. I told them I didn't want to worry you while you healed, and I didn't want to lead some other poor girl on. I told them the same thing I told you. I don't want to work with anyone else, ever. This is only until the price is off your head and you're fit to fight. Though strictly speaking we don't need an official partner for our new posts with Elita."

I had no words. Tears fell freely.

Talon sat beside me, wiping them away. "I hope you don't really think so little of me."

"I actually couldn't believe you'd take another partner. But Omri wouldn't lie, even to spare my feelings. Why didn't you tell me yourself?"

He ran a hand across my cheek. "Because I thought you might take the news this way. You only woke up yesterday. I didn't want to stress you out." He glared back at the door. "Thanks to Omri for helping me out."

"Speaking of Omri, Talon, could you please bring him back, so I can apologize."

"Why? Look at the way he left you."

"I wouldn't let him finish. I probably cut him off before he got to the part about your partner being a guy."

Talon frowned. "He should expound less and highlight the important parts first. But yeah, I'll go get him." He started to get up but stopped and looked me over. "How are you feeling today?"

"My throat hurts. I've never felt this stiff and I ache on the inside, but not too bad. My body feels abused."

"Geez, I wonder why? But I'm glad to hear you're not in any real pain."

Suddenly, Talon pinned me against my pillows. His chocolate brown eyes stared at me. He kissed me. Not the careful, sweet kisses I'd received from him since I'd woken up, but something far hotter. The machine began to beep as my pulse skyrocketed.

Talon yanked the band off me. "I'm not hurting you, right?"

I gave a shuddering breath and a shake of my head. He went back to kissing me and his hands ran up my body, starting at my hips. At a knock on the door he was sitting demurely beside me. I had no idea how he managed not to blush when the nurse walked in.

"We lost your vitals." The nurse gave my face a close look. "We should take your temperature as well. You look quite flushed. We don't want you getting an infection."

"Oh, I'm sure she's infected," Talon quipped. "Probably contagious, too." He gave the nurse a cheeky wink and she shooed him out with a smile.

Chapter 18

Talon returned later in the afternoon with a hesitant looking Omri in tow. I apologized, and he gave me a real smile. Talon on the other hand gave him an impressive lecture about the manner in which he delivered information. Elita brought dinner for all of us to have an impromptu picnic in my room and the nurses let Ferika visit for the meal.

Things were awkward with Ferika, or maybe the feeling was all mine. After all, I had killed her brother. Whether I was alone in the feeling or not, I didn't like the nagging in my gut. On my third day awake I got permission to leave my bed. I waited until everyone else had gone, and snuck over to Ferika's room. The interior surprised me. She had a large feathery mat on the floor, but then again, we were in the Borderlands. A dragon would never fit in a regular bed.

"Ferika?"

She looked up from her mat and smiled. "You heard I'm being discharged?"

"Actually, no. But congratulations. Can we talk for a bit?"

"Sure."

I stepped inside the door. "I . . . I'm sorry. About your brother."

She let out a sigh which carried a wisp of smoke. "I wondered if that's what was bothering you. Don't worry about what you had to do. You heard him. He didn't care for me. You lot are the first ones who ever have. I only mattered to him for lineage reasons. Family pride. He never would have let me live a peaceful life. I'm free and I'm dragon enough not to be bothered by what it took to accomplish my goal. Rather, I'm grateful for the service you provided me. Your motives don't matter."

I nodded. "I think you've covered everything I might have used to hold onto guilt. I'm glad you're not mad at me."

She nodded knowingly. "Yes, you have enough enemies without being the source of a dragon's grudge."

"Not for that." I gave her an exasperated look. "You're my friend. I don't want you to be mad at me because I want to continue being friends."

She gave a purr which vibrated the floor. "I keep forgetting things work this way with my new friends. It's so different from my previous life."

I smiled at her. "To some extent I know what you mean. Having been isolated amongst humans, unable to fully be myself and now this. I didn't realize an imp could have six friends. But now . . ."

Ferika gave another purr. "Since you're finally out of bed, stay and tell me about life amongst humans. I mean, before all this happened?"

She scooted herself into a coil and motioned for me to take the middle. Heat radiated inside her coils and she kept up a thrumming purr which made me want to close my eyes and nap. But I answered all her questions and asked her lots of my own. I took my time and reveled in quality girl time I never knew I wanted or needed.

~ ~ ~

I stood at the door to my hospital room in my normal clothes, waiting as Omri lectured me on the terms of my confinement to the palace grounds. I only half-paid attention. After spending three and a half weeks total in the hospital I needed to go. Besides, the rules were easy enough to understand: I wasn't allowed to leave. Period.

I followed Elita through the palace as she chattered and pointed out portraits of her ancestors, family heirlooms, the locations of various things like the dining hall and the council chambers. I peeked in at the council chambers, the legendary room where the Fairy Synod met. All my assignments had come from there. They ruled everyone's everyday life. The chamber was disappointingly boring, full of long tables and stiff-looking chairs.

I'd only ever been inside one palace in the Borderlands and only seen one bedroom, the one Zaemon had locked me in. Though that room had been used for actual living creatures, it wasn't much better than a cell and it had stunk of sigbin. My new accommodations, in the Lord High Governor's palace were light and airy and contained a fluffy bed, flowers on the nightstand, TV, and bookshelves. I would be comfortable here. Eventually, the space might even become a home.

"Well?" Elita bounced on the balls of her feet in excitement.

"I love it."

She pounced on me. "I knew you would." She pointed to a door on the far side of the room. "That's your shared bathroom. The one on the other side is usually mine." She heaved a sigh. "But Daddy thinks it's best if I'm not in my regular spot, just in case. So Omri and Ferika are staying in there. I'll be directly across the hall and Talon and the new guard are sharing the quarters next to mine. Have you met him yet?"

I shook my head. No point in trying to talk, she wouldn't let me get in a word edgewise, anyway.

Sure enough, Elita plowed on. "You'll get a chance to meet him tonight. I'm having a small dinner party in my room for all of you. It's a 'hurray you're well' for you, a 'welcome' for Ferika and Lynx, and I have some big news to announce."

"Lynx?"

"He's Talon's new partner. He's . . ." She cocked her head and gave me a veiled smile. ". . . tasty. Are you sure your heart's set on Talon?"

"Yes."

Elita shrugged. "Well, you're not bound. You can always change your mind. I know Ferika wants to eat him."

"Not that Ferika's picky. I've seen what she eats," I muttered.

"You're so sweet and innocent." Elita patted my head condescendingly.

Before I'd figured out what we were talking about she gave me a little wave and pranced out my door hollering over her shoulder as she went. "My room, five o'clock."

I checked my clock; the numbers said three. I poked around my new home to kill the time. The closet contained a full array of impractical clothing. I'd have to order some more. I'd never asked Elita what my salary would be. I hoped these were either gifts or returnable. A tap at the door drew my attention.

"Livy? It's Talon."

I dashed for the door. I couldn't think of a better way to kill two hours than to hang out with Talon. Yanking the door open I stopped and gaped. Talon stood outside my door, white teeth in his smile contrasting with his green skin. But the two figures behind him had me gulping. One had Talon's green skin, the exact same shade. He stood about an inch shorter than Talon and had a white tuft of hair in front of each ear which matched the shocking mop of white hair on his head. Next to the man stood an unmistakably human woman with Talon's mischievous dark brown eyes. Oh my God. I was meeting his parents.

Talon pushed his parents inside and mouthed "Sorry" at me. Out loud he said, "Olivia. These are my parents, Inessa and Dagger. Mom, Dad, this is Olivia. My partner.

Or she was going to be. Only now we're both Elita's new bodyguards. Or we will be once things are settled with . . ." He trailed off.

I knew exactly what he meant. Not needing a partner felt like a piece of my identity had disappeared. Assassins worked in pairs. We bonded through partners. The lack of needing him in the usual way left things feeling far too wide open.

Suddenly, I realized Elita had been right. Talon and I had no claim on each other now, besides our feelings. Our feelings were strong, and we were attracted to each other, but we'd only begun to test those waters. The hospital isn't the most romantic setting. Were we attached enough to pass someone else by? What if Talon met another girl? Not needing a partner opened up a whole new selection for him to choose from. I gulped as tears stung at my eyes.

Talon grabbed my arm and pulled me over to the far side of the room. "What's wrong with you? Seriously? My parents made you cry?"

"Why did you even bring them? We should have talked about this. I . . ." A rush of nervous energy something akin to adrenaline surged through me. Usually I let the fight instinct have the upper hand. This time flight dominated.

"They want to meet you." Talon gave me a strange look. "You saved my life. Remember your mom and the embarrassing display of gratitude I received? My parents are like that, too."

I fidgeted. "Um, if you're sure. I don't know what to say."

"In this mood, it's probably best if you don't say anything." He shook his head. "You're acting like I'm introducing you as my fiancé or something."

"Your *what*?"

"It's just an expression. You're obviously not . . . I mean . . ." He hung his head. "This is *so* not going the way I meant. Please?" he asked without looking up. "Go say hi and let them thank you."

I nodded and sidled over to them. "Hi," I gasped out. "Nice . . . nice to meet you."

Dagger roared with laughter. "I assumed Talon had gone nuts. He told me when he first met you he wanted to protest his assignment to the Synod and said you were underqualified to be an assassin. I figured any girl who could dive under a dragon had to be blatantly proficient and my son was too stupid to see it." He leaned in and gave me a conspiratorial wink. "He can be sometimes, my dear. But in this case, I should have had more faith in him. If it weren't for all the accolades lavished on you by the Lord High Governor, I'd be inclined to agree with his initial assessment."

I stammered and blinked up at him. Talon was obviously this man's son. I couldn't tell if his comments were meant as insults, teasing, or real disbelief. Such infuriating men in this family. His mother laid a gentle hand on my head. The power reserve hummed in her the same way it now hummed in Emmett.

"Thank you, Olivia." She kept her voice soft and soothing. "For saving my son's life. I am in your debt."

"No need." I dropped my gaze to the floor and wondered what color I blushed now that my skin was buttercup yellow. Did I blush orange?

I hoped they'd take a hint and leave but Dagger got some sick enjoyment out of watching me squirm. They stayed all the way until ten-'til five.

"Talon, Elita expects us for dinner in ten minutes and I still need to change."

"Me, too." His relief at the excuse to get his parents out shone obviously on his face. I received a hug from Inessa on her way and got a wink as cheeky as Talon's from Dagger.

I tapped on Elita's door and Emmett opened it. Of course, he would be here. But . . . Since a relationship with her wasn't mandatory, where exactly did that leave the two of them? I needed to get him alone at some point, so I could ask. He said he liked her, but did that mean *like*? I had no experience with romance and I'd never be able to tell by watching. They were quite kind to each other but nothing obvious, at least to me. As opposed to Omri and Ferika who were almost disgusting to be around.

"Wow, Livy. You look . . ." He blushed. "I had no idea you were such a . . . girl."

"I don't know if that's a compliment or not."

He took my hand and pulled me inside. "Compliment for sure. Elita's raking the staff over the coals because they mixed up everyone's dinner. But she'll be thrilled. She's been dropping hints about your outfit for days but refused to tell me more. Hey, Talon."

Talon turned, and his jaw dropped. A warm tingle ran through me. He started wandering over, looking dazed but someone else had caught my attention. On the other side of the room stood a young man who had to be Lynx. I don't know what Elita meant by "tasty" but he was the most gorgeous male I'd ever seen in real life.

Lynx had shimmery gold skin, hard muscles and thick gold hair. Not human blond, gold like metallic threads. His eyes were the most unreal shade of apple green and his smile would melt steel. He smiled at me and my knees went weak. How could I possibly be worthy of this angel's attention? Lynx brushed past Talon and approached me. Part of me registered the look of hatred on Talon's face, but only a small part. The rest of me tingled at the possibility this divine creature sought my company.

Lynx took my hand and kissed the back of it. Somehow in one simple gesture he took my ability to speak. "Ah, the dragon slaying imp. A pleasure to meet you. You are quite renown."

My brain whirled as I tried to remember what the word renown meant. Talon stepped up beside Lynx and gave me a disgusted look.

"He's flattering you about being famous. Don't trust him. He's a makhai."

This time Lynx shot Talon the dirty look.

"Wait." I shook my head. "How's he a makhai? Aren't they classified as demons?"

"Technically, yes." Lynx's voice was beautiful and deep and masculine in a way which made my stomach thrill. "But we're also classified as malevolent, not evil."

"Meaning he's sneaky and can change his allegiance to suit his own ends," Talon spat at him.

Lynx eyed him antagonistically. "I'm in the same classification as your dragon friend. You don't seem to have a problem with her."

Talon flushed with anger, then quickly let his color drop, stepped from beside Lynx to my side and slipped an arm around my waist. "Our partnership is not a measuring contest," he said coolly. "It's about team work. And yes, Ferika's infinitely preferable to work with than you. Surprising a dragon would make a better team player, but watch her. You might learn something." He bent and pressed a kiss to my temple. "Yumiko wants to see you but can't call. You forgot to look around."

I blushed and started toward the waving Yumiko but Talon caught my arm and whispered in my ear.

"Watch out for Lynx. Makhai dazzle on the battlefield, it's one of their skill set. But in day to day terms that means they use their power to always stay on top in a group and they pretty much always get their way with the opposite sex. You have to outsmart the feelings he causes. Don't lose your true feelings."

"Oh? And what would those be?" I teased. I did feel much more like myself since we'd left Lynx behind.

Talon squeezed my arm. "I'm serious, Livy. Watch yourself. I'll only forgive so much. I don't want to be mad at you or hurt him, or both."

I took Talon's hand, pulling him over to a secluded corner behind a bookcase. "Why are you fighting so hard? We don't have to be partners anymore. You never have to steal again. I never have to kidnap. We're like Yumiko and Omri. We're free to be with whoever we want now."

Talon hit the wall, looking like I'd slapped him. I hesitated, a fiery feeling of guilt and fear buzzing through my body knowing where I intended to push this.

"If you only liked the way I fight. I mean, I know you like Ferika's looks better than mine. You don't have to be with me."

His expression flipped between devastated and furious. "Are you not interested?"

"No, I—"

"Then what are you getting at, Livy?"

My eyes filled with tears. "I only meant—"

"Whatever, Livy. You seem to be trying to find reasons for us not to be together. So, have it your way. Have Lynx, or whoever else you want. I'm not going to force you. Be happy on your own." He turned and stalked off.

Every step he took away from me burned harder in my chest. The pain went from hurt, to aggravation, to all out anger. I leapt, tackling him and landed on his back, pinning his arms behind him.

"Look here, you insufferable toyol. I don't want to be on my own."

"Get off, Livy."

I shoved his chest into the floor. "No. You got your chance to tell me to shut up and listen. Now it's my turn. I wasn't trying to run you off. I want to make sure you aren't staying because you feel obligated. I need you more than you need me. I drove in the sword, but you came up with the plan to kill Farak. You were my eyes in the tunnel with the sigbin. Everything people are proud of me for, you're behind it. You like the way Elita and Ferika look. I know I don't compare. Between the two why would you want me?" The last part came out with a bit of a sob.

Talon got his knees under him and I let him sit up, sliding down his back to the floor. He twisted and took my face carefully between his hands, giving my head a gentle shake from side to side.

"I'm only going to clear this up once more, so get your head out of the sand and pay attention. I still want us to be partners. Not because we have to be but because we're better together. Do you think I would have lived through the fight in the tunnel without you at my back? Do you think my plan would have amounted to anything without you to kill Farak? I can't do these things by myself. I need you. Protecting Elita may not be so adventurous once Zaemon is in hand but there's no one else I want at my side."

He leaned to kiss me, but I dodged. "What about my looks?"

He sighed and let his hands drop. "My feelings aren't based on comparisons. I want the package deal. The perfect girl for *me*, not some homogenized ideal. And that girl is *you*."

He tried again for the kiss and I dodged again. "Everyone is watching," I mumbled.

Talon caught my face and squeezed my cheeks into fish lips. "Let them. Our friends don't care, and I want Lynx to see this." He pressed his lips to mine and I relaxed, accepting the kiss.

"Is the dinner show over? Everyone's good?" Emmett smiled down at me and offered a hand to help me up.

"Yeah. I think we're good."

Emmett ruffled my hair. "You should have a higher opinion of yourself. I agree with Talon. You've done some pretty amazing shit the past few weeks. No one here thinks you're a one-woman show, but we all know who's got balls of steel."

I scowled at him. "I'm a girl, remember? I don't have balls."

"It's an expression." He winked at me. "Now. I think Elita's tired of having her thunder stolen. Let's not piss her off."

Elita ignored Emmett's teasing and directed us all to a table she had set up. I'd been seated directly across from Lynx with Yumiko and Talon on either side of me. Yumiko had her little tablet next to her and I slipped it onto my lap and scratched a note to her.

What do you think of Lynx?

Narcissistic, but serviceable.

Elita indicated she found him attractive but she wanted me to make a move on him, why?

She wants to live vicariously. Elita won't make a move. She's got a *real* crush on your friend.

Emmett?

Yes. But as far as I know she hasn't said anything to him.

I thought Elita planned on bonding with him.

Sort of. The old Elita was going to force the pair-bond, but this new Elita is somewhat lost I think. She still wants to be with him, but she doesn't know how to start up a real relationship. How about Emmett? Has he spoken to you?

No. I don't know how he feels. Emmett probably doesn't either. He's the kind of guy who really likes to think things through before he speaks or acts. The more important the decision, the longer he'll brood. Do you know why Talon hates Lynx so much? He said it's because he's a makhai, but I wonder if there isn't more. Should we trust him?

Yumiko gave a silent laugh. Talon's completely green with envy. You were practically drooling on Lynx.

Talon's green anyway.

You know what I mean. Yumiko rocked with her laughter this time. Talon's jealousy has not been helped by the fact Lynx made a public announcement he intends to win your affection and pair-bond with you. He spouted some crap about you making a worthy partner to his illustrious self after all your heroic deeds. She rolled her eyes.

Elita stood and tapped her fork to her glass. "I'm glad to see everyone enjoying the food and getting to know one another. But I have an important announcement. Most of you know the agreement between Omri and Ferika. Father has decided the wedding should commence at once." She gleamed at us all.

Everyone clapped and the two shone with pleasure, but I felt confused. I poked Yumiko and whispered, "Why the rush? Aren't we in sort of a precarious position? Is now really the time for a wedding?"

She scribbled a reply. From the Lord's point of view, now's the perfect time. In part because it shows Zaemon we won't be threatened. And in part because dragons are incredibly loyal to their mates. The Lord doesn't doubt Omri's loyalty and as Omri's mate Ferika will protect him ferociously. A pair-bond locks her to our cause.

I nodded, my mouth in a silent "o". So, the wedding wasn't a party. It was a political maneuver. I listened more intently as Elita gave the date for one week out and informed us all we would be a part of the wedding ceremony. I sighed. Wasn't there an evil creature I could fight instead? I did not want to be dressed up and put on display for the elite of the Central Borderlands.

Ferika gave us a huge, dragonish grin and picked demurely at her scales with one claw. Next to her Omri's white lion tail swished behind him and I giggled. Once again, the strangeness of the pairing struck me. Everyone had started talking at once and Elita immersed herself in the thick of the chaos, obviously reveling in her role as wedding planner.

"Don't even ask." A sensual voice came from next to my ear.

I jerked away from the face and Lynx's eyes sparkled at me.

He winked. "You were giggling about the happy couple. I don't need to be an oracle to figure out what set you off and trust me, you don't want to know."

My blush crept across my head, even under my hair. "You're too close."

He gave me his most melting smile. "Not close enough for me." He put his hands on my shoulders. "I find you . . . intriguing." He breathed the last word out.

I had no idea how that word became so sexy, but holy wow. I shook my head to clear it at the same time I took a swift kick to the shin under the table. I glared at Talon but snapped out of Lynx's spell. Scooting my chair back I stood, excusing myself. "I need to go offer congratulations to Ferika and Omri."

I scurried around the table and away from Lynx. Once he stopped using his powers of attraction, my feelings did a complete flip: I hated him. I kept a wary eye on him as I hugged Omri and Ferika, but he sat down to a fairly amiable looking conversation with Emmett. I really didn't need him sneaking up and surprising me. If I planned to keep my head around him, I needed to see him coming.

Chapter 19

I lay in my comfy new bed letting everything run around in my mind, but mostly luxuriating in the first real bed I'd slept in for weeks. I'd forgotten how nice they were. Made even nicer by the nuzzle at the back of my neck. I stopped short of rolling and scolding Talon for sneaking in. The body behind me was the wrong size.

I slipped my hand under my pillow at the same time I giggled. I wanted to keep the intruder from paying attention to the fact I now gripped the hilt of a dagger I'd stashed. One doesn't sleep unarmed when they're at the top of a demon lord's hit list.

I rolled at the same time as bringing the hilt of the dagger up and into the face of the intruder.

"Ow. That's not the welcome I hoped for."

"Lynx?"

Lynx lay along the length of my body. I sat up and scowled at him. He shot me what I assumed was supposed to be a sexy smile. But I had been so afraid and now felt so angry his charm wasn't affecting me at all. I punched his gut, hard.

"Get the hell out of my bed."

He kept grinning. "Ah, but aside from the welcome, I like it here."

I slipped out of the bed and to the adjoining door. I raised my hand to knock but based on the noises coming from inside, trying to get their attention would be a waste. "Fine. You stay. I'll go." I left for the hallway.

Counting doors, I opened the one I hoped led to Talon. Good thing the moon shone brightly through the sheer curtains. I recognized the green tail hanging out of the bed.

Tiptoeing up to the side of his bed I whispered, "Talon?"

He grunted.

I poked again. "Talon."

He caught me around the waist and tossed me over him into the center of the bed. "To what do I owe this pleasure?" he purred.

"Shut up and listen. This isn't a conjugal visit. It's business."

"Too bad," he mumbled into the pillow.

"Lynx was in my bed."

His eyes flew open and he scowled at me. "And why would you think I'd want to know that?"

I sighed and rolled my eyes at him. "He wasn't invited. And I thought you'd want to know because you seem to be the most likely to believe how slimy he is."

Talon sat up rubbing his eyes. "You don't have to sell me on his slime. Do you think slug bait would work on him?"

"Talon, please. Stop joking and help me figure out what to do. I can't take this."

"Neither can I. Since everyone else seems to tolerate him at least, let's go the easiest and least offensive route. We'll talk to Elita tomorrow and see if he can't be reassigned. If not, we'll try to get him caught so the others will see the slime, too." He gave me a hug. "You don't have to fend him off alone."

"Thanks." I wiggled. "You can let go now."

"Where are you going to go?"

"With Elita?"

"And what would her father say about you bunking with her? We're lucky he's been permissive enough to let us all stay in the same wing. But she's upper crust and you're hunted."

"I don't want to go back to my room, what if he's still there? And I can't go to Ferika. She and Omri are"—I flushed—"busy."

"Stay with me."

"I can't. You're a guy and we're . . . you know . . . sort of involved."

He laughed. "I also happen to be a bodyguard. And I'd rather be very involved rather than sort of. You staying here would help accomplish that."

"What do you mean 'very involved'?"

He leaned toward me. "Omri and Ferika style."

I fell back. "Not happening."

"Why not?" He gave an exaggerated pouty lip.

"Stop, please. I just escaped one guy coming on way too strong. I'm not saying never. But not tonight. Not with the mood I'm in."

"Okay." He opened his arms wide. "I'll behave. I promise."

I snuggled in next to his chest and fell asleep before I had time to dwell on anything.

~ ~ ~

"What's the point of giving you your own room and guards?" Elita stood over me looking irritated.

Talon stayed curled against my back.

"Some guards," I griped. "Lynx attacked me last night and they were too involved with each other to help. Hence my current location."

"Lynx attacked you?" Elita asked, completely dumbfounded.

I yawned and sat up. "He's a sexual predator. He snuck into my room, climbed in my bed and tried to molest me."

Elita raised an eyebrow. "And the problem is? Who wouldn't want to be in bed with him?"

"Me. I'm not interested, and he won't accept *no*. Can we please replace him? He makes me uncomfortable."

"I doubt it." Elita finally took on seriousness. "He passed Daddy's screenings and it's a rare man who's willing to partner with another man. There's hardly a que of replacements waiting."

"Your father is the Lord High Governor." I was getting close to whining and checked myself. "Being Talon's partner is a cushy job, surely someone else wants it. Hell, I almost think I'd rather Talon partner with a girl at this point."

"All right, if Lynx bothers you so much I'll see what I can do. But Daddy's really busy so it might take me a day or two to even see him."

I wrinkled my nose. "You won't see your own dad for two days? In the same house?"

Elita tipped her head up and I saw her chin quiver. Suddenly her quirks and her previously crappy personality all made sense. I scrambled out of bed and hugged her.

"I'm sorry. I know you said Omri and Yumiko were your family. I just didn't fully understand why."

"Sometimes he goes months without actually seeing me." Her voice sagged. "I always got everything I wanted, but . . . it's not the same."

"You know what, don't worry about Lynx. I'll find a way to deal with him. Will your father be upset if I maim the creep?"

Elita giggled. "I'll talk to Daddy for you. I don't care, but if you have to hurt him, spare his face."

I rolled my eyes. "How about I off him and have him stuffed as a throw rug for you? Then you can sit and gaze at him all you want. And he'll never move or speak again. Everyone ends up happy."

"Geez," Talon yawned. "Remind me never to get on your bad side. I don't want my head mounted above the family fireplace."

"Actually," I mused. "I have to admit Lynx has some serious talent. At your most aggravating I never felt like actually snapping your neck. He's lucky I thought you were sneaking into my bed, otherwise I'd have slit his throat first and asked questions later."

Talon gave an exaggerated fake gag. "Even in the dark I don't know how you could mix the two of us up."

I grimaced back at him. "It's hard to tell one type of snake from another when you don't have night vision. You're both after the same thing, predatory, really. You're lucky I like you."

"And that's my cue to leave." Elita headed for the door. "You guys are free to do whatever until eleven, then Talon needs to come with me."

My stomach gave a huge growl. "Breakfast?"

"Not yet." He hopped out of bed and started to dress. I hadn't meant to peek, but I noticed his boxers had a tidy slit in the back out of which his tail poked. His jeans had the same. His tail threaded itself through of its own accord. Mine must do the same because I'd been pulling my pants on without thinking about it and I'd never squashed my tail.

"See somethin' back there you like?" He waggled his butt at me and I slapped it.

"I was watching your tail. It seems to have a mind of its own."

"That it does." He smirked as the tip of his tail took aim at the gap in my cleavage.

I grabbed his tail and pulled. "Watch it."

Talon whirled, stopping very close to my face. "If you're gonna flirt rough I'll forget what your surprise is and keep you here instead."

I hopped from the bed. "A surprise?"

"Yeah but we need enough time to properly enjoy the treat, and I have to be back here in time to go with Elita. So, get a move on."

I hesitated at my door. "Come with me. I don't want to go back on my own in case Lynx sees me. He'd probably peek at me changing."

Talon's face darkened. "Unacceptable. He'll never get to see you naked before I do."

I stuck my tongue out at him, but held out my hand. Talon led the way and opened the door, but my room looked the way it had when I left the night before, minus Lynx.

I went into the bathroom and changed as quickly as I could. Talon led me to the end of the hall and up several sets of winding staircases. At the top a small door stood shut and bolted, nothing else around it. Talon unlocked the door and opened it. Blinding sunlight flooded the stairwell.

At midday, the sun wasn't so much red but electric strawberry. He led me out along a roofline access path to the peak. From our vantage point the whole palace spread below us. Beyond were gardens and pools, courtyards and secluded patios. Outside the palace wall forest spread as far as the eye could see to the left, and beyond the dark blanket of trees, shimmered ocean to the right.

"It's beautiful."

"I thought you'd like the view." He inched in behind me and put his arms around my waist. "We'll do more of this kind of stuff now that we aren't running for our lives." He ran his nose along my neck, brushing with his lips as he went.

"You're distracting from the scenery," I whispered, chest burning.

"I'm admiring other things." He lifted my hair and kissed the back of my neck.

I leaned back into his chest, despite desperately trying to find an excuse to put distance between us. I couldn't think of any which made sense to me. Tipping my head back onto his shoulder I gave up. No point trying to kid myself, I wanted this. A romantic relationship was new and a bit frightening, but I trusted Talon. Besides, if I wanted to keep him in the capacity of being a couple, I probably shouldn't run every time he tried acting romantic.

Talon squeezed until he'd smooshed me against his body and began tracing the neckline of my dress with delicate strokes of his fingers. I should have been embarrassed at the way I pressed back asking him to go a little lower . . . to do a little more. He ran one hand up my neck tilting my head so he could find my lips. I'd largely let him lead with kissing up to this point, but this time I let my feelings go and kissed him hard enough to show him how I felt. He gave a happy sigh.

Unfortunately, I didn't find out what came next. His phone chirped, and Talon stepped back with an entirely different sort of sigh.

"That's Elita's ringtone. She needs me. I've gotta go. Work." He pecked a last kiss on my cheek and disappeared through the door.

I stood, giving myself a moment to catch my breath. Once I had control of myself, I turned to go back to the door, but a mellifluous voice caught my attention. I recognized the voice. Lynx. But if Talon had been called, why hadn't Lynx? I followed the sound of his voice. Spying on him meant I had to leave the safety of the path and shimmy down the tiled roof to a dormer below where Talon and I had been. From my new perch, I spotted Lynx on a balcony below me. I couldn't imagine how he'd squeezed out there. I wasn't sure I would have been able to stand next to him. He pressed a finger to his ear and spoke, almost like using a headset.

"No. You're going to have to trust me on this." He paused for a few moments. "It's what you're paying me for. Am I or am I not a professional?" He let out a low growl. "I'll see she's safe." He paused again as the other person spoke. "Best laid plans . . . Everything else went so well for you.

So, trust *me* this time. I promise I'll earn your faith in me for giving me the job and my payment for seeing everyone safely through to the other side."

He stalked off the balcony and a glass door got slammed hard enough to break the window, but somehow didn't. What had I heard? I couldn't imagine anyone talking to the Lord High Governor that way. But the conversation had to be with his employer who was the Lord High Governor. Nothing about his phone call made sense. Not to mention the sick feeling in my stomach he always left came roaring back. His conversation hadn't come across as threatening, so why did I mistrust him so badly? Was the sour taste he left only because of the way he treated me?

Looking back up the roof, I knew I couldn't go up the way I came. Going down wasn't an option either. Below me opened a good twenty-foot drop to Lynx's balcony. A drop from this high would break something if I tried jumping. My palms had started to sweat with building panic. A soft swooshing noise caught my attention and Omri landed gently on the roof next to me.

"You are in a heap of trouble," he scolded. "You wandered off without telling Ferika and I. We—"

"—were too busy last night to help when Lynx accosted me in my own bed." Omri looked suitably appalled so I blazed on. "I had to take refuge in Talon's room to get him to leave me alone."

Omri snickered. "That must have been rough."

"Stop it." I slugged his shoulder. "This is serious. We didn't do anything. I didn't want to be touched at all after Lynx took liberties. He's slimy and I don't trust him. That's what I'm doing stuck out here on a ledge. After Talon left when Elita called him, I was surprised to hear Lynx out here on the phone. He ignored her call. He seemed to be on a headset call with someone else. The conversation had to be with his employer, but I can't imagine anyone snapping at the Lord High Governor the way he snapped at the caller. Something's fishy. I don't like him."

Omri sighed and put a hand on my head. "Okay, I get your dislike in reference to yourself and I don't blame you. But overall I think you're letting your emotions and all your previous traumas cloud your perception."

I grabbed his hand and stared into his eyes. "Omri, you're a sphinx. If you tell me his heart is clear and you trust him, I'll let everything go."

Omri blushed and glanced the opposite direction. "I can't read makhai. Their ability to influence others to their own ends clouds my vision of their hearts. I've got nothing on him except what he wants me to see. All I know is he's not as spotless as he presents himself to me. But I only know so much because of his treatment of you. If I hadn't seen some of his shameless behavior and had you tell me the rest, I'd think the same as everyone else."

"Okay, then I hold to my original protest. I don't trust him. And I don't think you guys should either."

"Noted." Omri sighed. "I'm sorry about last night. How can we help?"

"Obviously he can get past locks because my room was locked." I hesitated and gave him a desperate look. "Can I borrow Ferika?"

Omri wilted in disappointment. "Yes. If she's willing."

"Oh, don't look like that." I poked his waist making him chuckle. "You guys are only a week from being pair-bonded. Aren't you supposed to wait for the big night or something?"

"Human custom. But our neglect of you caused this so we will fix the situation. However, I'm sending you to Talon on our wedding night."

"Deal." I gave him a hug and happened to brush the fur at his waist as I did. Fascinated I stopped and pet his hip like a cat. "You're way softer than I thought you would be. You know at home, cats lick themselves to keep their fur clean. Do you?"

He shot me a look with one eyebrow raised. "I should think not. I'm not the only creature with fur. We have special hair driers for such things here."

Omri stood and picked me up by the waist, hanging me over his hip like a naughty child. "Your parents dropped off a stack of homework for you this morning. I saw enough work to keep you busy for quite a while. They said you are now nearly six weeks behind."

"Crap. They brought six weeks' worth of work? On second thought leave me on the roof. I'll be fine here."

"Nope. You are already displeased with me for slipping in my duties with you. I won't fail again." He gave me a wicked grin. "Since you are so anxious to start, how about we go down the fast way."

He tightened his grip and leapt off the roof, spreading his wings to catch us as we fell. I couldn't help screaming like a little girl. Omri simply laughed and took us down to a large terrace off the third floor.

"This leads to Elita's room. You'll find Emmett there, already working on his homework."

"You're mean and . . . and you have a sick sense of humor and . . . and . . ." I stuck my tongue out at him and stalked into the house.

Chapter 20

For the two days after the incident with Lynx's phone call he'd been so good I found him more suspicious than when things were obviously fishy. I kept myself braced for continued attempts at me but received nothing more than brilliant smiles. I'd almost reached the decision to set my apprehensions aside when I happened to be walking past the doors to the grand ballroom. Strangely, the door was cracked. I peeked inside.

Lynx slowly wandered the perimeter of the room, his finger pressed to his ear in conversation again. I watched as he examined windows and doorways, running his hands over pillars and running his eyes across the ceiling. When he came toward the exit I ducked away and down a side corridor. The ballroom would be where the bonding took place. What did he need in there, alone?

I got so lost in thought, mulling over his motives, I never noticed the Lord High Governor, until a hand grabbed me, pulling me to the side. A bodyguard had stopped me from running into him. He gave me a short nod and kept walking. Wait. The Lord High Governor hadn't even been holding his phone.

I couldn't catch Lynx to verify my suspicion he was still talking, so instead I wandered aimlessly, thinking. I supposed Lynx could be on the phone to anyone. I tried not to let my imagination run away with me, but the strangeness of the phone calls kept nagging at me. Finally, I couldn't stand it anymore, so I found Elita and told her about what I'd seen.

She smiled at me. "Yes, he told me he intended on doing that." She flipped back a lavender curl.

"He did?" I deflated. "What he was doing looked so . . . sneaky."

"Lynx told me he wanted to confirm the safety modifications. I guess Daddy agreed to one last check."

I frowned. "Did you confirm with your father?"

Elita put a hand on my back, pushing me toward the door. "Don't worry so much. You're afraid of shadows at this point. Daddy has plenty of security. You're safe. Let yourself relax."

I nodded and left her room, but didn't go back to mine. Instead I chose to wander and brood. I couldn't relax or let my suspicions go. Once again, I wasn't watching in front of me and I ran straight into a fluted pillar. I rubbed my nose after connecting with the pink marble. Suddenly, Lynx had me in his arms. I opened my mouth to protest but he swung me off to the side. He yelped, falling flat as a massive statue of pink marble hit his shoulder on its way to shatter on the floor.

I kicked pieces of marble out of the way and turned him face up. Lynx grimaced in obvious pain.

"You saved me?" I sounded as flabbergasted as I felt.

"Uh . . . Can we discuss this after you help me to the hospital?"

"Oh, my goodness, yes." I helped him to his feet. "I mean, if I knew which way."

"The right-hand corridor," he gritted out.

"Why would you save me?" I helped him down the hall he'd indicated.

"That's the kind of stuff they hired me to do, remember?"

"I know. But you've been so . . . aggressive with me. I have to admit, you made me doubt you."

He gasped at the pain as I readjusted my grip on him. "I know you don't like my style, but your dislike of me doesn't change the fact *I'm* interested in you. I'm lost as to why you are so hostile toward me. And I have no idea where you came up with the idea I wouldn't save you. That should be a given."

"I guess you're right. Sorry."

I pushed open the swinging doors to the admitting room. Despite having a dislocated shoulder and cracked ribs the nurses had him healed and discharged two hours later. Why couldn't I have healed so quickly?

"We're an extra hardy breed," Lynx explained on our way back to our wing.

I had no idea why I'd stuck around, probably guilt. I felt horrible about suspecting him now. He still raised my fur, so to speak, but he *had* saved my life. How embarrassing would that have been, to survive a battle with a dragon only to get squashed by my own klutziness?

Lynx stopped and pulled his phone out of his pocket. "You're on your own from here." He flashed me a text. "Elita calls." He dashed off in the opposite direction, leaving my head spinning.

~ ~ ~

I kept Ferika close. I still didn't want to be alone with Lynx, but her company meant more than just protection. I'd come to need my female friends: Yumiko, Ferika, and on occasion, when her schedule allowed, Elita. We could talk about things I might not have even shared with Emmett. They schooled me in clothing. My appreciation came slowly. We talked about boys. Those discussions made me blush. I was surprised to find myself by far the most innocent. Even Yumiko, who I would never have expected it of, had dated a couple of the palace guards and one of the gardeners.

Ferika and I got very close as we now shared my room and we stayed up far too late giggling and talking in my bed. Elita's station kept her slightly apart from all of us, despite her desire to be a part of the group. She had difficulties fitting us in as she bustled to and from obligations and duties. I was coming to love her, too. But she wasn't part of my world in the same way. And no matter how great my newly found fame, I would never be a part of hers. I actually wished we could go back to Earth. We'd been equals there. I knew the distance hurt her more than she let on.

In a blur, we found ourselves the day before the wedding. After lunch, a gleeful looking Elita kicked all the boys out of her room and told Ferika she'd arranged for a surprise for us. She bolted for the door at the first knock and opened it to the centaur from the spa and three others. The room filled with tapping hooves and swishing tails. Excitement thrilled through me as the centaurs set up portable massage tables.

Elita grinned until her face might split. "I booked us a private spa session for a bachelorette party," she trilled.

My centaur, a palomino whose human hair gleamed sunny blond, ran a gentle hand across my scar. I flinched as he reached the front of the scar beneath my breast.

"Would you like me to take care of your disfigurement for you?" he asked in a deep, rich voice which reminded me of dark caramel.

"Yes, she would," Elita answered without lifting her head. "Don't worry, Livy. Centaurs have magic perfectly suited to cosmetic stuff. You're in good hands." She giggled at her own pun.

I shook my head. "No. Not unless they do Talon before they go, too."

"He's a guy. He doesn't care," Elita said.

"I do," I explained. "His scars are my fault. I don't feel right having mine fixed and leaving him the way he is."

"Who is this Talon?" the centaur asked.

"My partner. I know you've heard about all the things I've done. Everyone seems to have. But I couldn't have done any of it without Talon. He was injured protecting me. And if he keeps his scars, so do I."

"I will stay and heal him as well," the centaur announced.

I gulped. "How much? I'm not earning a paycheck yet."

The centaur chuckled. "From the slayer of Farak I can ask no payment. I will do this for your partner as thanks. Zaemon frequently turned Farak loose on Setmyth Forest. My wife and foal live there. While eating sentient beings is against the Synod's laws, Farak never abided by those laws. He had a particular fondness for centaur. I sleep easier knowing my family is safe. I am happy to give such a small service to you in return."

Warmth spread through my chest. "I didn't realize. I mean, I never set out to do something noble. But I'm really glad."

"One rarely knows how far a single good deed can reach, nor how many lives will be touched. Now, lay still."

I put my face back against the table and the centaur placed his hands on my scar. The magic he used chilled me like ice and the tissue realigned itself along the length of the scar. I would have expected the sensation to be unpleasant, but it wasn't. The repairs felt like things were righting themselves, which of course they were.

He made three passes across the scar before he gave my head a gentle rub. "I can't erase all signs of the damage. Your scar is nearly invisible to the eye now, but should you spend time in the sun in a bikini the scar will darken a different color than the rest of your skin. An over the counter fading cream will take care of any discoloration from here on out."

I reached around and felt for the scar but met smooth skin instead. "That's so cool. Thank you."

After the massage we were all rubbed in oils which smelled like exotic flowers, buffed, polished, and then led off to be waxed and trimmed in places which made me blush. If Lynx had touched anywhere near those spots I'd have put my dagger to his throat, but the centaur I trusted. Once again, my strong negative feelings toward Lynx left me wondering. Did I loathe him just because of his perverted tendencies or was there something more?

The centaurs excused themselves and Elita hurried to get us dressed.

Someone knocked. "Can you get the door, Livy?" Elita asked me.

I opened the door and Talon pushed it wide, a huge grin on his face.

"I love seeing you all dressed up, Livy."

"Talon." I reach for his now smooth neck. "He really did fix your scars for you." My voice failed as I caught sight of his ear. The point was still missing. "Oh, your ear."

Talon rubbed the spot. "Yeah, he said he can't regrow flesh which no longer exists. But he smoothed the edges a bit for me."

I ran my fingers across his ear and down his neck.

He closed his eyes and tipped his head into my touch. "Thank you for sending him. He said you insisted." Talon's hand wandered to the open back of my dress. "You can't even tell you had a scar," he marveled.

"Talon." I blushed as his hand wandered toward the front of the missing scar. "The others."

As if on cue Omri came through the doorway followed by Lynx and I felt the conflicting emotions he now brought to the surface every time I saw him. The urge to run, the urge to growl at him, and the urge to blush and say "hi" all mingled and mixed so I simply got overwhelmed.

The next afternoon I paced my room in my bridesmaid gown: a ridiculous rendition of cotton candy, just as fluffy and nearly the same color. The shade had to clash horribly with my buttercup skin. My hair hung in goldilocks style curls picked out with pink flowers. Ferika had been decked out with flowers and ribbons since a dress would never have fit her dragon body.

She glowed with anticipation. But my body hummed with nervous energy I couldn't explain. This wasn't my wedding, why be so nervous?

I mulled over the mundane to amuse and distract myself as I waited for this shindig to get underway. So far, I wasn't impressed with weddings. Maybe when the time came I'd elope. Or get married in Vegas. Wham, bam, thank you minister. None of all this hype, and waiting, and nervousness.

Finally, the moment had arrived. Elita led the way out to the isle. Yumiko followed, and I came after. Talon caught my eye and winked. Omri stared at Ferika, his eyes shining. Emmett drooped, bored, but Lynx stood strangely tense. His expression was mellow, but every muscle corded up, ridged. Strange. But I had no sense of an evil aura. Talon acted relaxed. And the Lord High Governor's heavy guard encircled the room. I tried to force myself to relax as well.

That stupid pervert, Lynx was probably pissed he and I weren't getting married. After all, he went and announced he'd take me as a wife before I even woke from my coma. He probably thought not only should this be his moment, but now he wasn't getting any action tonight either. Not that he would ever get *that* from me.

I took my place beside the alter and tried to keep my expression pleasant. I couldn't let my nerves spoil Ferika's special day. At this point the union became more interesting. Instead of busting out a bible or some other inspirational text the minister took out a set of golden blades and lay them on the table.

I squirmed. This would be a bond sealed in blood. Divorce didn't exist amongst magic folk the way it did for humans. I'd already known that. But I finally understood why. You were permanently linked to your partner. Yikes.

I took a sideways glance at Talon and felt ill. Did he hope we'd do this someday? As an imp was I even capable of such commitment?

I scanned the audience hoping to distract myself and my eyes landed first on my parents and then Talon's. My stomach settled a little. They were bonded and happy and they were like me. A pair-bonding would work out. As long as I picked wisely, I could be happy like them.

Omri and Ferika were finishing up a long and boring vow. I now forced myself not to yawn. The minister pointed them both toward the alter and took up the first of the sacrificial knives.

A slow clap echoed through the otherwise silent hall.

"Is this where I say I object?"

My stomach turned inside out. I'd heard that voice once before and I'd never forget the paunchy little owner who scared the crap out of me. Lord Zaemon.

As if on cue the ceiling crumbled inward and screams echoed through the ballroom as people were crushed. Roaring which brought down more debris filled the hall and heat blazed as dragon fire herded the survivors into the center of the room.

Rough hands grabbed me and pulled me against a solid chest. I struggled, but Lynx was stronger.

"Let me go. We need to help."

"I am helping. I'm helping myself to my payment. Just wait for it. There's still a pair-bonding to happen and then we can enjoy ourselves."

"I'm *not* bonding with you."

He gave a cruel laugh. "I don't want to bond with you. I might have at the start, to play nice, but all I need from you is children. I don't have to be married to you to make that happen."

I struggled again and gasped. "I don't understand."

"That's because you're stupid, shortsighted, and entirely too noble," he growled. "The wedding is for Zaemon. He'll be taking Elita. You're my payment. In order for a makhai to successfully reproduce the woman has to meet a set of very strict criteria. Makhai have no females, so finding a suitable vessel can take some time. I got lucky. You're perfect. After you've popped out a couple for me, I might do you the favor of ending your life swiftly. But fight me on this and I may simply keep you around for the pleasure of trying to break you."

I didn't bother fighting the sick feeling in my stomach and took pleasure in puking all over Lynx's arms and feet. He rewarded me by shaking me roughly, but the pain of my neck snapping back and forth was worth the small measure of justice. Once he stopped, I took a quick glance around the room which had filled with complete pandemonium. Dark beings overran the hall, killing at their leisure.

Lesser demons, their red skin and black hair nearly glowing with their internal hellfire were rounding up what I assumed to be members of the Synod. The people they were targeting were all older, upper crust, and stuffy looking. The demons kept the fairies unharmed. But then if I'd understood the gist of Zaemon's plans from before, he wanted to rule supreme. To help legitimize his coup with the common people it would be faster to have the Fairy Synod still in place, but dancing to his tune.

The rest of the guest were lambs for the slaughter. Another flock of Stymphalian birds were picking at the lifeless bodies like gruesome vultures. When they switched victims, the sight churned up my already tender stomach. Various bits of gore stuck to their razor-sharp feathers and went with them in a vomit-worthy display.

I struggled but Lynx kept his grip and I could do nothing. He forced me to watch the devastation unfold. The makhai must be trained in torture, as well as combat. I scanned the hall, looking around for faces I knew. Maybe I would see some shred of hope. The only ones I could pinpoint in the chaos were those who had been near the alter with me. I knew everyone else was still there, somewhere and hopefully alive. A huge, dark green male dragon guarded the doors while a smaller, poisonous green female, had squared off with Ferika.

Talon kept shooting me distraught glances as he tried to pull his parents out from under the rubble. I couldn't find my parents anywhere. A small group of guards had backed together, trying to protect the Lord High Governor but they were only managing defense.

Another group of guards, led by Omri were guarding Elita. They had her tucked back against the alter and they bristled with swords pointed out. Zaemon looked them over and gave a four-note whistle. A chill ran through the room and the glass of every window blew out. In through the empty frames floated a nightmare, wraiths. Like grim reapers in smoke they floated to the floor, killing anyone unfortunate enough to get caught in their mist. The guards around Elita paled as the wraiths tightened a circle around them. Out of the group Omri was the only one brave enough or smart enough to create a torch. Only fire would drive back the killing mist.

One of the other guards went pale. His weapon clattered to the ground and he fled, screaming in terror. His foot caught the edge of their mist and his lifeless body toppled to the floor with a thud. The rest of Elita's guard panicked and ran leaving her with only Omri. A Minotaur swiftly caught her and drug her to the alter and the waiting Zaemon.

I hung my head as I, too, got hauled toward the alter.

"Be grateful," Lynx sneered. "You get a front row seat to the dawn of darkness. Under Zaemon's rule we'll use Earth as we ought to. Life will be a lot more fun."

Screams and crying echoed around me. People were dead and more groaned as death crept up on them. Tears blurred my eyes. Evil wasn't supposed to win. How had this much evil even gotten past the guards? We should have been safe. There should have been help. But if the rest of the guard wasn't here by now, they weren't coming. They must have been decimated, too.

My chest burned as reality set in. Life would never be the way it was before, as if fun and joy had somehow died today, as well. Even if things ended this very moment, so many lives were ruined. I cringed as a bang like a gunshot through sheet metal rang through the room. Ferika growled and crouched in a growing pool of her own blood, hissing at the other dragoness. We'd lost. We had no more time . . .

I gasped. That was the solution!

Imps had one skill in their arsenal most probably didn't even realize they held. I might not have even remembered the talent myself if I hadn't overheard my parents talking about it in the not so distant past. The night on which all of this had started. Practically a lifetime had passed since I'd heard my father and mother preparing for their mission to Siberia. But they had given me my solution.

I could stop time. For ten seconds or so. I had no illusions. I'd heard my parents clearly. This method was a death sentence for the imp using it. Stopping time drained so much magic even intervention and infusions might not work fast enough.

I scanned the room again. My friends and family were dying. Lynx had his hands on me still. My life would be a living hell from here on out. My resolve solidified. I would end this. I had the power and the skill. Everything I loved was being exterminated around me. Life wasn't worth living in this new world, anyway. I had no idea how to do this. But Zaemon held the sacrificial knife over his head. I had to act now or never.

I dug inside myself and let instinct take over. The magic roared out of me with a flash and a silent explosion which rocked the room. Everyone stood frozen, statue-like. Only I was left moving.

Ten: I slipped out of Lynx's arms.

Nine: I grabbed one of the sacrificial knives off the table.

Eight: Diving in, I slit Lynx's throat. Deep enough I knew there'd be no helping him.

Seven: I hurried the few steps to Zaemon.

Six: I slit his throat, too.

Five: I placed the point of the blade at his ear.

Four: I drove the knife upward and inward, twisting as I went. Even a demon lord dies if you scramble his brain.

Three: I'd begun to move sluggishly. I still wanted to help Ferika.

Two: I wouldn't make it to her. Blackness surrounded me.

One: The last thing I felt was the slap of tile on my face.

Chapter 21

I had thought death would be more exciting. But nothing surrounded me except blackness. At least I felt warm. Strange that I could think. I still seemed to be me. Would I spend eternity with my disembodied thoughts for company?

Suddenly a jolt of something which burned ran through my body. Funny. I didn't think dead people had bodies.

Another burning jolt. This time I wanted to scream but I couldn't. My mouth wouldn't obey. Why? Why couldn't I die in peace?

Again, with the burning. This time I screamed, but my body wouldn't move to thrash like I wanted to. Now I heard voices, though I couldn't get my eyes open.

"Omri, do you have any more?"

"I'm out. Someone get more."

"Olivia. Hold on."

Sobbing.

I knew those voices, but I couldn't put names or faces with them. My mind filled with darkness once again. The world of pain began to fade, and I knew those had all simply been pieces of memories. The comfortable blackness swiftly returned.

The burning came back. This time I thrashed and screamed and fought against hands which tried to hold me. "Let me die," I screamed. Something horrible awaited outside the blackness. I knew it.

"Livy, *please*. Don't give up."

The voice cut through some of the blackness because of the heartbreak it held. Somewhere deep inside I wanted to make the owner of that voice happy. I screamed as I took another jolt, but this time I stayed in the world of the broken voice. Every inch of my body burned so badly I wanted to find water and become a part of it.

My eyes flicked open to chaos. People rushed at me, yelling my name and pulling at me. I couldn't get my bearings. Someone shoved all those people away and Talon's deep brown eyes looked down at me. Talon. He was the owner of the worried voice I'd wanted to comfort.

"Thank God." Talon cradled me gently in his arms. "I thought I'd lost you again."

Suddenly everything came rushing back and I pushed away. "Elita? Ferika?"

"They're fine," Talon soothed. "As soon as Zaemon went down, every available healer went to work."

"I saw you pulling your parents out."

"My mom has a fractured pelvis. Dad has a couple broken ribs and a concussion. But they'll live."

"My parents?" Bile gathered in the pit of my stomach.

I was met with silence.

I grabbed his tux jacket. "Talon. Where are my parents?"

Talon's head drooped, and he silently pointed to the row they'd been sitting in. Pieces of stone the size of small cars, from the collapsed roof and buttresses lay over their row and the ones surrounding it. Nothing but complete devastation in that section of the hall. The world spun and went dark again. All the noises seemed to come from far away.

Talon stroked my cheek. "I'm so sorry, Livy. Yumiko found them while Omri gave you the power infusions. They don't know if your parents will survive." He pulled me to his chest. "Your dragons took them straight to the hospital. I'll take you to see them once you're up to it."

I blinked at burning tears. "What do you mean, my dragons?"

Talon rubbed nervously at the back of his head. "I'm not sure now's the time to tell you. You pretty much died and your parents . . . I think you've got enough to process right now."

"I don't want to process." I rubbed my eyes. "Distract me."

"Well . . ." He sighed. "You're kinda the new demon lord."

"I'm *what*?"

"The contract is a lot like the magic governing a werewolf pack, which I'd guess you're familiar with. You know, kill the alpha and you become the new alpha. You killed the demon lord so . . . I know you're not a demon, per se, but since imps are classified as malevolent, the magic still works on you. Velor and Vixaria were Zaemon's new dragons. Their allegiance falls to you, since you're the demon lord. So, you see, they're your dragons."

"I don't want to be the bad guy."

"You don't have to be."

I stared up at the owner of the unfamiliar voice and shock prickled through me at the sight of the Lord High Governor.

"Three demon lords govern their own districts in the Central Borderlands. Under normal circumstances they rank between me and the members of the Fairy Synod. Two of the three were happy with that arrangement. Zaemon clearly wished for a different role. But you can serve in a competent capacity like the other two. Only a handful of magic creatures are truly evil. As an imp, you ought to understand you are what you make of yourself."

I gasped. "I'm supposed to rule a district?"

"Once you reach your majority. Yes," Lord Feéroi answered. "Until then I will appoint a regent to assist you. Though I will take your opinion on the regent."

"Really?"

He gave me a sharp look. "I believe you were the only one who spent the last week trying to warn my daughter and her bodyguards about Lynx. You've proven your intelligence."

"Yeah. But I'm confused."

"He was a plant. He managed to slip past my screenings and scramble Omri's skills. You seemed to have a better measure of him. He worked for Zaemon in return for—"

I held up my hand feeling queasy again. "I heard his plan. Let's not go there again."

"Anyhow, Lynx sabotaged the defenses and set up Zaemon's attack on the wedding. Today would have been a total loss without your willingness to sacrifice yourself. You're a lucky girl Omri has the talents he does. We very nearly lost you. And we are certainly lucky to have you."

The rest of the day passed in a blur. I went from elated to miserable by turns but I never got a moment alone. I wanted to decompress and visit my parents, only now I had dragons awaiting my orders and servants pestering me.

Talon showed up at the door to my new quarters with a wheelchair. I glared at him from the bed.

"What are you planning on doing with that?"

"Taking you to visit your parents. Your mom just got out of surgery."

I crossed my arms. "I'll walk. Thanks."

"It's not your choice." The Lord High Governor stepped inside my new room and gave an appraising glance over me. "I ordered the chair. You *will* use it. I need you up and on your feet in three days."

"Three days?" Talon didn't sound pleased. "Why the rush?"

"Don't panic, dear boy." He lay a hand on Talon's shoulder. "I simply need to present her to the Fairy Synod and the other demon lords. But I assume she'll feel more dignified on her own two feet at such a meeting. Better to use the chair now and rest. It's not every day one gets drug back from the jaws of death." He smiled at me. "Speaking of which, you seem to end up there more than most. Let's not make that a habit, shall we?"

"O . . . okay." I still hadn't found my voice when he disappeared.

The Lord High Governor had just spoken to me. Not simply in passing, but conversationally. Like I knew him, or I mattered. Weird.

Talon shook his head as he helped me out of bed and into the wheelchair. "Imagine being on friendly terms with the Lord High Governor. Not even a demon lord for a day and already I feel beneath you."

I gave his fingers a tug. "You'll never be beneath me."

"Too bad." Talon nipped my earlobe as he pushed me out into the hall.

I wanted to flirt back, but I couldn't. We were on the way to see my parents. With all the people fawning all over me, no one had yet assured me they would be all right. My fears were confirmed as I passed through the door of my father's room. He lay motionless on the bed, a breathing tube protruding from his mouth. I grabbed Talon's hand and looked up at him, blinded by tears.

"Go on," he said gently. "Just talk to him. It helps a little. I talked to you every day when you were in a coma. I'd have gone crazy if I hadn't."

He left the chair beside the bed, so I could reach my father and ducked out the door. I took my father's limp and battered hand, pressing my cheek into it. I expected the bubble welling up inside me to bring tears. Instead it brought flaming anger. The rage must have been tied to my new demon magic, because I'd never felt this burning before.

"This isn't going to happen again," I promised my father. "You, Mom, all the other innocent people who were hurt or killed. I won't let it be for nothing. You guys raised me with a code of honor. We never hurt bystanders. Zaemon was the exact opposite. For the last month I've known the fear and heartache he's inflicted on his district for who knows how long. But that ends today."

I straightened up in the chair. "I'm going to clear out every last bit of evil. Then you and Mom and everyone else can live peacefully. I'll even give you magic rations, so you don't have to keep kidnapping or taking assassinations. If I don't have to be the bad guy simply because I'm an imp, then I don't have to be evil because I'm a demon lord. I'll be a new kind of demon lord. The best kind.

"Please don't leave before you see what I can do." I rubbed a tear on his hand. "Talon? I need to go."

I knew if I didn't I'd start bawling. He took me to my mother next. She lay in a recovery bed, machines beeping.

The nurse shot me and then Talon a look. "Do you think she really ought to be here?"

Talon shrugged. "You tell her to go. She was stubborn enough before. But I'm not going to be the one to give a demon lord bad news."

The nurse looked frightened. "Okay. I was only checking. Your mother is still coming out of sedation. But she was conscious before, she'll probably be able to interact some. She had tearing on several internal organs and her leg was completely crushed. But she'll live. Assuming she has the will."

I took several steadying breaths. When I looked around I was alone. I wheeled my chair over to my mom's bedside and lay my head alongside her.

"Don't listen to the nurse, Mom. You'll be fine. I'm not hoping you have the will. I know you do. You and Dad are twice as tough as I am, and I'm still here. I mean, I'm your child. I had to get the drive from somewhere." I snuggled my face into her side. "I wish you were awake. I really need you. I know I should be taking care of you, but I need your ear."

I got a soft pat to my hair. "I'm here, baby."

"*Mom.*"

I burst into tears. Everything I'd been holding in from that horrible day came flooding out through my eyes. I soaked the spot on her bed where I'd laid my head. I never wanted to lose the feel of her hand on my head.

"Are you all right?" I asked through the sniffles.

"Drugged. Can't tell."

I gave something between a chuckle, a hiccup, and a sob. "I've been so worried all day. I still am. I just saw Dad . . ." I trailed off as I realized my mistake.

"What about Arsen?"

Shit. No wonder Omri and the others had such a hard time talking to me in these situations.

"He's still unconscious?"

Crap. I hadn't meant that to be a question. Now she'd be even more suspicious. I looked up into her bruised face.

"Just tell me, Livy. The truth can't be worse than what my imagination will cook up."

"No. That's the truth. He really is unconscious. I only left out the part about the nurses being unsure of . . ." I gave a shrug. "I'm sorry. I suck at not worrying you."

Her lips were too swollen to smile, but I heard it on her voice. I felt it in the pat on my cheek. "I always worry about you. You're my daughter. It's part of being a mom."

I caught her hand and kept it on my face. "I . . . Can I still be your daughter? Really?"

"Of course. Why would you ever think otherwise?"

"Because . . ." How did one tell their parents they now ruled as a demon lord? I felt hands on my shoulders.

"Hi, Mrs. Skotadi." Talon gave me a rub at the same time he gave my mom a smile. "Livy's just a little worried about how you might take the news. She's the new demon lord."

The machines screamed as my mom tried to sit. "She's *what*?"

"Talon!" I saw red. He'd upset my mom.

He grabbed Mom's shoulder and pressed her gently back down. "She's the biggest hero of all. She paused time and killed the demon lord. She saved the entire Central Borderlands. But the magic and the throne got passed to her. I'm not really sure why she was afraid to tell you. Of course, as her parents you'll be busting with pride over what she's done."

My mom's mouth flapped and with her yellow skin she reminded me of a goldfish. "You're not hurt, are you? How did you survive the magic loss?"

"Omri and some others saved her. She's got great taste in friends." Talon patted my mom and put his hand back on my shoulder.

Mom shook her head slowly. "My baby is a demon lord?"

"Yeah," I whispered. "You're okay with that, right?"

Her eyes glistened. "I'm *so* proud of you. I can't believe you saved . . . *everyone*. When your father and I go home—"

"You're not going anywhere." That fierce determination roared up again. "I'm a demon lord. I'll take care of your magic rations, so you can stay here. I get to pick my household, right?"

Talon smoothed my shoulders. "I'm sure you do. You're supposed to be resting, too. Just relax, Livy. You'll have plenty of time to do all those things later. You should say goodnight to your mom. You both need sleep."

I opened my mouth to protest.

"You can come back tomorrow. All you have to do is order someone to take you." He grinned at me.

I stood and waved off Talon's protest at me being out of the chair. I needed to hug my mom. I touched her as gently as I could, so I didn't hurt her.

"I'll see you tomorrow, Mom." I kissed her cheek. "I love you."

"I love you, too, Livy."

Her eyelids were already sagging as I sat back down. After such a horrible day I took solace in the idea of going to bed. But even bedtime had changed. As the new demon lord, my lodgings were now in the guest wing: a lavish room meant for VIPs. Velor and Vixaria were curled in my room like massive, scaly guard dogs. Talon had to go back to the far side of the palace with Elita and my friends.

A sob hitched itself out, opening the door for a flood of tears. I curled around my pillow and let my misery out. A huge scaly head came to rest on the bed and I bit back a scream.

"Mistress." Velor's snaky tongue flicked at me as he spoke. "You are an entirely different kind of mistress than I am accustomed to. However, my duty is to see your needs are met as part of the terms of my contract with Zaemon. I will be honest. I know you are unhappy, but I have no idea what you might need."

"I need my parents," I yelled at him. "You and your old master nearly killed them. If you think I'm going to be thrilled I'm stuck with you, I'm not. You can't possibly fix what's wrong."

Velor cocked his head to the side. "I am unfamiliar with such attachment to one's parents. Do imps not eat their young?"

I pounded his face with my pillow. "*No.* I love them and they love me. And now they're stuck in the hospital. My dad is in a coma and who knows if my mom will ever walk again. And don't tell me your kind doesn't understand love. Ferika has many different types of relationships and she loves them all in different ways. I don't suppose it would do any good to order you and your sister to learn *that,* would it?"

He blinked a very black eye at me. "If you wish. Strange request, really. Wouldn't you rather put us to work eating your enemies?"

I glared at him. "*You* were my enemies. But since I'm now in charge of my enemies, I guess I don't have any—at the moment. I'd like to stay that way. So, you two have to play nice."

The door opened and Vixaria slunk back in. I hadn't even noticed she'd left during my conversation with Velor.

"I brought something to make you feel better, mistress." As her tail cleared the door Talon stepped inside.

"Talon." I scrambled out of bed and into his waiting arms, where I promptly burst into tears again.

~ ~ ~

When I woke the next morning, I had to rub the grit from my eyes. Too many tears the night before. Talon slept beside me, his chest rising peacefully. A strange feeling welled in my chest. Pride and honor. I couldn't imagine what I'd done to deserve a friend like him.

Trying not to wake him, I slid quietly from my bed. Restlessness had settled over me, and I needed to walk. Slipping on my loose clothes and Hermes shoes, I tiptoed out. Once in the hall I decided to head for the gardens. Maybe hanging out with the plant life would help clear my head.

Two of the Lord High Governor's uniformed guards appeared in the hall before me. Damn it. I didn't want to work this early. Behind them sunlight shone on emerald hedges. I couldn't see a way to dodge them and make it to the gardens.

"Lord Olivia?" The taller guard spoke hesitantly.

"Yes?" Something about his expression made me pause.

"I . . ." He paused.

The second guard swallowed hard. "We have some bad news. Perhaps you'd like to go somewhere else."

My stomach filled with cement, hard and uncomfortable. "Tell me now. I don't want people coddling me. I wish you guys would just spit news out."

He shifted uncomfortably. "I'm sorry. Your father . . . passed away last night."

The hallway spun, and I staggered to find support against the wall. "What?"

"Your father—"

"Shut up," I screamed at him. "I heard."

My knees buckled. I slid down the wall, unable to will my feet to hold me. The guard reached for my hand to help me up. Instead of taking it, a red rage boiled up from within me. I slapped his hand away, snarling. Shame took the place of the rage. I pushed myself to my feet and bolted for the garden.

I lost myself in a maze of fragrant hedges. The blossoms, which should have smelled delightful were cloying. The rage still nagged at me, as if it had its own voice. A voice which scolded me for not punishing the guard for the death of my father. So, I punished the flowers for their scent. Rippling demon fire scorched the delicate petals, leaving them as withered as my innards felt.

Stumbling my way to a bench, I let my sobs tear from my body. By the time I felt relief, the sun had risen high and warm. I had purpose again. I needed to find my mother. Bonded partners tended to die if one was lost. I had to remind her my father wasn't the only one in her life. She had me, and with my new job as demon lord, I needed her now more than ever.

Giving myself a mental once over, I seemed to be in good shape. Or at least good enough to help my mother. My heart still burned for the loss of my father, but the rage had gone. I'd never had such a volatile temper before. But my life had altered significantly, and I held a whole new source of magic. Needing time to adjust seemed logical.

I'd almost pacified myself to the fluctuation in my power. Until I stood to find my mother. The metal bench I'd been on had twisted into an unrecognizable lump. Had I done that? Adrenaline, pushed by fear pulsed. I . . .

"Olivia?" Talon called from across the garden.

I didn't want to talk to him yet. And I certainly couldn't let him find me by the melted bench and the scuttling ashes of the flowers. I fled the scene of my deviance. I needed to find my mother and have a conversation before people began cramming condolences down my throat. I'd worry about myself later.

My mother lay so still in her hospital bed, I thought I'd come too late. I'd growled at several nurses on my way, demanding privacy. Being a demon lord seemed to carry the perk of getting your way. Not a single one argued with me.

I took my mother's hand. The flutter of a pulse sent shivers through me. I buried my face in her chest and sobbed.

"Thank God, you're still alive."

"Don't cry, Livy." Mom's voice came out so soft I had to lean in to hear. "I want to know you're happy. That you're going to be all right."

"I'll be all right if you stay with me. I need you, Mom. I don't know anything about ruling a district. I haven't even come of age."

She cupped my cheek. "You're growing into a beautiful, strong, resourceful woman. You've learned more about friendship in the last weeks than I could ever teach you. Take that knowledge and let it grow in your heart. Then apply it to every creature who lives in your district. Your father and I lived in the shade. But you have the chance to blossom in the sun. You can become more than any other imp in history. From here forward you will write the story of our kind."

A fat tear dripped down my cheek, stopping on her fingers. "You said 'lived'. You're still alive. I want you to see all that. I want you to see my district. Stay with *me*, Mom."

Her hand slid from my face and she placed it over one of my own. "I'd like to. But you know how these things go. It's a rare partner who survives the other's passing. With your father gone, I feel cold and empty inside. I miss the taste of his magic already."

"I'm never going to pair-bond. If this is the result, then I'd rather live alone."

"It's not so bad, Livy." Mom squeezed my hand. "Our life together brought me so much joy. My biggest being you. To see you poised on the edge of your new life and knowing your heart as your mother, I'm sure you and the world hold great things for each other. But don't let what's happening now cheat you out of part of that.

"Find love, be it Talon or whoever makes you truly happy. Have a family. I promise, every tear, every moment of fear, every struggle, even these goodbyes are worth it. Just the memory of your smile is enough to sustain me as I prepare to join your father."

"What's going to sustain me?" I choked out.

"Your wonderful tenacity. And your friends. You have been blessed in a way few imps get to experience. Draw your strength from them. You already know how. It's how you got where you are today."

She drew a shuddering breath. Her eyes slid shut.

"Mom?"

"*Mom.*"

"Still here . . . Livy," she whispered without opening her eyes. "I love you."

"I love you, too."

Those were the last words she spoke to me. I lay with my head on her shoulder for the whole afternoon and evening. Stars winked outside her window when one breath no longer followed the next.

I screamed for the nurses to save her. I still screamed as Talon carried me from the room. He took me to an empty waiting room and pressed me into a chair, holding me there.

"There's nothing they can do, Livy."

"Magic . . ."

He shook his head. "I'm so sorry. This is how—"

"Don't tell me this is how things work. It's a stupid way for them to work. If she couldn't survive without my father's magic, then just give her more."

"It's not just his missing magic." Talon caught my eyes with his. "That's the depth of their love. Can't you imagine being that in love? Wouldn't you want to experience that?"

I shuddered. I couldn't imagine. The idea of such love frightened me. A horrifying thought occurred to me. What if that's what Talon wanted?

~ ~ ~

The day of my presentation arrived too swiftly for my comfort. I couldn't find any joy. I'd spent the previous day in solitude. If you count the fact my dragons had insisted on staying on the far side of my room. Without my parents I felt lost.

"I've been before the Synod lots of times." Elita chattered as she slicked my hair back into an intricate twist. "Don't be nervous. You rank higher than them. You won't even see them after this unless it's a formal state occasion. Or if something comes up that you can't handle in your district."

"Do I have to do this?" I could already feel sweat on my palms.

"You'll be fine. Besides, you'll want some idea of who they are and how things work. After all, you're a demon lord now. This is your job."

I closed my eyes and drew a deep breath.

"Geez, Olivia. You've faced dragons and demons. You can face a room full of old men and ladies." Elita pushed me out the door and into the hall.

We were followed all the way to the council chambers by Talon and my dragons. They would have to stay in the hall, news which had come as a relief to me. The dragons still made me nervous. Talon gave my nerves a workout for a whole different reason.

Elita took me inside the room, showed me to a chair just in front of the doors and went to the far side to sit behind her father. I tried not to show any fear, but next to me sat a demon with dark gray skin and black hair which matched the crow-like wings folded on his back. He smiled and offered a hand.

"Drix. Demon lord of the eastern most district."

"Olivia. Newest demon lord."

He chuckled. "Of course you are. News this big travels fast. I—"

Feéroi, the Lord High Governor stood and raised his hands for silence. He had translucent green butterfly wings with the same design as Elita's. I'd caught a pattern over the last few times I'd seen him. He always wore a vest and a pocket watch. With his straight, shoulder length white hair, he reminded me of Alice's white rabbit.

"Welcome. Thank you all for making this emergency meeting of the Synod. As I'm sure you've all heard, we've lost Lord Zaemon. We're here to install his replacement. I've had the privilege of watching the new Lord Olivia at work for the previous few weeks. For those of you who were not keen on Lord Zaemon's methods, I think you will find Lord Olivia a most refreshing change of pace.

"My biggest concern is her age. She—"

The doors beside me burst open. "Oh, really? Her age is your biggest concern?"

I gawked at the new arrivals. A man with glowing garnet hair, like dying embers had entered beside the speaker. The speaker was impressive. Tall and lean with a regal manner. Like the other man, his hair appeared to be on fire. His flickered a pale yellow. They both dressed in embroidered silk robes. I'd never seen a creature like them.

"Akuma," Drix hissed. "What do they think they're doing here. The borders are closed."

Lord Feéroi frowned in their direction. "These proceedings are for members of the Central Borderland's government only. I also don't recall you asking permission to cross closed borders. Is it your intent to start an international incident?"

The speaker raised his chin, making him look all the more austere. "I could ask the same of you. Are you trying to start an incident by seriously installing an imp in the role of a demon lord?"

"She's malevolent enough for the magic to accept." Lord Feéroi puffed himself up. "The magic chose as it has always done."

"And you could find a replacement for her and transfer someone qualified into the position."

Sweat beaded up on my forehead. What they were discussing meant killing me.

"Hi there."

I looked to my side. A third akuma crouched beside me. The man next to me both terrified me and left me breathless. Akuma were fire demons. They headed the demon family tree, if I remembered the lessons my parents had given me correctly. He would be very powerful. Aside from that, I'd come face to face with Lynx's replacement as the most gorgeous male ever. Orange flame hair flickered softly over spring green eyes.

"Don't mind my father and Lord Shandian. They take demon purity very seriously." His grin contained gleaming white teeth and sent a flutter through my stomach. "Besides, they're old and they don't like change. An imp as a demon lord is a big one. But I think you're fascinating. Imagine an imp taking out a demon lord."

He glanced back up at the others. After a moment I got my gaze to follow. Though, I really wanted to touch his hair to see if it was hot. And what made it dance like flames in the still air of the council chambers?

"We're not trying to install her on one of your thrones." Lord Feéroi's tone bordered on undiplomatic. He scowled at the akuma. "We wouldn't dare meddle in the governing of Hakushi. This is most disrespectful."

"So is having an imp wielding demon magic. Once this blows up in your face, perhaps we can provide you with a capable replacement. A proper demon." The yellow-haired akuma spun so his robe swirled around his feet. "This is what you get for kicking us out and tricking yourselves into believing no rational demons exist. Good luck with your foundling." He stormed from the room.

The garnet-haired demon paused near me on his way. "Come, Iya."

"Hang in there, sweetheart," Iya whispered softly. He stood and flashed me another grin.

I couldn't be sure, but it looked like he mouthed the words "good luck" on his way out.

"Well."

Lord Feéroi did a lot of huffing. What had started out as a seemingly formal introduction turned into a simple vote to keep me. Thankfully the vote turned out unanimous. Most of the Fairy Synod had been in the room when I'd killed Zaemon. At least I had nothing to prove to them. While they rambled about dealings of the Central Borderlands that I probably should have been listening to, I gave myself up to thought.

This incident just steeled my resolve to see through the promise I'd made my father. I'd show those biased akuma what an imp could do. Besides, who were they to judge? After all, they were demons.

My first act toward cleansing my district was to get the palace into a habitable state. I sent Velor and Vixaria ahead of me with orders to purge it of all evil. And to wash anything which smelled of sigbin. I sat on my bed with Talon, attempting to focus even though he kept trying to kiss me. I swatted him away.

"Seriously, Talon. I have to pick someone for regent. I've put off taking my throne for as long as I can."

He hopped over, so he straddled my legs, half-sitting on my lap. "I have some cool news on that. My parents applied to be your legal guardians until you reach your majority, since you still have a full year. But this way it would be pretty much like having family rule with you." He scowled. "Dad's told me several times he'd rather have you as a daughter."

I raised an eyebrow. "I'd be your sister? Really?"

"Gross. No. You'd be their ward. But it's only a little over year."

"Be your sister ward still doesn't help."

He ignored me. "I thought you could nominate my dad. I'll vouch he won't do anything weird with an advisory position. My parents love you. I mean you saved me and all, but they think you're the best thing since furrberry jam. I have a feeling they'll just offer advice when you need it. But you're smart, for an imp and they know that." He gave me a teasing look.

I sighed. "I'd appreciate having someone in the role who wasn't on a power trip. Sure. I'll tell Lord Feéroi at lunch."

He shook his head at me. You talk about the Lord High Governor so casually now." Talon gave a shifty look around the room. "So where are your dragons?"

"Getting my new palace fit to inhabit."

"Any meetings?"

"Not until after lunch."

He turned on me, eyes narrowed. "Perfect."

I was swiftly attacked. I forgot how fast he could move. I'd also forgotten he could rob you blind while you watched, until my shirt had disappeared. "Hmm." He looked me over.

"Princess Prissy Pants is still picking out your clothes, huh? I like this bra, but it's about sixty-years too young for your taste."

"Talon, give me my shirt back!"

"Not a chance." He buried his face in my stomach and blew, making me shriek with laughter.

~ ~ ~

The red sunlight shimmered in a trail across the water. "Mistress. We should really be heading home," Vclor said.

I rubbed at my eyes and nodded to Talon. We scrambled back to where my dragon waited to carry us home. He'd brought me out to the seaside cliff where I'd spread my parents' ashes. I'd used the past six months to clean my district and come to terms with my new life. I wanted to make good on my promise to my father. To honor his memory. Now I could finally say goodbye to my parents and get closure. I knew I'd always miss them, but I also knew they wouldn't want me to dwell in the past.

What a district it had become, thriving and vibrant. My district had the best sand beaches in the Central Borderlands. As soon as the area became evil free, it took on the new role of a vacation destination. Some of those holiday goers played on the sand below us as we flew back to the palace.

Talon's father proved a capable advisor and I already had plans to keep him on after I reached my majority. His parents were easy to love and before I knew it, my impish heart added them to my growing family. I now believed the idea an imp only loved the precious few was wrong. I not only had my friends as my mother had said, I had a whole district I cared about. Learning to reach so far outside myself had taken work. But work which rewarded me every day.

My dragons had followed my orders and after spending much time in Ferika's company they were beginning to get the hang of reigning in their more vicious tendencies. Their growth proved my theory about myself. Ferika and I weren't freaks outside the nature of our kind. We simply expanded on ourselves. If my dragons could do it, too, I knew anyone could.

Velor landed on the terrace to my suite of rooms, let Talon and I slide off, then left to see to his duties. Talon put a hand on my shoulder, stopping me.

"You know, you kind of rushed over here and spent the last six months driving out all the evil creatures who had called this region home. I thought we were going to have a break from hunting vicious beasts."

"The hard work is done now. Vixaria confirmed finishing the last mission this morning. She rounded up the last pack of blood bats in Setmyth forest and relocated them to the far end of the mountain range."

"I heard. But once upon a time, I told you I'd take you away to a beach where all you had to do was lounge around."

"Talon, I can't."

"I know. So how about this instead? Since evil is thwarted for now. Let's have dinner in your room without all the formalities. I'll properly welcome you to your new home and new life."

"I'm sure whatever you have in mind is certainly not proper."

He sighed and nuzzled my neck. "I understand you've been busy, but haven't you given any thought to us? Taking things further? Bonding? I'm falling for you. Have your feelings for me grown at all?"

The air left my lungs at that. "I . . . I'm not ready. I . . . haven't been thinking about stuff like that. As you said, I've been busy."

I looked up into those brown eyes which were now such a part of me. He'd truly become my partner, but I still wasn't sure exactly what that meant to me. Guilt tickled my stomach. I owed him more than evasive answers. He meant the world to me.

I kissed the tip of his nose. "Now that all the evil is gone, I can focus on us for a change. Let's start with a quiet dinner, which sounds awesome by the way. We'll see where things go from there. Do a little dating, you know, now that I might have free time."

"Sounds like a good place to start." He swept me off my feet and carried me through the door. "Welcome to your new life, demon lord."

CPSIA information can be obtained
at www.ICGtesting.com
Printed in the USA
FFHW02n0553151018
48775396-52887FF